THE TROUBLE WITH MIRACLES

<u>The Trouble with Miracles</u>

*The ancient secret of fusion energy is
rediscovered in a breathless thriller
about the magic and mystery of the
Easter Island statues.*

To MARJORY —

Best wishes + HAPPY READING !

Stephen Steele

Other Books by Stephen Steele

THE TROUBLE WITH MIRACLES
Book One: *The Cannastar Factor*
Book Two: *The Organ Grinder Factor*
Book Three: *The Trouble with Miracles*

THE TROUBLE WITH MIRACLES

<u>The Trouble with Miracles</u>

*The ancient secret of fusion energy is
rediscovered in a breathless thriller
about the magic and mystery of the
Easter Island statues.*

Stephen Steele

SPEAKING VOLUMES, LLC
NAPLES, FLORIDA
2022

The Trouble with Miracles

Cover design by Hannah Linder

Maps by Steven Bates

ISBN 978-1-64540-810-9

For Beverly
whose fearless editing,
cooking and scooping of the kitty
litter box made this novel possible.

Preface

The Cannastar Factor is the first in a 3-volume series entitled *The Trouble with Miracles*. Alex Farmer, M.D. is a former drug addict trying to put his tortured life behind him. Cyd Seeley is a botanist and rancher in dire financial straits. They are inadvertently thrown together when a mutual friend is murdered after developing an inexpensive, organically grown cure for viral diseases.

The miracle plant is called Cannastar and it cures all manner of viruses from Coronavirus and cancer, to HIV and herpes. Cannastar costs next to nothing to grow, returns the hopelessly ill to good health, and threatens to bankrupt the pharmaceutical industry. Big Pharma will stop at nothing to keep it off the market.

Aided by faithful Native Americans in Montana and Arizona, Cyd and Alex fight to grow Cannastar and distribute it to a desperate world. Their harrowing and perilous journey ranges from the Rocky Mountain wilderness, to the political corruption of Washington D.C., to the jungles of Mexico, to the deserts of the Southwest. Filled with mystery and suspense, *The Cannastar Factor* is part adventure and part love story; a timely thriller that unfolds with endless surprises and heartwarming relationships; an epic novel about the resolute passions of two people who stand against a broken world.

***

The adventures of Alex Farmer and Cyd Seeley continue in *The Organ Grinder Factor*, Book Two in the 3-book series *The Trouble with Miracles*. Based on true events, this timely thriller ranges from the real-world horrors of child slavery in Africa to the ongoing Israeli/Palestinian conflict in Israel.

In desperate search of a place to safely grow their miracle cure for viruses called Cannastar, Alex and Cyd shipwreck off the west coast of Africa and wash ashore in the drug and war-torn nation of Guinea-Bissau. Fleeing for their lives, they arrive in Senegal where they become involved in the country's real-life child slavery problem and barely avoid execution.

They find refuge in Israel where they meet the inventor of the Organ Grinder, a 3-D printer that replaces diseased and damaged human organs without the need for surgery. The experimental research is funded by a ruthless billionaire with a violent and secret past who becomes Cyd and Alex's investor in their vast new Cannastar plantation.

While living in Israel, Cyd is badly wounded in a Palestinian rocket attack. Her only chance of survival is the Organ Grinder—which has never been tested on a human being. Meanwhile, Alex is taken hostage by Palestinian terrorists and spends weeks living in fear not knowing if Cyd is alive or dead.

In the end, Cyd and Alex are married in a beautiful Montana wedding. After the ceremony, Clarence Bigfoot pulls them aside. The big, affable Native American was their ardent supporter in the first book in the series, *The Cannastar Factor*. His geologist son Robert is in Chile surveying the vast mineral deposits unearthed by the recent intense earthquake activity down there. The earthquakes are exposing a strange phenomenon as well: intense lights, bright as the sun, flashing out of the ground and disappearing again as quickly as they came. Clarence wants to sponsor an expedition to Chile to investigate, and asks Cyd and Alex if they will lead it.

Cyd's insistence that they have come home to start a family falls flat. Alex lies when he says he is looking forward to becoming a country doctor. Restless for adventure, fascinated by the possibility that an ancient civilization may actually have held the secret to fusion energy . . . they nonetheless refuse Clarence's offer.

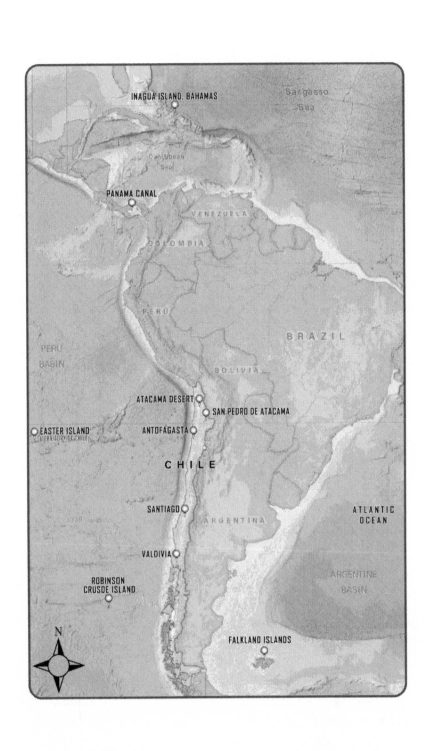

Chapter One

January 10th

The sun burned bright and hot on this steamy summer day in January as the Boeing 737 from Los Angeles turned onto its final approach and settled into a long glide path into Chile's Santiago airport. Out the left side of the plane, the passengers admired a view of the towering Andes that soared close by and ran the full 2,700-mile length of the long, narrow country from Peru to Cape Horn. Out the right side of the aircraft, they caught glimpses of Chile's 4,000 miles of glittering coastline. And far out to sea beyond the horizon, unseen, lay the Chilean territory of Easter Island where mysterious stone statues stood as silent guardians of lost secrets that would soon be told.

Cyd leaned over Alex to look excitedly out the window on the other side of the plane at the white-frothing blue of the Pacific Ocean, then turned back to watch out her window as the plane sank below the 20,000-foot peaks of volcanic mountains that seemed so close she could almost touch them. In her enthusiasm she woke Alex up. He made an impatient sound, resettled himself and went back to sleep.

Before leaving Montana, she had been ambivalent about the idea of going all the way down to Chile on a wild goose chase to find the source of some mysterious underground lights that may or may not be coming from a new form of energy. That was then. Now that the plane was about to touch down in Santiago, she couldn't wait for her adventure to begin. She looked over at Alex's sleeping form curled comfortably in the seat beside her and smiled to herself thinking how lucky she was to be sharing this amazing life with such an amazing partner.

It was a relief when she learned that their friend Clarence, the tech millionaire who was sponsoring their trip, had bought them first class plane tickets. Alex would have been miserable back in coach with his long legs pulled up under his chin for fourteen hours.

She smiled again remembering Africa and how much she loved watching Alex treat their patients in the clinic they had in Senegal. His rapid, gentle, fluid movements were like watching a ballet performed in hospital scrubs. She marveled at his quiet resolve once he made a medical diagnosis, at the absolute confidence with which he administered treatment. It was as if his training and intuition were always working hand in hand. Beyond that, she loved his almost child-like wonder at the world around him. He was a different person when he wasn't with patients: curious, bold, unafraid. It amazed her how he could be so decisive as a doctor and so completely accepting and nonjudgmental about everything else. His patience amazed her, especially since she had so little of it herself.

At thirty-four she had outlived the idealism and moral outrage of her youth. The world had moved on and so had she. The polarizing propaganda that had everyone hating each other back home, the violence and the double-talk in the media, made her never want to see another television news program again as long as she lived.

She thought of Cannastar and their efforts to bring their organically grown cure for viral diseases to the world. It pleased her to think it was relieving so much pain and suffering, so much death. It frightened her as well. With so many more people in good health, she was afraid they would use their newfound vigor and vitality to create even more chaos and destruction in the world. Fewer people dying meant more people living longer, and there were already too many people pursuing too few resources. *You let one species overrun a planet*, she thought, *and they'll destroy everything.*

Before leaving Montana, Helmut Stein had called from Israel. The inventor of the Organ Grinder was thrilled to report that the money from

Cyd and Alex's Israeli Cannastar Grow that funded his research was being put to good use. His 3-D printer had recently replaced vital organs in a dozen primates in a row without a single failure. Human trials, he added enthusiastically, were scheduled to begin next year.

Stein's ongoing success triggered yet another fear in her. They were tampering with the primal forces of nature, and in the process once again helping to overpopulate the world. The thought was depressing and brought back the memory of the time they were driving to Bethlehem and their car was hit by a Palestinian rocket. It occurred to her then that thanks to the Organ Grinder, the world was currently overpopulated by one Cyd Seeley, and that thought improved her mood considerably.

Her decision at the last minute to come on this trip, however, was based on something else entirely. Truth be told, she hated routine, hated chores, hated the idea of getting up in the morning and doing the same thing day in and day out. After all she and Alex had been through, after the dangers they had faced and the challenges they had overcome, she thought she wanted nothing more than to go home and lead a dull, domestic life. She had tried it for about a week after the wedding and realized she was bored to death. She simply wasn't the domestic type and that was that. A restlessness burned deep inside her, a need to learn and have fun, to search out new and broader horizons. And if she could help make the world a better place in the process, well, she had to admit she wanted that too. She wasn't so much of a cynic that she was ready to give up on the human race just yet. In spite of everything, she still had hope.

Out both sides of the descending airplane, the passengers now had a good view of Santiago's closely packed high-rises sticking up like shiny spears out of a dull brown urban sprawl that housed some six million people.

From the cockpit, Captain Daniels had the airport in sight. An air traffic controller's voice crackled over his headphones:

"American one three niner cleared for landing, runway one seven right."

"Cleared for landing one seven right, American one three niner," Daniels responded in his best pilot's voice. His copilot lowered the landing gear, startling the passengers with a shuddering thud as the gear locked into place.

Captain Daniels prided himself on his soft, smooth landings. "Greasers," he called them. An early career as a Navy pilot taught him to bring a plane in hot and level on carrier decks that were pitching like a bull at a July rodeo. Gliding a 737 into an international airport with barely a brush of its tires on the asphalt, especially on a sunny, windless day like this, was a piece of cake—and still a thrill, even after all these years. A good landing never failed to make him smile.

The number 17R loomed up in twenty-foot letters at the end of the runway as the big jet thundered down. The moment its wheels hit, a 7.1 earthquake centered 150 miles off the Chilian coast struck Santiago. The sensation was like landing on a field of boulders.

The airliner pinballed down the runway, bouncing from side to side with terrified screams coming from the cabin. Captain Daniels reversed thrust and the loud, whining rush of air, combined with the plane's violent movements, only made it worse for the panicked passengers in back.

"Brace for impact!" a flight attendant cried over the intercom, and a moment later was thrown forward so violently in her harness that she broke a rib and was left gasping for air.

Captain Daniels stomped his foot brakes in a frantic effort to slow the plane. As he did, he saw a deep crack opening up in the runway dead ahead. He released the brakes and slammed the throttles forward to try and loft the aircraft over the crevasse, but only managed to raise the nosewheel. The main landing gear disappeared into the hole and was immediately sheared off. The plane dropped onto its belly and began a sickening slide down the runway, careening along the asphalt in a shower of sparks. The tortured screeching and scraping of metal, the howling protest of the engines, the blinding confusion of noise and speed sounded like the end of the world to the horrified passengers.

Deprived of its landing gear, the plane skidded off the runway, dug a wingtip into the dirt, spun violently around and came to a shuddering halt with the ground still shaking beneath it. Back in the fuselage, the desperate passengers bounded out of their seats in a panicked rush to get out.

"Evacuate! Evacuate! Evacuate!" The captain's urgent shout over the intercom only added to the hysteria. People started climbing over one another in a frantic effort to escape. A crush of bodies piled up in the aisle trampling one another underfoot as panicked flight attendants struggled to open the doors.

Cyd lunged to her feet and Alex grabbed her arm, forcing her to sit back down.

"Wait!" he said. "Not yet."

"What about fire?" she cried.

"We're not on fire."

"You don't know that!"

"If we were on fire, we'd be smelling smoke and seeing flames."

"What if we *do* see flames?"

"Then," he smiled grimly, "we panic."

The earthquake was shaking the plane so badly that nobody could keep their footing. Alex pushed a man away who had been flung on top of them by the mob, and the man disappeared into a panicked wall of writhing bodies.

Cyd made another effort to get out and Alex restrained her. "Listen to me," he hissed. "You can't force your way out of here. You'll only make things worse and get crushed in the process. Sit tight a minute and we'll be alright."

She gritted her teeth and forced a smile. "Is the minute up yet?"

It was several minutes before they managed to squeeze out the door of the plane. A wall of hot, sticky air hit Cyd in the face. She stood blinking in the brilliant sunlight. Then someone pushed her from behind—a stomach-churning fall—and Alex caught her at the bottom of the slide.

"What are you looking so mad about?" he asked, amused at the anger on her face. "We made it, didn't we?"

She was furious. "I must have been out of my mind wanting to come here! This is a horrible place! I mean, look at that will you? They don't even try to hide it!"

He looked where she was pointing and saw a colorful banner hanging from the terminal roof that read, "Welcome to the country at the end of the world".

"Good place for it, the end of the world," she remarked, bending to help an elderly woman who had fallen to her knees and was gasping for breath.

The ground stopped shaking, but nobody trusted it not to start up again. Someone threw blankets over their shoulders and was ushering them along amid the pandemonium of flashing red lights, dazed and traumatized passengers and fire trucks screeching to a halt at odd angles around the plane.

Helmeted men in heavy clothing jumped out and began stretching out hoses.

Cyd was a nervous wreck now that the danger had passed. "Where's Robert?" she cried, casting about with her eyes. "He was supposed to meet us here. I don't see him anywhere!"

Alex threw off his blanket. "Worry about Robert later. Right now, we have to help. They're going to need all the doctors and nurses they can get."

Chapter Two

AFTERSHOCK

It was late by the time they finally managed to get from the airport to their hotel. They hadn't been in their room five minutes when Alex looked over and saw Cyd had fallen asleep on the bed still in her clothes. He sat on the edge of the bed and with one finger gently moved aside the cascade of dark hair that covered her face. Her beauty, even after an ordeal like this, never ceased to amaze him. He carefully pulled a blanket up over her.

The next morning when Robert still hadn't appeared or contacted them, they became worried. Was he injured or worse, dead under the rubble from some building after yesterday's earthquake? Before leaving home, Clarence told them his son had taken a new job with the Chilean government locating and evaluating recently uncovered natural resources on government owned land. He gave them a piece of paper with the address and phone number of the Chile's Ministry of the Interior in Santiago that oversaw its mining operations.

Alex fished the paper out of his pocket, picked up the phone and tried calling the number Clarence had written only to be met with a cascade of indecipherable Spanish followed by a babble of what sounded like Chinese. He hung up and told Cyd they were going to have to go there to find him.

Following a hurried breakfast of coffee and toast, they caught a cab. It was a warm, humid morning and the old Spanish city was already alive with activity. The cab headed up a wide, busy boulevard with a center divider lined with palm trees, then turned down a tree-filled avenue crowded with cars and busses.

Broad sidewalks on either side of the street teemed with people hurrying past rows of tidy vendor stalls arrayed with colorful crafts and cheap foreign goods under the shade of tiny tents. A low, constant hum of vehicles and voices, haunting Peruvian flutes and the unintelligible, electronic pounding of Latin rap music filled the air. Everywhere they looked in the vast city they saw modern high-rises encroaching on centuries-old Spanish buildings and ornate Catholic cathedrals that inevitably gave way to ugly, low-rise structures painted in the explosive colors of frenetic street art. Passing a forested park, they saw a white-faced mime jump out from behind a tree and begin intimidating visitors with robotic-like movements and mechanical gestures.

Street crews were rapidly cleaning up the rubble from yesterday's earthquake, broken store windows were being replaced and road crews were swiftly filling in the latest cracks in the streets. With so many recent earthquakes, it was a fair assumption that most of what was going to fall down had already fallen down, and anything that hadn't was safe from any but the deadliest of quakes. The population, with typical Latin fatalism, didn't seem in the least concerned. The earth moved all the time down here. *Y qué?* (So what?) And those strange lights that were appearing out of the ground high up north in the Andes when *los terremotos* came? A collective sigh implied that the lights were just another mystery in this land of endless mysteries.

Had Cyd not been so worried about Robert, she might have been a little more enamored with Santiago's esoteric delights and ethnic eccentricities. As it was, she saw the city only as a crowded, bustling metropolis with a high crime rate. She had tried repeatedly to reach Robert on his cell ever since they arrived, or rather crash-landed, in Chile, but her calls had gone directly to voicemail. She was hoping the Chilean government headquarters where Robert worked would at least know his whereabouts.

Minutes later the cab entered an industrial park on the outskirts of town and pulled up in front of a maintenance yard filled with mining and oil exploration equipment. Shovels, dozers, hauling trucks and loaders the size of apartment buildings were crowded in together apparently waiting to be serviced in the compound's huge warehouses. Another portion of the yard was devoted to towering drilling rigs and grasshopper pumps drawing oil out of the ground. Chilean workers in grimy clothes were servicing the equipment. Chinese supervisors, carrying clipboards and mobile phones, walked among them wearing matching coveralls and hard hats with red stars on them.

A high security fence encircled the entire area, blocking it off from the street. Attached to the fence was a large, official-looking sign at the top of which was a government seal for the Department of Natural Resource Management. The seal was encircled in words that read, *Ministerio del Interior, Chile*. Below the seal was an important message written in elaborate Spanish script, and below that, in English, were the words *China Mining and Energy Co., Ltd.*

The cab driver, in broken English, interpreted the Spanish for the benefit of his passengers. "Sign say national headquarters for management of national resources has moved. It say all business now being conducted out of new downtown offices. It give an address. *Nosotros vamos* (We go)?"

Cyd and Alex exchanged a concerned look. The unexpected news gave her a knot in the pit of her stomach. Alex turned to the driver. *"Sí,"* he confirmed. *"Nosotros vamos."*

Twenty minutes later they were back in the heart of the city. The cab honked its way across three lanes of bumper-to-bumper traffic and stopped in front of a towering glass skyscraper that blazed with sunlight and impaled the sky with its pointed spire. They got out and Cyd noticed two workmen installing a bronze plaque on a wall next to the building's enormous glass entry. Alex finished paying and tipping their driver and Cyd touched his arm, pointing to the plaque. Embossed in bronze were the words *China Mining and Energy Co., Ltd.*

They entered the harsh expanse of soaring glass and steel that enclosed the building's lobby and Cyd shivered. It was like going from a sauna to a refrigerator. Alex approached a row of Chinese security guards in military uniform seated behind an enormous reception desk. One of them looked up in response to his request for directions to the head offices for Chile's natural resource development and pointed to the elevators. "Top floor," he said in clipped English.

The elevator ride to the top felt like a ride in a vacuum tube at the drive-up window of a bank. The doors whooshed open breaking the seal, and they stepped out into a modern reception area the size of a basketball court. Hard, uncomfortable-looking furniture softened by pale pastel fabric was arranged at a distance that made conversation between the pieces impossible. More pastels softened the cold, hard surfaces of the walls. Windows two stories high looked out on the sprawling city and windows on the opposite side of the lobby looked inward at an indoor rainforest of plants and trees.

Cyd and Alex walked over to a tall, apparently-deserted reception desk. On the high wall above the desk was an enormous TV monitor that was changing images every few seconds. A picture of a copper mine with a hole in the ground the size of a giant meteor strike gracefully dissolved into a picture of a huge oil field dotted with busy drilling rigs and bobbing grasshopper pumps. That image was followed by one of gigantic holding ponds full of milky white brine baking in the desert sun. Behind the holding ponds, at the far edge of the desert, a ragged spine of towering volcanos lined the sky.

Alex looked over the top of the counter and saw a tiny Chinese woman seated at a computer monitor. She smiled up politely. "*Buenos días. Puedo ayudarlo?* (Good morning. May I help you?)" Her Spanish didn't sound at all like Spanish.

"Looking for one of your employees," Alex smiled. "Geologist by the name of Robert Big Foot."

The receptionist spoke quickly into her headset in Chinese, listened and smiled back up at the visitors. "Someone be right out." Her clipped English wasn't much better than her Spanish. Cyd had to replay the words in her head before she could understand what the woman had said.

A door opened and a Chinese man the size of a nine-year-old boy stepped out. He too was overly polite. "You will follow, please." His diction was better than the receptionists, but delivered just as rapidly. He led them past a room full of Chinese office workers engaged in feverish activity. The din of spoken Mandarin sounded like the buzzing of flies. No one looked up, but Cyd had the feeling they were being closely watched as they passed.

Their guide showed them into a glass-walled conference room, indicated they should sit at a long, varnished table, and with a slight bow abruptly left. Cyd and Alex sat looking at one another in constrained silence. The door opened again, a line of three men in identical business suits filed in and sat in unison on the other side of the table.

Cyd smiled to herself thinking they looked like a collection of Chinese dolls. Alex returned their formal nods with his easy smile.

The one on the right spoke first. "Identification, please."

They slid their passports across the table. The small stiff booklets were quickly examined and returned.

"How you know Robert Big Foot?" the one in the center asked politely.

"We're friends of the family," Alex answered.

"We've come all the way to Chile to see him," Cyd added.

"Robert Big Foot missing," the one on the right informed them bluntly.

"Missing?" Alex probed anxiously.

"He due back at mine headquarters one week ago. Not heard from since."

Cyd's heart sank. "Mine headquarters?"

"Salar de Atacama in Atacama Desert."

"Which is where, exactly?" Alex asked.

"You would perhaps like some tea?"

The visitors impatiently shook their heads. The three Chinese were clearly educated men. Judging from their command of English, it was a fair guess that they probably all held degrees from an American university. They were cordial enough, but there was no emotional connection talking to them, no space between the words for feelings.

"Fifty-five kilometers south of San Pedro de Atacama," the gentleman in the middle replied evenly.

"Sixteen hundred kilometers north of here," the one on the far right added, then saw he had confused his guests. "One thousand miles," he amended.

"What was Robert doing when he disappeared?" Cyd asked with growing apprehension.

"His job. Geological exploration."

"And your search parties have turned up nothing?" Alex inquired.

"Big desert. Robert never tell anyone where he go."

The indifference Cyd heard in his voice angered her. "You must have thousands of employees," she declared in frustration. "How would you even know that Robert works for you, let alone anything about him?"

Her question was met with silence. The executive on the left steepled his hands. He looked to be twice the age of his fellows and up until now had not spoken.

"So sorry," he smiled smoothly. "Robert *vely* different from other geologists. *Vely* important to company."

"How so?" Alex asked.

"Make many discoveries of natural resources. Company fortunate to have him."

"So why aren't you out looking for him then?" Alex pressed.

"It is harsh and hostile land. Thousands of square kilometers of empty desert and some of tallest mountains and volcanos on earth. Robert always work alone. Claims only way he can find things. Against company policy, but he make many important finds, especially after recent earthquakes, so we let him break rules. Always he come back before. Perhaps this time he may also return safely."

On the surface he sounded compassionate, but Cyd could sense his evasiveness and it angered her. He knew more than he was saying, she was certain of it. "We understood Robert was working for the Chilian government," she pressed. "How did he come to be working for you?"

The senior executive smiled proudly. "China now in partnership with Chilean government. They welcome our managers, our engineers, our expertise. Good for everybody."

"And the government, they allowed you to just come in here and take over?" Alex appeared amused, but the idea angered him.

"Chile and China friends since new administration voted in." He stood abruptly and the other two stood with him. "You will please to leave address of where you are staying with receptionist. We will inform you of any news."

The tiny man who escorted them in reappeared and escorted them out. They crossed the lobby and entered the elevator. Cyd pressed the button for the lobby, the doors started to close, a battered leather brief-case was inserted between them and they quickly reopened. A rumbled Chilean of about sixty walked in, the doors closed behind him and the elevator began its descent.

Cyd turned to Alex, beside herself with anger. "We just got brushed off," she fumed. "That makes me so mad!"

Before he could respond a heavy jolt shook the elevator and it came to a shuddering halt. Cyd cried out as the lights dimmed and came back on at half strength.

"It is just another aftershock," the other passenger assured them in perfect English. He was a stoop shouldered man in a wrinkled summer suit with dandruff on the shoulders. Intelligent eyes twinkled behind his sleepy eyelids. "Happens all the time in my country. We will be on our way again in no time."

Cyd was too frightened to hear his assurance. "I mean, what the hell is China doing in Chile in the first place?" she demanded nervously.

The dumpy little man smiled compassionately. "Allow me to intro-duce myself," he said in the calmest of voices. "My name is Juan Luis Morales. I am lead council for China Mining and Energy here in Chile."

Alex smiled and shook the hand that Cyd ignored.

The attorney regarded Cyd kindly. "It is public information, *señora,* that China paid over four billion dollars for a twenty-four percent stake in Chile's lithium mine in the Atacama. The Chilean government retains seventy-six percent ownership of the mine and gets residuals on every-thing taken out of the ground. Chile gets the benefit of unprecedented Chinese management, as well as the world-class expertise of their U.S. trained engineers."

"Sounds more like the early stages of imperialism to me," Alex said.

Just then the power came back on, the elevator jolted and continued its smooth descent. It reached the lobby, the doors whooshed open and

Cyd and Alex stepped out. The stoop shouldered man in the wrinkled suit stepped out after them. "People think countries rule the world," he said with a curmudgeonly smile. "Countries don't rule the world. Money rules the world."

Cyd watched him shuffle off, then followed Alex to the curb where he hailed a cab. A taxi screeched to a halt and they got in the back. Alex gave the driver the name of their hotel and the driver forced his way back into traffic.

"So, Chile is selling off their natural resources to China?" Cyd said, still a little shaken from the elevator ride. "What are they thinking?"

Their driver overheard her remark. "It is new day for Chile, and China part of it," he responded before Alex could answer. He was a young man with thick black hair who was driving with one hand while casually diving in and out of traffic. He shifted his position to shake his fist out the window at another driver, and they caught a glimpse of the writing on the back of his red shirt. It said, *"Partido Communista de Chile"*. Below that was a red and blue circle encircled in a gold leaf garland. Inside the circle in white was a Russian hammer and sickle.

Cyd and Alex exchanged a look of dismay. "A new day for Chile, you say?" she asked, gripping Alex's arm in response to his erratic driving.

"The voters, they vote seventy-eight percent for new progressive constitution that return power to the people." He swooped in front of another car and there was a sharp, metallic click as their bumpers touched. "Conservatives, businesses, the military, no longer are they in charge," he continued. "We have new social order now that will be model for free world."

"A seventy-eight percent margin," Cyd repeated. "That doesn't make you just a little bit suspicious?"

"Free healthcare, free college, free everything! I am suspicious of anyone not happy over that."

"What's your major?" Alex asked, assuming he must be a university student.

"I have degree in political science." The driver's repeated honking was creating a chorus of noisy responses from the other cars. "I do thesis on how capitalism enslave common man."

"I see," Alex said. "And in Chile, do cab drivers work for the government, or are they independent contractors?"

"Independent contractors," the driver replied indignantly. "Nobody boss of me."

Alex smiled at Cyd's incredulity and looked out the window at the park they passed earlier that now had several white-faced mimes jumping out and confronting visitors.

Cyd turned to him anxiously. "Those Chinese we met with were so evasive, so noncommittal. I don't trust a thing they said."

"They're hiding something," he agreed, "that's for sure."

"They don't want us to find Robert," she concluded. "That makes me want to find him all the more."

"He may just be lost."

"Or he may be in serious trouble. We need to at least try to find him. We owe his parents that much."

Alex nodded thoughtfully. "I'll see if I can't book us a flight to— what was the name of that place again?"

"San Pedro de Atacama. Absolutely. Only I'm not getting on another plane. I haven't gotten over the last landing."

The driver turned to speak over his shoulder and they saw in his eyes that he was far younger than they imagined. "They have wonderful buses here in Chile that go everywhere," he said enthusiastically. "Very cheap, very comfortable."

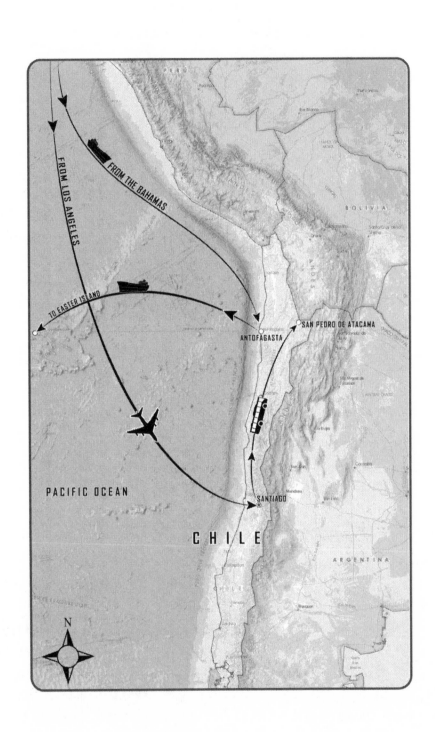

Chapter Three

WELCOME TO MARS

Cyd and Alex arrived back at their hotel and found the airline had delivered their luggage from the crashed plane. Alex checked on busses to San Pedro de Atacama and learned the next one left at 7am the next morning. He booked the best seats which cost a little over 55,000 pesos, or about $75 dollars each. It was a twenty-three-hour ride so they went to bed early and the following morning they were heading north aboard a large, luxurious coach.

January 12th

Throughout the day they passed through cities that came and went in a colorful architectural blur of the old and the new. On their left rolled the white-foaming blue of the Pacific and always on their right soared the jagged, unbroken spine of the Andes. The bus had a commodious restroom so stops were few and far between with barely time enough to grab a handful of snacks.

To try and get some idea of where they were going, Cyd burrowed into her recliner seat and studied the travel guide she bought at the bus station before they left. The Atacama Desert was the driest place on earth, according to the guide. Nearly a thousand miles long and six hundred miles wide, parts of the barren wasteland had not seen rain in forty million years. The desert lay between two mountain ranges, the Andes to the east and the Cordillera de Domeyko, on an *altiplano* (high plain) that was itself two miles above sea level, to the west.

Fifty million or so years ago the Pacific Coastal Plate burrowed under the continental shelf and lifted the long spine of the Andes over twenty-two thousand feet in the air. The newly formed mountains created a barricade that effectively blocked the humid air from the Amazon from flowing westward and produced what scientists call a "rain shadow" or dry area on the leeward side of the range. Recent reports indicated that the plates were still shifting and that the same inexorable, rock-crushing party that built the backbone of the continent had accelerated. They speculated that it was most likely the cause of the big earthquakes that Chile was currently experiencing.

Beyond the mountains west of the Atacama Desert, the icy waters of the Humboldt Current flowed north from Antarctica, cooling the oceans off South America. The cold water was prevented from evaporating by the hot air mass coming off the land and this, the guide explained, was what created the permanent high-pressure ceiling over Atacama's "absolute desert".

The daylight faded and the scenery disappeared in the dark. Cyd's eyes grew heavy from reading and she dozed off. Late that night the bus lurched and halted in the port city of Antofagasta for fuel and a driver change. Her eyes fluttered open, she stood stiffly and got off to stretch her legs. Alex followed her off the bus and disappeared into the darkened terminal in search of food.

While he was gone, she wandered across the street to a narrow, grassy, well-lit park that was bordered by the street on one side and a high seawall on the other. Going to the rail, she looked out at a shoreline that curved to the north and formed the harbor. Countless high-rises crowded the shore outlined in lights. Below her a huge freighter flying a Chinese flag was tied up to a long pier taking on cargo under bright loading lights.

Walking back across the street, Cyd boarded the bus and found the new driver settling himself behind the wheel. For the moment, they were the only ones on the coach.

"Speak English?" she asked the driver.

"Sí señora. Very good English speaker."

"That Chinese freighter in the harbor. Do you know what cargo it's taking on?"

The driver smiled proudly with a mouth full of gold teeth. "Lithium carbonate from Salar del Carmen plant just outside of town," he explained. "All lithium from Atacama Desert is refined right here in Antofagasta."

"Does it all go to China?"

"Sí señora. To make the batteries for the electric cars."

Alex came back carrying an armload of junk food and they returned to their seats to enjoy a messy late-night feast of sugary treats.

"Four more hours to go," he assured her.

She rolled her eyes in exhaustion and opened a package of cookies with her teeth.

From Antofagasta the big coach turned northeast on *Ruta* 25 and began a steady climb. Cyd forced herself to stop eating before she gained ten pounds, picked up her guidebook, opened it to the place she left off and switched on the overhead reading light.

The Atacama Desert, she read, was breathtakingly beautiful. She looked out her window. What little she could see in the shadows made her doubt there could be anything of beauty where they were headed. What intrigued her were the myriad secrets that the desert was said to hold. According to the book, an hour and a half drive from San Pedro was El Tatio Geyser Field where a geyser called El Jefe let loose a spout of boiling, white-plumed vapor every 132 seconds, 655 times a day. El Jefe's eruptions had supposedly been going on like this for thousands of years and every time they did, 80 of its mates whistled, hissed, spurted and gushed in approval. At a place called Cero Unita visitors could stare in wonder at the world's largest anthropomorphic figure resting on a

21

gentle hillside. She turned the book sideways to study a picture of the stone outline of a 390-foot body gazing up at the stars with outstretched arms. Inca legend claimed that a race of giants had once walked this land and that their lost city still existed somewhere deep inside one of Atacama's volcanos. Just north of the city of Calama, where they would soon be turning south, was the vast Chuquicamata open-pit copper mine with a hole so deep in the ground it was said that the skyline of Shanghai was visible from the bottom.

She wanted to see it all, but they hadn't come all this way to go sightseeing. If she could see only one thing, she wanted it to be the brilliantly pink flamingos that inhabited the saline lagoons of the desert. Her book claimed that the brine shrimp in the lagoons ate pink algae and that the Flamingos devoured the shrimp, sometimes kicking them up out of the milky water in a kind of flamenco dance. It was the keratin in the algae that turned them pink. She started to eat the last piece of the red licorice that Alex had bought, paused with it half way to her mouth, and put it back in the package.

Three hours later they had gained over 7,400 feet. Their bus passed through the city of Calama, gateway to the Atacama, and turned southeast on *Ruta* 23. It was that time of morning when the top of the sky is still dark and the bottom is turning blue and life stands still in a ghost world in between.

Alex had slept in his big recliner, but woke up stiff and tired. "I know Robert was once your fiancé," he said, staring out at the waking desert.

She stirred and stretched. "What?"

"Do you still have feelings for him?"

"It wasn't like that," she yawned. "More like brother and sister, like best friends who liked to hang out together. I thought he was exotic.

Maybe because he's half Native American, maybe because he always seemed to have secrets he wasn't telling. Robert is complicated."

"Do you still love him?"

"He was my first love. I'll always love him." She saw his constrained expression and smiled. "You jealous?"

He refused to answer.

"Good," she laughed.

He loved to hear her laugh. It was always so spontaneous, so genuine, so musical.

After a full day and night of traveling, their coach was finally approaching San Pedro de Atacama. Cyd looked out in the early light and gasped at an endless alien landscape of rust-streaked hills and stark, barren, bone-dry sand. To the southeast along the distant edge of the desert, three gigantic, closely spaced volcanos dominated the horizon. The one on the left was lazily spewing a plume of dirty white smoke that hung in the air like a towering cloud.

"The only thing this place lacks are dinosaurs," Cyd remarked, looking across at the primeval volcanos.

Alex nodded, imagining the monsters that might have populated this alien world. "Welcome to Mars," he muttered.

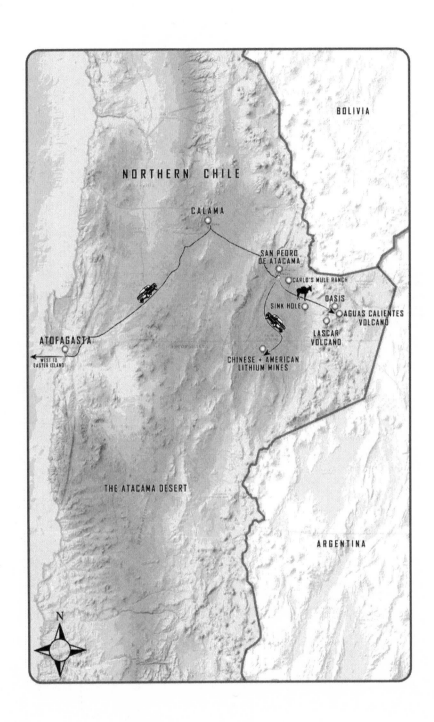

Chapter Four

SAN PEDRO DE ATACAMA

January 13th

The bus hissed to a stop in the village of San Pedro de Atacama and the passengers disembarked. Cyd and Alex stood looking down a narrow dirt street shielding their eyes from the brilliant morning sun. The heat was already oppressive and they shed the sweatshirts they had worn on the air-conditioned bus. Low, squat, mud-brick houses lined the street with doors and shutters that hung from their hinges at odd angles. The front walls of some of the houses had endured an attempt at being whitewashed, but the painters had apparently run out of paint because the brown mud was showing through. Halfhearted displays of souvenirs were draped on wooden ladders that leaned against the front walls of a few of the houses to tempt the tourists. The sunburnt empty fronts of the other houses attested to the fact that their owners had no real interest in the retail trade. A scattering of tourists, out for a morning walk before it got too hot, strolled along the street trying to look interested.

Shouldering their backpacks, Cyd and Alex went in search of a place to stay. On the outskirts of town, they were stunned to find a dizzying array of four-and-five-star resort hotels. Picking one at random, they entered a cool, luxurious lobby of towering green plants, running waterfalls and rich wood finishes to rival any resort in Latin America.

"I know this is the premier tourist destination for northern Chile," Cyd said as they checked in at the elegant reception desk, "but it feels like Fantasy Island got built in the middle of a stone age desert."

Robert's father Clarence, in sponsoring their trip to Chile to investigate the source of the mysterious lights that Robert couldn't stop talking about, had given them a credit card with the instruction not to worry about expenses. Alex handed it across the counter to the cordial desk clerk. "The lithium mine where Robert works and the other one owned by that American company are both near here," he said. "I'm guessing these hotels cater to a lot of business traffic as well as tourist traffic."

Anxious to start their search now that they know Robert is missing, they dumped their things in their room and head out to find transportation to the mine. Cyd, desperate for a bath, looked back longingly over her shoulder at their plush suite with its commodious bathtub as Alex closed the door on it.

Shuttle buses and tours ran from the hotels to all the points of interest in the region including out to both lithium mines. An hour after checking into their hotel they stepped out of a van at the vast mining complex in the middle of the Atacama Desert co-owned by the governments of China and Chile. Spread out on the desert floor were the ponds of milky white brine they had seen on the video monitor above the reception desk at the mine's Chinese headquarters back in Santiago. The shallow pools were laid out in endless checkerboard squares the size of small lakes. The tiny figure of a man in hip waders stood in one of the ponds taking samples. At the edge of the ponds sat a low-rise complex of dull metal industrial buildings shimmering like baking ovens in the desert heat.

Cyd and Alex had to sit thirty minutes in a dusty, stuffy waiting room until a Chinese secretary showed them into a glassed-in conference room. The conference room windows looked out on a warehouse full of white-coated men. Some sat at drafting boards, others stood at long lab tables filled with test tubes and microscopes, and the rest sat at metal desks with people talking on the phone or doing paperwork. Most of the workers looked to be Chilean, the ones in charge appeared to be Chinese.

The conference room door opened and two Asians and a Chilian entered. One of the Asians wore a Chinese military uniform. The other wore a severe brown Mao jacket, had an officious, off-putting manor and was clearly in charge. The Chilean that accompanied them was in his late twenties with a pleasant smile and handsome, delicate, almost feminine features. The uniformed soldier stood to one side at stiff attention. His two companions took off hard hats with red stars on them and mopped at their foreheads.

"I am Qiang Wáng, director of facility," the one in the Mao jacket said in clipped, staccato English. He was smaller even than his bosses in Santiago with slitted eyes so narrow it was hard to imagine how he could see out of them. "You would be the Americans looking for Robert Big Foot. Head office say you might come." He turned to the handsome Chilean. "This Robert's friend, Mateo Rojas. Geologist also. He last one to see Robert."

Mateo shook Alex's and Cyd's hands warmly. "So happy to meet you both," he said in a Spanish-accented lisp. "Robert has told me so much about you. I know he's been looking forward to you coming. We're all so worried. It's been over a week now and not a word."

"Any idea where he might have gone?" Cyd asked.

"Robert not like other geologists," Qiang Wáng interrupted. "Never tell anyone where he is going. We allow because he make so many uncanny discoveries."

"He's always disappearing like this," Mateo lamented. "I don't know why he has to be so mysterious about it. I've warned him time and again how dangerous this desert is, but he insists he has to be by himself to do what he does."

"Do you at least know the direction he went?" Alex asked.

Qiang Wáng again spoke before Mateo could answer. "Security say he go west toward coastal range called Cordillera de Domeyko. So sorry. He will be missed."

"So sorry?" Cyd was incensed. "A key employee disappears after wandering off alone and all you can say is you're so sorry?"

"Atacama Desert over forty thousand square miles. Easy to get lost." The director made a small bow. "Now if nothing else, *vely* busy."

Mateo caught Alex's eye with a slight movement of his head to indicate he wanted to talk privately.

"You've been very kind," Alex smiled. "Thank you for taking the time to see us."

Cyd gave him an angry look for giving up so easily.

"One thing more as long as we're here," Alex added. "I'm something of a scientist myself. Your lithium mine is fascinating. I'd love a personal tour of those holding ponds we saw on the way in. Got anybody who can explain the process to us?"

"Any friends of Robert are friends of mine," Mateo responded quickly. "I'd be happy to show you around."

Qiang Chen's expression froze. "By all means, Mateo, give our guests a tour. Just make sure they don't miss last bus to town."

"Appreciate it," Alex smiled. He and Cyd turned to follow Mateo out, and the stoic Chinese soldier followed close behind.

***

Cyd and Alex stood with Mateo on a rooftop observation platform overlooking an enormous checkerboard of milky-white holding ponds laid out on the desert. The Chinese soldier took up a position to one side where he could watch them carefully. Heat was coming off the barren wasteland in shimmering waves. Three miles away they could see the holding ponds of another lithium mine, and far away in the distance, tall and foreboding, rose the soaring brown slopes of two closely spaced volcanos with a high-altitude saddle connecting the two in between. Dirty smoke was pouring from the smaller summit cones in the saddle and fouling an otherwise pristine blue sky. A little further to the east, the extinct summit cone of a third volcano towered even higher than the two conjoined volcanos on its right.

Cyd, looking out at the great expanse of desert between the holding ponds and the volcanos, felt the platform's hot metal floor through the bottoms of her sandals and shifted her weight uncomfortably.

"Salar de Atacama is the world's largest source of pure lithium," Mateo announced with a dramatic sweep of his hand that encompassed the vast salt flats. "Not only is this the richest lithium mining area in the world, it is also the most economical to operate." He cast an uneasy glance in the direction of the stoic soldier who stood close by listening to his every word and went on in a lisping monotone. "A vast reservoir full of lithium-rich salt water lies deep beneath the desert floor in this area. We pump the brine to the surface where it is left for months to evaporate in the sun. Those great piles of dried white powder you see are the result. They will be trucked down the hill to Antofagasta and refined into pure lithium carbonate."

Alex could tell from Mateo's sideways glances that he was anxious to speak with them alone. Playing along, he pointed to the cluster of lithium holding ponds in the distance. "Is that mine over there part of your same operation?" he asked innocently.

"There are two lithium mines in the Atacama," Mateo replied. "This one is a joint venture between China and Chile. The one you are pointing at is larger and owned exclusively by Albemarle, an American company out of South Carolina."

"American?" Cyd asked incredulously.

Mateo glanced sideways at the soldier, saw he was still being watched, and replied with formal authority. "It may interest you to know that the largest hard-rock lithium reserve in the world is located just outside Perth, Australia. That one is jointly owned by China Mining and Energy and your American company Albemarle."

Their military escort got a call on his cellphone and turned aside to talk.

Mateo lowered his voice and went on rapidly. "Meet me in town to-night at *La Tortuga Salada*," he said. "The Salty Tortoise Cantina. Eight o'clock. I have word of Robert."

The Chinese soldier interrupted his phone call and quickly turned back thinking he heard something other than company propaganda.

"It takes twenty-two pounds of lithium to power the battery pack in a single electric car," Mateo announced loudly. "The world needs all the lithium it can get. China is meeting that need with its fifty-one percent ownership of the world's supply."

Chapter Five

THE JOURNAL OF ROBERT BIG FOOT

July 11th—Six months earlier

I begin this journal because of the extraordinary search I am about to undertake this winter. I have no idea what will happen, if my explorations will produce anything of value, or even if I will survive, but I have seen visions of what I am looking for and they fill me with wonder and excitement.

I am Robert, only son of Clarence and Mary Big Foot, from the Flathead Indian Reservation in Montana. I am thirty-four years old, stand six feet tall and have the same high cheekbones, narrow eyes and long black hair as my Salish Indian father. He wears his in a ponytail, I wear mine long to my shoulders. Thanks to my Caucasian mother, a retired ballerina with a pencil-thin figure, I'm not as fat as my pops.

Back home I am also known by my spirit name, *Speaks with The Earth*. Indian children are given spirit names based on their personalities at Native naming ceremonies. As they grow older and their personalities develop and change, they are often given new names. That was never the case with me. I was *Speaks with The Earth* then, and I am *Speaks with The Earth* now.

Growing up it took me a long time to come to terms with who I am. I hate labels like psychic, clairvoyant, soothsayer. The mental images I get of underground things are not magic or supernatural; on the contrary, they are as ordinary as the dirt I see through. And they come with a price. From the age of five I have had migraine headaches. They feel like someone is trying to drive a nail through my skull, and always they predict an earthquake.

The first time it happened I cried to my mother that I was seeing the earth move and grind up rocks with terrible force, and not long afterward Montana shook like a bowl of Jell-O. After that, whenever I fell on the sofa clutching at my temples, my mother would run around the house pulling anything breakable off the shelves. She was also the one who taught me how to deal with my headaches. Instead of resisting the pain, I learned to lie down and relax into it. The pain then has a chance to say what it came to say, and having said it, moves on.

There is another aspect to my so-called gift that is more annoying than painful although it hurts like hell for a moment. I get shooting pains in my head that bring flashes of random things that exist underground. These are pictures, or snapshots if you will. It doesn't always work, and I usually have to be alone in a desolate place, but I have seen veins of gold and silver, deposits of copper and coal, even reserves of oil. At other times the images come out of nowhere. I have witnessed hidden rivers rushing through rock ravines and underground seas washing up against stone shores. I have glimpsed the prehistoric ocean of lithium-rich brine beneath Salar de Atacama. Sometimes the sharp pains are accompanied by pictures of whatever is directly beneath my feet. It is very distracting to be talking or eating with friends, get a stabbing pain and see a boiling cauldron of scalding hot lava a mile or more straight down. I'm told that the look on my face when this happens can be quite unsettling. They ought to see it from my side.

There is an explanation for all of this, or at least I like to think it explains a few things. I am a Two Spirit person, born with the spirit of both a man and a woman. Among Indian Nations Two Spirit people are revered as having a dualistic connection with land and spirit. We are thought to have a sort of mana or spiritual power. In most tribes, Two Spirit people are not seen by their sexual preference, they are seen as friends, as human beings with extra knowledge and an extra spirit.

Women with a male spirit were often helpful in war parties. Two Spirit people over the ages have become shaman and healers because they have a knowledge of both sides. Among the Diné (Navajo) Two Spirit people are regarded as holy.

Me, I'm a geologist. I made a profession out of my passion for rocks so I wouldn't be considered a freak by the outside world, and so people on the res would stop trying to turn me into their shaman. Should anyone ask, I hold a master's degree in Engineering Geology from Montana Technological University in Butte, and a Ph.D. in Earth Sciences and Engineering from the University of Montana in Missoula. None of my training has prepared me for what I believe lies ahead, however. Or perhaps all of it has.

I love living and working in the Atacama Desert because the earth energy here is so strong. Soon after I arrived in Chile the powerful earthquakes began that brought the mysterious lights that lit the sky. My migraines at the time were terrible, but in the midst of the pain I started seeing images of the ruins of an ancient city. Not a city buried in the jungle or hidden on some remote mountaintop, but the ruins of a civilization lost inside a vast volcanic cavern.

The blinding light that accompanies the earthquakes has become an obsession with me. I believe it is like a lighthouse warning sailors of a danger, or in my case leading a sailor home. My mind's eye reels with images of towering structures made of boulders weighing thousands of tons, of vehicles that float on air, of an energy source of such unimaginable power that it can still put out a light that can be seen from the heavens. There is something to be discovered here, something more important than all the natural resources I have discovered in my professional career, and I must find it.

Even my best friend and partner Mateo, who I love above all else, does not understand. It saddens me to think that he does not see the importance of my search, saddens me even more that we have been having such terrible arguments over the dangers he imagines I face. The fights have gotten so bad recently I've simply stopped sharing information with him—which only makes things worse.

Chapter Six

THE SALTY TORTOISE CANTINA

Night of January 13th

Cyd and Alex found the mud brick cantina on the third unlit side street they went down. A weather-beaten wooden carving of a salt-crusted tortoise hung drunkenly from its one remaining chain over a doorway lit by a single lightbulb. The rest of the pub's exterior lay outside the circle of light shrouded in darkness.

They entered the cantina and stopped, staring apprehensively at a barroom straight out of a spaghetti western. The rough-sawn wooden walls were unpainted, the wood floor marked with boot heels, the thick slab of wood that served as the bar was more beat-up than the floor. Local drunks and assorted reprobates sat at wooden tables drinking and gambling. A pair of wide-eyed tourists had wandered in and sat craning their necks like hapless flamingos. The music was harsh and loud, the laughter cruel and dangerous.

Cyd wrinkled her nose. "I love the smell of urine in the evening," she said in disgust.

A figure at a table in a darkened corner waved them over and motioned them into rickety chairs. Mateo, dressed in local peasant garb that only slightly disguised his delicate, urban, academic look, held up three fingers to an attractive young waitress who brought over three frothing clay mugs of flat, warm beer.

Alex, thinking she was too pretty to be anything but the owner's daughter, nodded thanks as she gracefully placed the tankards on their table.

"Cyd, Alex, this is Maria," Mateo said, smiling paternally at the girl. "Maria just graduated from the *Universidad de Chile* in Santiago with a degree in environmental sciences."

The girl smiled back with perfect white teeth. "Professor Rojas, he was my geology teacher," she said admiringly in perfect English. "I just love geology."

"There's certainly plenty of that around here to love," Cyd agreed.

Maria sobered. "Except for the mine where *El profesor* now works and the American mine. They are draining the water supply from beneath our desert that the people of the region desperately need. I've come home to help the group that's trying to stop them."

"A noble cause," Mateo agreed and lowered his voice. "Maria, see to it that we're not disturbed, please."

She gave him a conspiratorial nod and left to deliver more drinks.

Mateo searched for prying eyes. "Were you followed?"

"Why would we be followed?" Alex asked.

"These Chinese, they are dangerous. Robert has no business playing games with them."

"Games?" Alex prodded. "If the Chinese are so bad, why do you work for them?"

Mateo stiffened and dropped the slightly effeminate lisp. "The money they offered me was irresistible. Worst decision of my life leaving the university." A whimsical look came over him and the lisp came back. "Then again, if I was still at the college, I would never have met Robert."

Cyd smiled supportively.

"Listen to me," Mateo said, glancing around again before going on. "Robert, he didn't go west, he went east. Toward the Andes and the volcanos."

Alex scowled. "So, what's his name, this Qiang Chen, he was lying to us?"

"The Chinese are as obsessed as Robert is with those mysterious lights that show up every time there's a sudden shift in the tectonic plates."

"He's seen them then, the lights?" Cyd asked.

"We both have. More than once. Blinding flashes so bright they obscure the terrain for miles around. The Chinese try and follow him every time he goes to find their source."

"Then you *do* know where he's gone," Alex pressed.

Mateo nodded in despair. "The Láscar volcano, yes."

"The big one that's smoking?" Cyd asked in alarm.

"Chile has two thousand volcanos," Mateo moaned. "Five hundred are considered active and sixty have erupted over the last several centuries. Robert, he has to pick the most active one. Lascar erupted in 1993 after ten thousand years and it has erupted three more times since."

Alex scratched the back of his head. "What does he think he's going to find if he locates the source of the lights?"

"Who knows? There's no talking to him. He's convinced that lights that strong would have to be generated by some form of ancient alien technology like fusion. He thinks if he can find the power source, he can reverse engineer it and bring fusion to the world."

"How do the Chinese know what he's after if he won't even talk to you about it?" Cyd asked.

"I have no idea," Mateo moaned. "All I know is we keep having these terrible fights over it."

***

October 12th—Three months earlier

Robert's secretive activities over the past three months had alerted his Chinese employers that he was hiding something. Anxious to claim whatever it was he was looking for should he find it—he wouldn't be going to such effort to conceal his movements if the thing he was looking for wasn't extremely valuable—they hid microphones in the company-owned condominium he and Mateo shared in San Pedro and listened to their every word. The couple's arguments over Robert's obsession with finding what he was convinced was an ancient source of fusion energy were well known to them.

Mateo was preparing supper in the condominium's kitchen one night when the argument got particularly heated. "If there were any more lost civilizations to be found," he argued, "somebody would already have found them by now."

Robert tried without success to conceal his irritation. "South America is littered with ruins and artifacts of lost cities and lost civilizations, Mateo. Some wonderful ones like Machu Picchu and the Nazca Lines in Peru have been discovered, but satellite images show there are all kinds of ruins still buried in the jungles. What of the ones we don't know about? What of the ones still overgrown and lost in time?"

Mateo threw up his hands in frustration. "That doesn't mean aliens had anything to do with them."

"How can you say that? Petroglyphs and petrographs of what appear to be spacemen have been found all over the world. What about Puma Punku in Bolivia that dates back over fourteen thousand years and predates any known civilization in the area? How could those blocks of stone weighing tens of tons been moved into place, precision tooled to machine quality, drilled to perfection and fitted together like a jigsaw puzzle so tightly a razor blade can't be inserted between the joints? Did primitive people do all that by pounding on impossibly huge boulders with rocks? What about the walls of Sacsayhuaman in Peru with their towering doorways? How were boulders weighing between a hundred and two hundred tons transported there in a time that predates the Incas and then fitted together with the same precision as Puma Punku? Humanoid skeletons of giants eighteen, twenty, twenty-five feet tall have been found in various parts of the world. Like Hamlet said, 'There are more things in heaven and earth, Horatio, than are dreamt of in your philosophy.'"

Mateo, afraid for Robert's safety, afraid of the danger he was putting himself in, could listen to no more excuses for his irrational behavior. Crying out in fear that he was going to lose his partner, he threw what he was cooking into the sink and marched out of the room.

***

The Salty Tortoise Cantina
Night of January 13th

Maria came by their table, saw they were still engrossed in conversation and hadn't touched their beers, and moved on.

"I keep begging Robert to at least take me with him on his searches, but he is so secretive, so private," Mateo lamented. "He says the less I know the better if the Chinese should question me."

"He actually thinks a lost city exists inside an active volcano?" Alex scoffed.

"There's an Incan legend that talks about a lost city of giants inside a volcano," Cyd said with growing excitement. "I read about it in my guidebook."

Alex smiled patiently. "Folklore is fairytales for adults, Cyd."

Cyd ignored the remark and turned emphatically to Mateo. "But you believe him," she pressed. "You do, don't you? I can tell."

Mateo sighed. "All I know is, Robert and I are both geologists and scientists, and there is no scientific protocol for the way he makes his geological discoveries. If its underground, he somehow knows what it is and where to find it. I've never known him to be wrong."

Alex took a sip of his warm, flat beer and made a face. "What are the chances he's still alive?"

"We'll know more after we talk to Carlos. I just received word that he wants to see me."

"Who's Carlos?" Cyd asked.

"Some old Incan Indian Robert uses as a guide. He and Carlos have made three trips to Lascar together to search for Robert's city. Carlos has come back this third time without him."

Maria appeared at their table just then slightly out of breath. "Señor, señora," she whispered to Alex and Cyd, "you go now. The Chinese, they are coming."

"They must have followed one of us," Mateo said urgently. "We can't be seen together, they'll know we're up to something."

"This way," Maria said, heading for the rear of the cantina. Cyd and Alex came to their feet with a scraping of their chairs.

"Wait for me at your hotel," Mateo instructed. "I'll come for you as soon as it's safe and we'll go see Carlos together."

Maria led Cyd and Alex through the kitchen, out into the darkened alley at the rear of the cantina and gave them directions on how to find their way safely back to their hotel.

Moments later a squad of three uniformed Chinese, led by the stoic soldier from the lithium mine, entered the bar and stood surveying the room.

"More beer!" the peasant-dressed Mateo bellowed, banging his mug on the table and grinning drunkenly at the newcomers. "And a round for my Chinese friends here!"

The three military men gave the drunken geologist a disgusted look, turned on their heels and left.

Chapter Seven

LEGEND OF THE GIANTS

Robert's Journal
December 17th—One month earlier

All I knew was that the blinding light that lit the sky during the earthquakes appeared to be coming from the Lascar volcano. This was one search I could not conduct alone. If I was going to go climbing around on Lascar I needed a guide, someone who had lived in the Atacama all his life and knew his way around a volcano.

It is odd the serendipitous things that happen once a person gets clear about what they need. I was at a gas station in town fueling my Jeep Wrangler and telling the grizzled owner about the kind of guide I was looking for when an old Incan rode past on a mule leading a string of tourists on mules back from a desert tour. The station owner smiled confidently and pointed to the passing muleskinner. "Carlos there is our local historian. Some say he knows more about the Atacama than anyone. Others say the peyote has made him crazy."

I finished paying for my gas, caught up with the mule train and followed at a respectful distance. A short distance from town the mules turned down a rutted dirt drive that led to a dilapidated ranch set back off the main road. A splintered, sun-ravaged sign with faded lettering hung over the entrance to the drive. The words were in Spanish with an English translation underneath that read:

RANCHO SAN PEDRO
Guided Mule Tours
Experience the Atacama from the back of a mule
Carlos Roca, Prop.

I passed under the sign and approached a small, squat adobe house shaded by a crooked front porch held up by gnarled and crooked logs. Out back was a fallen-down barn and an old log corral where the tourists were climbing down off their mules, thanking their guide and tipping him. Between the barn and the house was a tangled garden of spineless cacti. I waited until the guests were gone before getting out of my car. The muleskinner was entering his house when I approached him.

He saw me and the deep wrinkles in his toothless face lit with a smile. Stout as a fire hydrant, he reminded me of one of those ten-thousand-year-old mummies that are so well preserved in the Atacama Desert's bone-dry climate.

"I have seen a man who looks like you in my dreams." His heavily accented English was spoken in a voice that came from deep in his throat and seemed to echo down through the ages. "A shaman who comes with a dangerous request I must refuse."

"Nothing that dangerous," I replied. "I just need you to help me explore an active volcano. And I'm not a shaman."

"Takes one to know one," he muttered as he stepped aside to let me in.

Maybe it's because I am part North American Indian and Carlos is South American Indian, but from the moment we met I felt like we had known one another forever. I am told such a thing sometimes happens when two people who have shared a past life together meet again. Be that as it may, I was not here to talk about past lives.

"Pisco?" he asked, pouring me a mug before I could respond. "Grape brandy I make myself."

I took a sip. "It's good," I said, looking around. Four adobe walls enclosed a surprisingly tidy one-room cabin with a clean-swept dirt floor, a wood stove in the kitchen, a neatly made bed and a battered sofa that sat in front of a TV set with foil-wrapped rabbit ears. We sat at a crude wooden table worn smooth from a lifetime of use.

"No family?" I asked.

"Children all grown and gone. My wife I bury in cactus garden out back. Her spirit is in the peyote. She never shut up in life. In my visions now and still she never shut up."

I suppressed a smile. "I've had those kinds of visions."

He raised his heavy eyebrows and waited for me to go on.

"I've seen a city inside a volcano. An abandoned ruin of an ancient civilization that held the secret to the power of the sun. Have you ever heard of such a place?"

"Shaman," he repeated under his breath before closing his eyes and rocking gently back and forth. "A race of giants live in Chile eight thousand years ago. They come from the stars. The natives, they killed them."

"They what?"

My shocked expression seemed to amuse him. He steepled his gnarled hands and went on. "Gorgons, they were called. Giants twenty feet tall according to legend. The natives resented the Gorgons for trying to teach them things they could not learn and did not want to learn. They resented that the giants had such a wonderful city full of such amazing things when they lived in grass huts. But mainly what they hated about the Gorgons was that they forbid the natives from killing each other. Natives back then loved killing each other more than anything."

I bent forward urgently. "Carlos, there is something in that city I must find. I don't know what it is yet. I only know that it's important."

"Inside *volcán* Lascar," he repeated slowly.

I nodded.

"*Pachamama*, she live in *volcán* Lascar. *Pachamama* not like visitors."

"Who?"

"*Pachamama* is ancient earth goddess of the Incas. Name means Mother Earth. Incans believe her home is in *volcán* Lascar."

"We'll take her an offering," I pleaded. "Tell her we mean her no harm. I need to find this city, Carlos. Will you help me? I'll pay you well."

The old Incan closed his eyes again and was silent a long time. I thought he had fallen asleep when his eyes reopened. "I not do it for money, shaman. It would not be right."

"You'll help me then? You'll do it?"

"As long as she is sleeping, *Pachamama* won't mind. If she wake up, we must leave quickly."

Over forty miles of burning desert lay between San Pedro de Atacama and Lascar volcano. Carlos wanted to go by mule, but I insisted we take my Jeep. The next morning, we loaded the Wrangler with food, water and camping gear and headed south. I trusted Carlos to keep me safe and he, I think, trusted me that I had seen my city.

Chapter Eight

THE EYE OF PACHAMAMA

San Pedro de Atacama
Night of January 13th

Cyd and Alex returned to their hotel after meeting with Mateo at the cantina and waited impatiently for him to appear so they could go and meet Carlos. Alex stood in the open patio doorway breathing the clean, fresh, high desert air and inhaling the fragrant perfume of the hotel's tropical landscaping.

"Cyd," he said, "in all the time you were with Robert, did you notice anything strange or different about him?"

"Everything about Robert is strange and different," she replied, brushing her dark hair with long, luxurious strokes. "He was always so mysterious. Like he knew things that either he didn't know how to say or was afraid to say."

"Did you know he was gay?"

"I didn't always want to know." She tilted her head and tossed her hair to the other side to brush it from underneath. "But I think I always did. I was young and he was so handsome and charming. I overlooked a lot of things back then."

"So, you never slept with him, even when you were engaged?"

She shook her head to indicate she never had. "All I remember is being devastated when he broke up with me without an explanation."

Birds were calling from the hotel garden in the quiet of the desert night.

"Mateo is a good man," Alex said thoughtfully.

Cyd smiled. "And a good friend."

It was after midnight by the time Mateo knocked softly at the door to Alex and Cyd's suite. They left the hotel and piled into Mateo's work-worn Land Rover. Silently, intently, they drove through the deserted streets of town and out into the desert.

A short way from the village they came to Carlos's ranch, turned down the rutted drive and passed under the splintered sign that advertised his guided mule tours of the Atacama.

A pale-yellow light lit the front window in the adobe house. Mateo knocked softly. There was no answer and he knocked again. The door creaked open, a man peered out and recognized the visitor.

"*Señor* Mateo," Carlos cried in relief. "Come in quickly." He saw the two strangers behind him and hesitated.

"Carlos, this is Cyd and Alex," Mateo said. "They're friends of Robert."

Carlos nodded, motioned them inside and passed around cups of Pisco.

"Where's Robert?" Alex asked without tasting his cup. "Did you leave him up there on Lascar?"

"Oh, no," Carlos replied sadly. "Not on *volcán* Lascar."

"Not on Lascar," Mateo repeated. "Isn't that where the two of you have been for the past three weeks?"

"Twice we search Lascar, *Sí*. First week west cone, second week east cone. We find nothing."

"What about week three?" Alex demanded.

"Third week I help Robert get a new vision before we go."

"A new vision?" Cyd asked suspiciously.

"Robert see orb and follow it. Find out *Pachamama*, she not live in *volcán* Lascar."

"Who the hell is *Pachamama*?" Alex asked in exasperation.

Cyd had read about the Mother Earth goddess that the Incans called *Pachamama* in her guidebook and explained to Alex who she was.

Mateo was both frustrated and confused. "What are you saying, Carlos? Is the legend wrong, or did *Pachamama* find a new home?"

Carlos shrugged helplessly. "All I know is she not live in *volcán* Lascar anymore, she live in *volcán* Aguas Calientes."

"What has that got to do with Robert following an orb?" Cyd insisted.

***

Robert's Journal
January 5ᵗʰ—Five days before Cyd and Alex arrived in Chile

After two weeks of scaling the steep and slippery slopes of Lascar's eastern and western cones, the terrain revealed no clue as to the source of mysterious lights. I was hoping to find a crack, a fissure, an anomaly of some kind in Lascar's brown and blackened lava that might be letting light escape from below, but I had found nothing. The only area we didn't dare go near was the elevated bridge between the two cones that was smoking dangerously. If there had been another earthquake with another light show while we were there, I might have gotten a new insight, or been better able to see where the lights were coming from, but no such luck. In the end, Carlos and I returned to his ranch with nothing to show for our two weeks of effort except sand in our hair and grit in our teeth. Dirty and exhausted, I told Carlos that I was going home to take a long bath and get drunk.

We were unloading his gear from my Jeep when he put a gentle hand on my arm. "Come back tomorrow morning," he advised. "I will show you a way to become one with *Pachamama*. She will clear your vision and give you new guidance." I stared after him as he walked away. "Eat a light breakfast," he added before disappearing into his house.

That night my refusal to discuss with Mateo where I'd been or what I'd been doing resulted in a terrible fight. I told him I'd thought about it and decided to go back in the morning to take Carlos up on a strange offer he had made me. Mateo's response was to storm out of the room, run down the hall, and lock himself in the bathroom crying.

The following morning, rested and refreshed, I had coffee and toast for breakfast and drove back out to Carlos's ranch. He didn't seem at all surprised to see me and led me around back where I was shocked to find he had a raised wooden bed full of hundreds of peyote buttons drying in the sun. Apparently, my trusted guide was also a commercial peyote farmer.

"Choose twelve that speak to you," he instructed.

"I don't do drugs," I said, suddenly frightened.

"Indians have been doing peyote for thousands of years to communicate with the life force, the Supreme Being, the Great Mystery."

He was right. In 1978 the U.S. government passed AIRFA (American Indian Religious Freedom Act) making it legal for Native Americans to hold peyote ceremonies to communicate with the Great Spirit. Immediately afterward, it was reported that peyote use on the reservations had spiked, but it was only because Indians were now doing openly what they had been doing privately for centuries.

"Peyote treat physical and mental ailments, pain and snakebite," Carlos went on. "It make crazy people sane."

"I'm not insane," I cried. "And I don't have snakebite!"

"You will go to divine place where spirits will guide you," he promised in a resonant voice that implied I had already agreed to this throwback-to-the-sixties hippie madness he was suggesting. "But first you must ask *Pachamama* a question. If question is brave and true and spoken from the heart, she will answer and guide you to where you need to go." He paused. "A peyote journey is best enjoyed out of doors."

"Out of doors? We're in the middle of a bloody desert!"

"You will see Atacama in a way you have never seen it before," he assured me.

I was skeptical, I was fearful, I was intrigued. My heart beat faster. I had planned on getting drunk anyway. Suddenly, peyote seemed the more interesting option. If Carlos was right and it could provide me with fresh clues to my lost city, or at least point me in the right direction to the lights, maybe I should give it a try. Half of me, the Indian half, was no longer afraid. The other half was scared to death. I reached tentatively into the wooden drying bed, fumbled around, and the twelve peyote buttons that were mine felt warm as they came into my hands. I handed them to Carlos and he washed them for me.

We sat on a blanket Carlos spread out on the sand. The blazing sun beat down. In front of me was his cactus garden where pods of flowering green peyote clusters lay growing on the parched earth. I prayed that his buried wife did not occupy any of the buttons I had chosen.

"Do not take them all at once," Carlos instructed. "Take three now and three more every half hour until they are gone. It takes two hours to feel full effects. Center yourself, clear your mind, chew each one thoroughly." Another pause. "They taste like shit, by the way."

"They what?"

"And don't forget to ask your question. Otherwise 'Mescalito', the spirit of the plant, will have no direction and might take you on a journey of fear and terror."

With that charming thought in mind, I sat cross-legged on the blanket, put on the broad-brimmed hat that had protected me from the sun on so many desert searches, and emptied my thoughts. "Where can I find the lights that come during the earthquakes?" I asked, putting the first button on my mouth and biting down. "What exactly am I looking for and where exactly is it?"

I never tasted anything as bitter and awful in my life. It was like eating dirt, only more disgusting. Carlos was chanting something under his breath as I chewed the second one and then the third. Eating out of a dumpster that hadn't been emptied in weeks would have been more appetizing.

Half an hour later when I took three more buttons, I was a little nauseous, then sweaty, then chilled. The sensations gradually passed and a feeling of peace and ease came over me. Things began to melt together and colors became more vivid. Another half hour passed with my senses steadily expanding and I swallowed three more. After an hour and a half, it was time for me to take my fourth dose—which I decided against. I had already ingested enough peyote for a trip to the moon and back. My senses were sharp and clear and I was very aware. An inner alertness filled my consciousness. Everything I saw and heard and felt I experienced intensely. I looked on the world around me with a gentle wonder. Mescalito was calling my name. *Speaks with the Earth,* he beckoned. *Speaks with the Earth . . .*

***

I stare at the cactus garden before me feeling light and tingly. The cacti have grown into a twelve-foot-high jungle and I am walking among the most amazing plants with tropical birds calling from the highest branches. The lofty garden of succulents is too real to be a hallucination. I look down and see my feet growing roots. Tentacles emerge from my toes and burrow deep into the ground until I am planted firmly in the earth. An overwhelming feeling of peace comes over me, then everything changes.

Millions of colored dots are carrying me skyward and suddenly I am flying. Ahead, leading me on between a sunbaked desert and a marshmallow sky, is a brilliant blue orb. I have no idea what it is, only that it is beautiful and I must follow it. The orb itself is about the size of a basketball and looks like the planet earth with oceans of azure blue beneath swirls of snowy white clouds.

The orb speeds ahead and I race after it as the twin cones and smoking bridge of Lascar come into view. This is our destination, I think, but we streak straight past. Spellbound, I wondered where I am being taken when another volcano appears close by that is taller and more perfectly formed than Lascar. We soar up its steep slopes and circle above its dormant cone. Looking down, I see the mirrored surface of a circular lake cradled in its cup. Suddenly a brilliant beam of light shoots out from the side of the volcano and pierces the heavens. The orb streaks down toward it with me in tow. We dive into its blinding stream and hurtle into a vertical shaft or well. Plummeting to the bottom, we burst out in my city.

The ruins of stone pyramids stand beneath a towering lava dome. A glowing light is coming from somewhere in the city and illuminating the ancient metropolis. The gaping mouths of tunnels ring its sparkling lava walls.

The orb races into one of the tunnels and disappears. I long to follow it, but there is a flash and I am back on the blanket in Carlos's backyard staring at the mules in his corral and thinking they are the most beautiful, intelligent creatures I have ever seen.

***

Carlos's ranch
January 14th, 2 a.m.

Despite Mateo's presence, Cyd and Alex's first meeting with Carlos was not going as well as they had hoped.

"He's alive then?" Cyd cried. "He's not dead?"

Carlos shook his head. "Ooh . . . I don't knooow."

"What do you mean, you don't know?" Alex demanded. "What happened after you got him stoned and he saw this orb thing?"

"We go this time to *volcán* Aguas Calientes and I run before Pachamama, she swallow me too. She angry, but Robert, he go down inside her anyway."

"How did *Pachamama* swallow Robert?" Cyd pleaded.

"There was terrible earthquake and she open her eye and Robert let her eat him."

"Then he's dead after all?" Mateo was almost in tears.

"Maybe, maybe not. I don't know."

"Take us there," Alex insisted.

Carlos stood squirming in indecision.

"Just show us the eye of *Pachamama*," Cyd urged. "Show us where Robert went. You don't have to do anything more than that."

"Carlos," Mateo begged, "we need a guide. Of course, we'll pay you, and you can come home the minute you take us to where Robert disappeared."

Carlos wrung his hands in fear.

"Carlos please," Cyd implored. "We have to find our friend. I think he's your friend, too. He may still be alive and in trouble."

"In trouble, *sí*," Carlos agreed.

"Then you'll take us?" Cyd said.

The Incan guide nodded reluctantly. "*Sí*, I show you her eye. But not if she opens it. Only if it is closed."

"I can have my Land Rover packed and ready to go by noon," Mateo said. "Will you be ready?"

"Oh, nooo," Carlos responded firmly.

"No?" Mateo challenged.

"Second time we go to Lascar we see Chinese following and watching us. Third time we go at night so Chinese they don't see. And not by car. Car have lights and make noise. Mules are silent and don't have lights."

"Láscar volcano is over forty miles from here and Aguas Caliente is three miles beyond that," Mateo argued. "You want to lead us across all that desert in the middle of the night on mules?"

Carlos nodded. "To where *Pachamama* live now."

"He's right about not wanting the Chinese to follow us," Alex said. "Carlos, can you be ready to go by tonight?"

"*Sí señor.*"

"Thank you," Cyd said, gratefully shaking his calloused hand. "*Gracias, gracias.*"

Chapter Nine

THE OASIS

January 14th

After meeting with Carlos in the middle of the night, Cyd and Alex went back to their hotel, got a few hours sleep, then spent the day buying supplies and stuffing them in their backpacks. Mateo picked them up at sunset and they drove back out to Carlos's ranch.

Four mules were saddled and waiting when they got there. Carlos took their gear and loaded it into panniers on either side of two pack mules. The tan and black animals stood patiently with their long ears pointing up while the boxes were then covered with canvas and lashed down.

"Mules," Mateo groaned.

"Mules!" Cyd cried in delight, picking the tallest one, making a little hop and vaulting into the saddle.

Alex smiled at Mateo's look of dismay. "When I first met Cyd," he recalled while helping the Chilean geologist struggle into the saddle, "I had to follow her on horseback over some of the most rugged mountains in Montana. Nearly killed me."

Carlos led them south from his ranch toward a horizon filled with mountains and volcanos. Darkness blanketed the desert and they rode in silence beneath its cover, four darkened figures on mule back silhouetted against a night sky bright with stars. Around them the vast and empty desert came alive with the tiny scratching sounds of rabbits and foxes and mice and birds foraging on a thousand busy feet. A pair of llama-like vicuñas, startled by the passing mule train, looked up and bounded soundlessly into the night.

The hours drug on. Near dawn the terrain dropped off in a sudden depression just ahead. A great hole, invisible in the dark, stood in their path like a black hole in the heavens that swallow stars. Carlos reined in overlooking the depression and Cyd started to ride past him.

"*Alto!*" Carlos cried, urgently raising his hand. "Stop!"

Cyd reigned in and looked around in alarm.

"You ride in there, you not come out," Carlos warned. "*Arena movediza!*"

"Quicksand," Mateo translated, coming up behind them in a state of exhaustion from the long ride.

"Quicksand," Cyd muttered under her breath. "Lovely."

"We camp here," Carlos instructed. "Tomorrow night we go around."

"Good idea," Alex sighed in relief.

They pitched their tents, hobbled the mules and Carlos made supper. No one spoke of Robert, but he was on everyone's mind. Some twenty miles away *volcán* Lascar clouded the morning sky with smoke. A little further east rose the dormant cone of Aguas Calientes. Their tents were like bread ovens in the desert sun. They tossed and turned all day, and after ten fitful hours crawled out of tents stiff, sore and unrested. The sun was setting as they ate a hasty meal and packed up their things. They mounted their mules, and Carlos led them safely around the sinkhole in the gathering darkness as an enormous moon rose in the sky.

The night passed slowly with the unusually bright moon lighting their way. Morning was still somewhere beyond the horizon when they passed beneath Lascar's smoking saddle. They were nearing the base of *volcán* Aguas Calientes when the moon began to turn from shades of white and gray to startling shades of red. Up ahead a small cluster of scrawny palm trees came into view in the crimson light.

Carlos pointed in relief. "Robert's mule still hobbled beside water-hole where I leave him."

Minutes later a small pond with a bubbling spring appeared. An unsaddled mule grazed contentedly on the abundant grass that grew around it. Behind the pond in silhouette rose the darkened slopes of the towering Andes.

"If he hasn't come back for his mule," Cyd said with forced optimism, "it means he's still up there on the mountain somewhere."

"And hopefully still alive," Alex added.

Cyd dismounted, flopped on her belly on the grassy bank and buried her face in the cooling water. "Heaven!" she exclaimed, turning her head to smile up at Alex. He squatted on his haunches beside her and splashed water on his face while their mules bent their necks to drink.

They made camp under the skinny, sparsely spaced palms in the light of the scarlet moon. Alex came up behind Cyd and put his arms around her waist.

"The moon!" she declared, looking up in wonder. "What's giving it that amazing color?"

He followed her gaze. The huge red ball was rapidly turning from burnt orange to the color of sangria wine.

Mateo overheard her question. "Total lunar eclipse," he said. "'Blood Moon' it's called."

"Blood Moon," Cyd repeated. "How absolutely beautiful."

Alex turned her to him. "Beautiful," he repeated, marveling at the beauty he saw in Cyd, not the moon. "Absolutely."

Behind them Carlos began to bark and howl like a dog while shaking his fists at moon. "The jaguar!" he cried. "He is eating moon! We must frighten him away before he turns and eats the earth!"

Alex was amused. "He wouldn't dare," he assured him. "*Pachamama* would run him off."

"Luna de sangre!" Carlos exclaimed. "Blood Moon is evil omen!"

Mateo, ever the erudite college professor whether anyone was listening or not, explained how during a total lunar eclipse the atmosphere bends the light and filters out all the colors except the red hues that are then reflected in the earth's shadow on the moon. "That's what turns its face from silvery white to copper."

As he was speaking, the ground began to shake and groan. An explosive boom shattered the stillness and threw them to their knees in the sand. The mules reared and screamed and kept on screaming as the shaking went on. Cyd held onto Alex with the copper taste of fear in her mouth. Somewhere behind them, like a disembodied voice in a foggy dream, Mateo was calmly explaining that earthquakes in this region are caused by the subduction of the Nazca Plate moving under the South American Plate.

"Make it stop!" Cyd cried in desperation.

Recent eruptions from Láscar's cone had ejected ballistic blocks of stone and thrown them in the direction of Aguas Calientes. The rocks lay in a great pile near the oasis where the earthquake was shaking them loose and sending them rattling down.

Cyd screamed and looked up. High on the slopes of Aguas Calientes beams of light, bright as the sun, were shooting out from the volcano and converging in a single beam that shot straight into the sky. She turned away to shield her eyes from the glare.

"El ojo de la Pachamama!" Carlos cried, pressing his palms together in frightened prayer. "The eye of *Pachamama!*"

Cyd squinted and looked again. The fading beam was withdrawing back into itself like a sword returning to its scabbard . . . and then went out. But she had seen it! It was far away, the intense light had washed out any detail making it impossible to pinpoint its exact location, but at least she now knew the general area on the immense volcano where Robert had disappeared.

Chapter Ten

VOLCÁN AGUAS CALIENTES

Robert's Journal
January 9th—The day before Cyd and Alex arrived in Chile

Native Americans, like myself, are supposed to know how to ride, but after a night of travel across the Atacama by mule my butt felt like I'd been sitting on a belt sander. Carlos and I reached the sinkhole at dawn and spent the day. That evening as night was falling we saddled up and continued our journey. At dawn of our second night, we arrived at the oasis at the base of Aguas Calientes. Its scattered palms and pool of cold, bubbling water were a welcome relief from the scorching desert heat.

I dozed off and on and crawled out of my tent as the setting sun was casting shadows across the desert floor. The brown and barren slopes of Aguas Calientes hovered high above me. If I wanted to make certain the Chinese couldn't see or follow us, we were going to have to climb in the dark. Carlos's determination not to abandon me at this point even though he was clearly frightened filled me with admiration.

We hobbled our mules beside the freshwater pond, and in the waning light I hoisted my monstrous pack onto my back. Carlos's pack was heavier than mine, but the rugged little man seemed to carry his with no effort at all.

We spent the night carefully picking our way over steep slopes littered with loose, slippery lava. Carlos was as surefooted as a mountain goat, but to me it felt like I was climbing on ball bearings. Near dawn I checked my altimeter in the light of my headlamp. It read fourteen thousand feet which meant we had gained six thousand feet in altitude overnight and the summit was still another six thousand feet straight up. Heat was no longer a problem here, but cold certainly was. I shivered and pulled on my parka.

We had reached the area where I had seen the light shooting out of the volcano in my peyote vision. We would make camp and come nightfall I would start my search for an anomaly in the steep terrain, some kind of irregularity or abnormality in the mountainside that might reveal an entrance to the volcano like the shaft I had seen the orb go down in my vision. Carlos waved me over to a saucer-like depression he had found in the lava. I joined him and saw that the concave hollow would shield us well from prying eyes below and keep us from rolling out and tumbling downhill while we slept, as well. I dropped my pack, lowered myself down and as I did, I brushed my hand against the rock. To my amazement, the lava here was smooth to the touch, not razor-sharp like it was everywhere else. Carlos had his little propane stove out and was beginning to boil water. Later on, we ate freeze-dried beef stew while watching the morning sun warm the desert below. The distant cones of countless dormant volcanos littered the landscape, and close by I could see the smoke rising from Lascar's saddle. The stink of sulphur coming from its vigorously degassing *fumaroles* combined with the fourteen thousand foot elevation was making it hard to breathe.

My attention drifted back to my immediate surroundings where I became suddenly aware that the hollow Carlos and I were sitting in was not the only one. I sat up quickly to take note. In all, I counted four more circles like ours that formed a larger circle roughly two hundred feet in diameter.

"My anomaly!" I shouted. "Carlos, we've found it! This is it!"

"What we find?" Carlos asked in alarm.

I had no answer to that. The seamless circle of depressions was a complete mystery. I was about to jump up and start exploring them when

61

I felt the mountain move under me. My heart raced, my mouth went dry, then the shaking suddenly stopped. My heart was still pounding when I realized I hadn't experienced one of my prophetic headaches. *How peculiar,* I thought. The shaking came again with a low-grade rumble that lasted a few seconds before stopping once more. A few miles away Lascar made a loud bang and I saw its saddle belch a great cloud of dirty black smoke.

"In my professional opinion," I told Carlos in a shaky voice, "our friendly neighbor over there is getting ready to blow her stack again."

"We wake up *Pachamama* from her sleeping!" Carlos cried, his eyes wide with fear.

"She probably just swallowed some lava that didn't agree with her," I assured him.

He apparently didn't appreciate my attempt at geologist humor because he looked like he was going to faint from fright.

The tremors ended as abruptly as they started. I leaned back against my pack and tried to slow my pulse. An hour later, I told myself that the event was over and was about to get up to begin my investigation of the indentations when a blazing headache doubled me over in pain. Massaging my temples in agony, an image flashed before me of the tectonic plates shifting somewhere off Chile's Pacific coast. Then the shaking began in earnest. Loose rock rattled down the slope from above like roof tiles from a falling building. I tried to stand and was thrown back down.

Oddly at that moment, I remembered that today was the day I was supposed to be in Santiago picking up Cyd and Alex at the airport. In my obsession over finding the source of the lights and my lost city, I had completely forgotten they were coming. Mortified to have neglected my friends, I hoped they had arrived safely, hoped I would live long enough to apologize and prayed they would forgive me.

The explosive shaking continued. Carlos was moaning softly nearby. Then something moved under my back and I sat up straight. The cup of lava I was in was shifting out from under me! I heaved myself to one side and with a mighty effort rolled out of the hollow. Clinging precariously to its rim, I saw Carlos do the same, then watched as a hole opened up and his backpack and mine fell through. One instant our gear was there, the next it was gone and I was staring down a circular shaft into a glowing abyss.

Carlos moaned louder as the shaking grew worse. I was shouting to him to hold on when a blinding light shot out of the hole. A beam as intense as the sun itself was suddenly burning my eyes. I turned away from the pain and caught a glimpse of the same light shooting out of the other four holes and washing out the detail of the terrain around me. Forcing my eyes to stay open, I watched as the five beams merged into one overhead, amplifying each other in a kind of exponential convergence of incredible intensity. Then it all went dark and I was blinded by pain.

The earthquake stopped. I rubbed my fists into my eye sockets and colored spots swam before me. I rubbed again and it only made it worse. My eyes were tearing badly when I saw the light began to fade. The five beams were slowly escaping back into their holes and the five apertures were beginning to close.

I panicked. If I let the hole before me close, I'd have no way of getting it open again and no way to investigate the light source. The mountain swam in my vision as I searched for anything I could use to jam in the opening. The hillside around me was littered with rocks and boulders that had shaken loose from above and rolled down. I put my arms around the closest one and tried to move it, but it was too heavy.

"Carlos!" I shouted. "Little help here!"

Terrified, he scrambled around the outside of the hole and grasped the rock from the other side. Together we heaved, moved it a few inches to the lip and rolled it over the side. The aperture closed on it with a terrible scraping and grinding of stone, then shuddered to a halt. We had managed to force it to stay open just as the others snapped shut, but for how long I didn't know.

The volcano had returned to its passive state—but Carlos was still moaning. I stared into the gaping hole I had wedged open with the rock and saw what appeared to be some sort of ladder that ran down into the shaft.

I laughed nervously at the magnitude of what I was facing, then I swallowed hard. *This is why I came*, I reminded myself. I'd found the access I was looking for, so what was I afraid of? *Everything*, I answered, *starting with death.*

Cautiously, I swung a leg over the side and put a tentative foot on the first rung of the ladder fearing it might be made of age-rotted wood that would crumble under my weight. It felt solid so I swung my other leg over, put my full weight on the crossbar and was relieved when it held. Glancing up, I saw Carlos watching me. His eyes were huge and his mouth was working open and closed, but nothing was coming out.

"You coming, or what?" I called.

My voice must have startled him out of his reverie because he turned and ran, fleeing down the mountainside in a mad scramble.

"Carlos, stop!" I yelled. "Come back!"

"I go now before *Pachamama*, she eat me, too," he wailed, slipping and sliding as he disappeared from sight.

I stood alone on the ladder watching the wind make little dancing swirls of dust on the barren slope around me, then looked down into a bottomless hole.

Chapter Eleven

THE LOST CITY

Robert's Journal
January 10th—The day Cyd and Alex arrived in Chile

I began my descent of the ladder fearing centuries of earthquakes had shaken it loose from its fastenings, but found it was still securely attached to the circular stone wall. The rungs were made of some kind of velvet-textured metal I had never seen or felt before, and they were three feet apart. After half an hour of lowering myself down on them, my arms felt like they were going to fall off—and there was still no sign of a bottom. I kept expecting it to get darker the further I went, but a soft white light lit my way. In my peyote dream I had followed the blue orb down a shaft like this. Was this the same one? Would I find my city at the bottom, or would I get trapped in here with no way out?

A thousand feet below where I started, I stepped off the last rung onto level ground. Looking up, the aperture I had forced open was a tiny pinpoint of light above me. It should have been cold and dank here, but it was quite warm. I quickly shed my high-altitude clothing and put on a t-shirt and shorts from my pack that lay with Carlos's at the bottom of the ladder.

The ladder well was obviously a light shaft. What else was it? An airshaft? An emergency exit? I was too nervous and excited to care. An extremely tall door was recessed into one wall. I hauled our two backpacks over to it, pushed it open, and drug them across the threshold. Outside, I straightened up, turned and stared in disbelief. This couldn't be!

I was on a bluff inside an enormous lava cavern. The mouths of tunnels ringed its sparkling black walls. Spread out below me on the floor of the cavern was an ancient city, my city, the one I had seen in my visions and my hallucination. A pulsing light was coming from somewhere in the distance and casting an eerie glow over towering, four-sided pyramids. Silence hung like a shroud, and I could hear my pulse pounding in my ears. I was seeing it, but I couldn't believe it.

Shouldering my backpack, I descended the slope and entered the city. Crumbling pyramids made of enormous stones lined the streets and towered hundreds of feet above me. Wide steps led up their sides to a succession of landings. Along the landings were rows of openings for doors and windows for what looked like apartments, and on top of the pyramids were flat plazas where other structures may have once stood. Staggered by the enormity of it, I continued on in the direction of the pulsing light.

Over the millennia, earthquakes had apparently taken their toll on the pyramids because the ground was littered with boulders the size of trucks and busses that had fallen down from their sides. The walls that were still standing were made of stones so huge it was impossible to imagine how the builders could have gotten them up the mountain, let alone fitted them together with paper-thin joints that followed the irregular lines of the stones with such precision.

I continued on down a canyon between two rows of pyramids filled with curiosity and anticipation. It was the discovery of a lifetime, and I still couldn't believe my eyes. The canyon ended, and I walked out onto a broad public plaza surrounded by even larger pyramids where my thrill of discovery faded and sadness came over me. Something tragic had happened here, a horrible calamity that still hung in the air like a silent scream. Then I saw what it was, and stood staring in horror.

The bleached bones of enormous humanoid-like skeletons, well preserved in the dry air, littered the plaza and the adjoining streets as far as I could see. Impossible as it seemed, the Chilean legend about giants that once lived in a volcano was likely true. Some of the dead had their huge heads bashed in while others had spears and arrows sticking out of their ribs. A massacre had happened here. The residents of this city had been overrun and slaughtered.

Badly shaken, I left the plaza and started down a wide avenue clogged with exotically shaped objects the size of delivery vans. Since they were abandoned in the street, and had enormous interior compartments, I assumed they must have been transportation devices of some kind. Laying inert on the pavers among them were long, oversized, sausage-shaped things with stubby handlebars and foot pegs that suggested they could have been motorcycles for giants to ride. Extending from the back end of both types of "vehicles" were two, fat, elongated glass tubes that reminded me of burnt-out florescent bulbs. Assuming these were in fact vehicles, where were the tires? Even an airplane needs landing gear. I walked over to one, peered inside and recoiled. Its operator lay dead behind some sort of instrument panel with a stone axe in his giant head and his skeletal mouth spread wide in a scream.

I hurried away feeling sick to my stomach. Further on, I came to a kind of central park that was run wild with long-dead trees and vines. I entered through a tall stone arch, and in the middle of the park found a freshwater lake that was the mirror image of the small round pond I had seen in my vision of the volcano's cone seven thousand feet above me. I dropped my pack beside the pool thinking I would camp here when I finished my explorations for the day, then walked on relieved not to be carrying all that weight.

Like any park, there were statues of dignitaries here and there. Approaching one that wasn't as deteriorated as the rest, I stood staring up.

He was a distinguished looking fellow, twenty feet tall at least, wearing a red lava cap that suggested rank or nobility. His head was half the size of his body with a huge square jaw, a long wide nose, and drooping ears. Long, slender arms hung at his sides. There was something familiar about him. I thought I'd seen statues like this before, but I couldn't think where. Were these the people Carlos called Gorgons? I remembered the name from my Greek mythology and wondered if the Greeks knew more than they were saying. The statue's gigantic head and narrow body certainly matched Carlos's description, and the skeletons in the streets confirmed its height, so I assumed I had met my first Gorgon.

I was leaving the park when I felt something watching me. I wheeled in time to see a shadow dart behind at tree. A rat? A mouse? Some hapless creature that had somehow found its way into the cavern? I walked on a little further and out of the corner of my eye saw the move-ment again. I turned, but there was nothing there. *Now you're seeing things*, I told myself in an attempt to calm my nerves.

The ghostly glow that lit the city was pulsing from somewhere just beyond the park and I made my way toward it. Rounding the corner of a pyramid, I came to a halt and stood gaping in shock.

A pair of gigantic cylinders rose a hundred feet or more in the air flickering with feeble light. They were identical to the smaller, depleted ones I had seen protruding from the back end of the "vehicles" in the streets, and reminded me of the enormous vacuum tubes in old radios. In the center of each cylinder was a black hole with thousands of lights like tiny suns rotating around it in a kind of death spiral. A circle of jagged lava pillars surrounded the entire installation looking like they had been erected as an anti-ram crash barrier.

Overwhelmed at the site of technology that was clearly not of this earth, I checked myself to make sure I wasn't still hallucinating. Had I found the thing I'd been obsessing over for so long? Was I staring at fusion in a bottle? Had the energy that powers the sun been somehow harnessed, captured in tubes, and made to run a city? If so, why weren't the cylinders blistering hot?

I approached one of the tubes and tentatively extended my hand intending to pull it back the moment I felt heat. Feeling none, I cautiously pressed my palm against its glass-like surface. The smooth, round tube was room temperature. Fusion supposedly involves millions of degrees of heat. How could something that hot be contained in a transparent cylinder that hadn't melted? *Cold fusion*, I thought? Science had thoroughly rejected the idea of fusing the nuclei of two atoms without employing unimaginable heat and pressure—but then again what does science know, it's only human.

Next to the cylinders was a large, awkward-looking apparatus that looked vaguely familiar. Looking more closely, I saw a drill rod that ran down into the ground and realized it was a pump jack of some kind, a head-bobbing grasshopper pump like the ones used on oil wells to draw oil from the ground. From its deteriorated condition—it resembled a piece of broken-down equipment abandoned in a scrap yard—it hadn't pumped anything in some time.

My incredulity turned to exhaustion, and I realized I hadn't slept in over twenty-four hours. Further exploration of the city would have to wait; I needed to get some rest. Returning to the park, I made camp by the lake. The limbs and branches of the tangled underbrush made poor kindling for a fire, and I had to keep stoking it because the old wood kept crumbling and turning to dust in my hands. I made a meal of smoked salmon and crackers while boiling water from the lake to drink. After supper my eyes grew heavy and I laid down on my sleeping bag looking up. The specks of glass in the dome of igneous rock overhead sparkled like fireflies in the light of the reactor. With all the excitement of my discovery I was afraid I couldn't sleep, but the minute I closed my eyes I was out.

***

I'm sleeping soundly. A blazing pain shoots through my head that doesn't wake me, an image of the blue orb flashes before me, and I realize I am having a hallucinatory flashback from the peyote. Pulsing intently, the orb hovers, beckoning me to follow. We fly out of the park, arrive at the towering reactor tubes and hover over the defunct pump jack next to them. The next instant the orb dives down the pump's motionless drill rod and I follow it underground.

In my hallucination, we come out on the banks of a sea where the ocean has retreated from the shore leaving the head of the drill rod stuck in the mud. Where once the rod had pumped water from the sea like a straw in a drink cup, the cup was now empty and the straw had nothing to suck.

The orb immediately streaks across the mudflats and out over what remains of the ocean. I race after it and together we fly over the green-glowing water. Out in the middle of the sea is a pair of drill rods three miles apart. We circled them, follow them up and burst out into the desert sun. Below, I see that one rod is attached to a grasshopper pumping brine into the drying beds of the Chinese lithium mine, and three miles away the other rod is pumping lithium-rich brine from the underground sea into the drying ponds that surround the American owned mine.

The orb streaks back to the lava cave where I'm sleeping and disappears into one of its tunnels. I am about to follow when I wake with a jolt.

***

I sat up on my sleeping bag with a racing heart. The Chinese and American mines were draining the ancient sea beneath the Atacama Desert of its hydrogen and lithium rich seawater just as Maria from the cantina had warned and just as Mateo and I suspected. The Gorgon's fusion reactor was sucking mud instead of the fuel it needed to run the city. Its light would soon go out, and the miracle of the Gorgon civilization would be extinguished with it.

Chapter Twelve

THE GRAVITYBIKE

Robert's Journal
January 11th

What was the blue orb? What did it do? Was it real, or was I losing my mind? It had shown me the city and how to find it, I reminded myself. Why would I doubt the reality of what it was showing me now?

I was pondering this while stoking my campfire, cooking bacon and drinking boiled black coffee that tasted almost as bitter as the peyote . . . when another peyote flashback hit me with a rush of frightening images.

***

Suddenly back in a dream state, I am following a Gorgon who is fleeing around the curves of a twisting lava tunnel clutching the basket-ball-size blue orb in his arms. Behind us as we run, I hear the sounds of battle and slaughter growing louder and closer by the minute. Up ahead I see a lighted chamber off to one side. We reach it and enter to find desperate Gorgons frantically hiding objects of great value in hollows carved in the lava walls. The chamber appears to be a makeshift vault for their most precious possessions, and the giants here look to be the last line of defense against the theft and destruction of their treasures.

My giant running companion removes a block of lava from a wall revealing a darkened hole behind it, inserts the orb and quickly replaces the block to hide it. Just as he does a mob of howling savages armed with axes and spears swarm the chamber. A feathered shaft pierces the back of the orb's protector and the giant falls dead on the ground.

***

The smell of burning bacon brought me to my senses, and I was back in my camp by the lake trying to rescue my breakfast from the fire.

I'm not losing my mind, I thought excitedly. *The orb exists and it wants me to find it!* I still had no idea what purpose it served. All I knew was it was calling to me—and that it hadn't bothered to show me which cave it was in.

I emptied my backpack and refilled it with only the essentials: my small pick and hammer for taking samples, my headlamp for searching in the dark, a drinking bottle full of boiled water, jerky and protein bars. My compass didn't work inside the cavern, so I left that behind along with the rest of my gear. The only other thing I added was my journal which I always keep with me for recording my findings, drawings and observations, as well as the things science can't explain like my dreams and hallucinations.

I was heading out of the park to begin my search of the tunnels when once again I saw movement in the trees. Startled, I turned and got a better look at it this time. It was a long-backed creature the size of a large dog. Feral, no doubt. I just hoped it didn't have fangs and wasn't hungry.

Exiting the park, I glanced back anxiously before heading down one of the broad avenues between a row of crumbling pyramids. The scientific and archeological communities would have a field day studying this place once they heard about it. Half an hour later, I reached the enormous lava wall that enclosed the cave, mounted the ledge that ringed the city and stood looking in confusion at the endless tunnel openings that ringed the cavern in all directions.

Picking one at random, I entered and was plunged into immediate darkness before thinking to switch on my headlamp. Tunnel walls of igneous glass glistened in the beam of my light. I hadn't gone far before my hands were full of tiny cuts from trying to steady myself on the sharp rock. After hours of hiking, I came to a gaping crevasse and almost fell in. The lava tunnel had come to an abrupt end and I had seen nothing that remotely resembled the chamber I had seen in my peyote flashback. I'd wasted a whole day going down the wrong damn tunnel. How many more would I have to explore before I found the right one? I retraced my steps and arrived back at my campsite frustrated and exhausted.

The stillness of the cavern and the dim light pulsing from the fusion tubes were oppressive. I crawled into my sleeping bag that night wishing I had something to ride instead of having to walk the tunnels. At this rate, it was going to take approximately forever to find what I was looking for.

Next morning, I was drinking a cup of my awful coffee and eating a piece of beef jerky while preparing to resume my search when I felt eyes on my back. Spinning around, I saw an animal of some kind hovering close by—and by hovering, I mean it wasn't touching the ground! I backed away groping for something to use as a weapon when I saw it was as frightened of me as I was of it. The creature darted into the brambles and poked its nose back out. I called to it in a coaxing manner and it slowly emerged, hovering shyly.

The remainder of my stick of beef jerky was still in my hand. Thinking the poor thing must be hungry, I held the piece of dried meat out to it, but it didn't respond. It was then that I saw it wasn't an animal or a creature, but a smaller version of the oversized, sausage-shaped devices I'd seen lying dead in the streets that I assumed were conveyances meant for giants to ride. My guess was that this one had been designed for a youngster to ride, and from the looks of its flawless, unblemished condition, it had never been used. It had a pair of telescoping lenses for eyes, a nose like a headlight and a tiny round mouth that could have been for hearing, speaking, ventilation, or perhaps even airflow, it was impossible to tell. Given that it was animated and self-propelled, I decided it must be a robot.

Amazed, I approached it cautiously. It darted away and stopped. Feeling foolish talking to a robot, I told it I wasn't going to hurt it and saw it quiver in fear. Extending my open hand in a gesture of friendship, I watched as it crept forward, sniffed at my fingers and recoiled. I reached again, it came a little closer, and this time I was able to pet its head. It cringed at my touch, then seemed to relax a bit.

Upon closer examination, it's so-called handle bars and foot pegs looked like the stubby horns on a giraffe. Along its back was a long, low saddle. It's slender, metallic body moved with the supple flexibility of a living body and for some reason reminded me of the shocking discovery of scraps of alien alloy with amazing properties from an alleged downed UFO at a Roswell, New Mexico ranch in 1947. A pair of dimly glowing cylinders with spiraling black holes in the center protruded from its rear end looking like smaller versions of the big tubes in the fusion reactor in the power plaza in town. And it was definitely floating on air!

This can't be, I thought. *Even if this was a Gorgon's idea of a motorcycle, motorcycles can't fly!* The moment I thought it, an image popped into my mind of a solid black cube, perfectly smooth on all sides, floating in the air before me. It didn't explain anything; I was as baffled as ever. The next instant the image disappeared and a single word whispered softly through my mind like the sound of the ocean in a shell: *gravitybike.* Was that what this thing was called, a gravitybike? For a moment I was frightened. Where had the word come from? How was it that I heard it in English? Was the bike telepathic on top of everything else?

I reached for the handgrips and it recoiled again. Cautiously, I gripped one handle and put my other hand on the saddle. The gravitybike shivered in place. I tested my weight on one of the foot pegs, and when the bike didn't move, I carefully swung a leg over its back. Nothing happened, so I gently eased my weight down on the saddle. Still nothing. There were no controls or throttle that I could see. Planting my feet firmly on the ground, I tried pushing it forward, but it wouldn't budge.

"*Go!*" I ordered mentally, and visualized the machine moving forward.

The gravitybike shot out from under me and I found myself sitting on my butt on the ground. The bike stopped a few feet away and seemed to look back in confusion. I struggled to my feet muttering to myself. It obediently backed up and hovered beside me.

"Let's try this again, shall we?" I said aloud, swinging my leg back over the saddle, grasping the handgrip and gently lowering my weight. "*Slow ahead.*"

The gravitybike inched forward and came to a halt.

"I didn't say stop!"

The bike shot out from under me and once more I was sitting on my butt on the hard ground. Determined not to let it get the best of me, I scrambled to my feet in frustration. What was I doing wrong? It was definitely a mechanical device, yet it looked and acted like a living creature. The only thing I could conclude was that it had to be some form of highly advanced artificial intelligence. No other explanation seemed plausible.

The gravitybike floated back and nudged me gently in the ribs. I reached for it and it shied away. I reached again and again it shied. *Now it's just messing with me*, I thought. *A gravitybike's idea of a childish joke?* The word 'childish' stuck in my mind, and suddenly I realized the thing wasn't built for a child, it *was* a child. And from its feral behavior, an abandoned one at that! My heart went out to it and I decided it should have a name.

"Lucky?" I asked. *"It's a stroke of luck we found each another. Can I call you Lucky?"*

Its fusion tubes glowed a little brighter and it floated a little higher off the ground.

"Lucky it is, then."

It relaxed and I relaxed, and I realized my obsession over finding the orb was making us both nervous. *"I'll try and relax,"* I promised, swinging a leg over its back and settling into the saddle. *"Now slowly and carefully, what do you say we go spelunking?"*

Lucky lifted its head as if pleased with itself for finding a way to communicate, proud to finally have a job and be useful, and away we went gliding soundlessly toward the caves.

I was to never know exactly why Lucky was the last functioning gravitybike in Gorgon City. Maybe it had been built or conceived right before the massacre and never commissioned or put into use. Maybe with everyone dead and gone it had powered down, settled to the ground and remained inert for thousands of years until its sensors told it someone or something had at last entered the cavern. Whatever the reason, its fusion tubes were still functioning and it hadn't completely run out of fuel yet. I was grateful to have found it, and it was apparently grateful to have found me. I couldn't imagine how desolate and lonely it must have been for something with such a high degree of artificial intelligence to lie dormant and abandoned over the ages with nothing to do and no one for company.

Chapter Thirteen

BLOOD MOON

Robert's Journal
January 14th

Lucky carried me on its back for the next day while we searched several more caves with no success. It was an indefatigable companion, but I was growing impatient. Over time, endless earthquakes had caved in the walls and ceilings of many of the tunnels. Piles of rubble were everywhere slowing our progress and making our search more difficult. Finally, tired of breathing stale air and longing for a glimpse of the moon and stars instead of staring up at a lava ceiling, I asked it a question. "Lucky," I said out loud, "there must be a way out of here other than the ladder shaft. Do you happen to know if there's a main entrance to this place, a front door?"

It apparently understood me because it nodded eagerly and the next day we started off in a new direction. Arriving at the wall that enclosed the city, we entered the gaping mouth of a lava cave the size of a subway tunnel. Lucky's headlight automatically switched on, flooded the way ahead with light and moments later we were hurtling around the curves of a massive lava tunnel. Piles of rubble from ancient cave-ins were everywhere, but the tunnel was so large we were able to easily maneuver around them. Sparkling walls flashed by and gaping grottos came and went looking more and more like all the other caves we had been down. The monotony dampened my spirits, my hope faded and I gave Lucky a command to stop and turn around—which it ignored. We rounded the next bend and the cave came to an abrupt end.

Lucky sat hovering with its headlight illuminating a solid wall of lava. I got off to stretch my legs, walked up to the wall, put my hands flat against its surface and lowered my head in despair. As I did, I felt movement under my palms and the wall began to move. I jumped back and out of the corner of my eye saw that Lucky had darted behind me as the wall slid aside and disappeared into a cavity in the rock.

Crimson light flooded the cave. Stepping out through the opening into the fresh air and breathing a sigh of relief, I looked up at a huge moon the color of blood hanging low in the sky. The Incas, I recalled, considered a Blood Moon an evil omen. I hoped for my sake they were wrong.

Taking deep breaths of the fresh air, I rejoiced in having discovered what had to be the main entrance to the city. The doorway itself was massive. I couldn't imagine designing something that large that looked exactly like the side of the mountain and still opened and closed. As I stood there my head began to ache with a pain that grew worse by the second. *Earthquake headache,* I thought, and felt the ground begin to shake. At first it was just a tremor, then the shaking became violent and rocks and boulders started tumbling down the hillside from above.

I ducked back inside the cave to keep from being crushed, and Lucky and I clung together in fear as a landslide of lava rock thundered down outside the entrance. The upheaval was so fierce it felt like the volcano was going to split open and swallow us up. The enormous entrance door must have thought the same thing because it began to close as quickly as it could to seal off the city.

The powerful shaking continued as the portal slowly ground along its track, then came to an abrupt halt. The door strained mightily, backed up, tried again to close and finally gave up with a screeching groan. A giant boulder had rolled down onto the track and jammed the mechanism. Not even something as massive as the door could move a rock that large. The entrance was wedged open, and the Blood Moon was shining through the gap.

The shaking continued and threw me to the ground. I covered my head as a nearby inside wall began to crumble. Rocks came crashing down exposing an opening that looked like it had been sealed over with boulders from a previous earthquake.

The intense vibrations stopped, I let out a shaky breath, the dust settled and I found myself staring into a newly exposed chamber nearby the jammed entry door. It was too geometric in shape to be a natural cavity. Was this the storage vault I'd seen in my vision? I scrambled to my feet and hurried toward it with Lucky close on my heals, then stopped in horror at a ghastly site.

The bleached and twisted bones of giant skeletons lay piled on one another like the murdered bodies I'd seen in the streets. Spears and arrows protruded from their ribs. Some had their enormous skulls crushed in. I shuddered to think of the slaughter that had taken place here, then saw evidence that the fallen had fought the good fight. The bodies of a few of their attackers, easily distinguished by their diminutive size, sloping skulls and protruding jaws, lay about with Stone Age clubs still clutched in their hands. No doubt the savages had won by sheer force of numbers, but there was carnage on both sides. The Gorgons assigned to watch over their civilization's most precious possessions had not gone down without a fight.

Lucky followed me inside the chamber and I saw in its headlight that everything was covered in inches of dust. My feet kicked it up as I walked and I had to cover my mouth with my scarf to keep from choking. Judging from the empty shelves and vacant alcoves, the room had held many treasures. Everything was gone and the recesses in the lava were stripped bare. My heart sank thinking that the orb had been plundered or destroyed in the carnage, as well.

Overwhelmed by the magnitude of the tragedy that happened here, I looked on in sorrow. A feathered spear sticking out of one of the Gorgon skeletons across the room caught my eye and I gasped. It was the body of the fellow I'd seen running with the orb and hiding it here in the wall. I was making my way toward him, stepping over and around his fallen comrades, when an aftershock hit that was almost as big as the original earthquake.

Lucky panicked, bolted for the exit and managed to escape the chamber just as the violent shaking brought down the roof of the tunnel outside the entrance. I watched helplessly as tons of lava came crashing down, trapping me inside. Horrified, I realized Lucky must have been crushed in the rubble that sealed off the chamber.

The room was plunged into total darkness, then immediately relit in soft light. I turned and saw that the shaking had exposed a hole in the wall. Inside the hole, illuminating the chamber with a lovely blue glow, was my orb.

***

The Oasis
Night of January 15th

Down at the oasis at the base of *Volcán* Aguas Calientes, the aftershock that trapped Robert in the chamber felt like another earthquake as big as the last. Cyd and Alex, still kneeling in the sand, held tight to one another. Carlos, staring at the Blood Moon in wide-eyed terror, began grabbing up his gear to flee.

"Carlos, stop!" Alex shouted. "You can't go! We need you!"

"Jaguar is eating moon!" Carlos moaned. "He will eat us next!"

Mateo went to him, put a reassuring arm around his shoulders and pointed up. "Calm down my friend. Don't you see? *La luna* has defeated the jaguar once again. She has stopped her bleeding." The red hues on the lunar surface had in fact begun to fade in the morning light and the moon was returning to its normal shades of white and gray.

Carlos looked where Mateo was pointing and nodded nervously.

"So, you'll stay?" Alex urged. "At least for now?"

Carlos gave another unconvincing nod.

Exhausted, they crawled into their tents to try and get some rest, but found the unnerving effects of the earthquake combined with the stifling heat of the sun made sleep impossible. Cyd lay on her back staring up. "I can't climb that volcano in the dark, Alex. I don't even know if I can climb it in broad daylight."

He drew her to him and kissed her. "Sure, you can. I know you can."

"I mean it. I'm not going up there if I can't see where I'm going."

He sighed. "Then I guess we better get started. I just hope Carlos doesn't abandon us."

"We're lost if he does. I saw the general area where the light was coming from, but he's the only one who knows exactly where Robert disappeared."

Alex began rapidly pulling on his clothes. "Anything beats laying here worrying about it."

They crawled out of their tent to find Carlos pacing nervously up and down.

"Carlos," Alex ordered. "Pack up. We're starting the climb now."

"Oh, nooo . . ." the Incan moaned, shaking his head vigorously. "Not in daylight."

"If Señor Robert is still alive, he's in trouble," Alex insisted. "Don't you think he'd want us to find him as fast as possible?"

"Oh, *sí* . . ." Carlos agreed, then paused in confusion when he realized he had just agreed to something he didn't want to do.

"We can't find Robert without you," Cyd pleaded. "Please help us."

"Just show us the last place you saw him," Alex promised. "Then you can leave."

"Señor Robert, he be angry when he find out we go during day."

Mateo overheard them talking and stuck his head out of his tent. "What's all the noise about?"

"We're leaving," Cyd said. "Let's go."

"Nobody's following us anyway," Mateo agreed, scrambling to his feet. "A few hours could make all the difference if Robert is hurt or trapped somewhere."

Leaving their mules safely hobbled beside the spring, they started up the volcano in broad daylight with Carlos leading the way. The higher they went the steeper and colder it got. Cyd stopped to put on her parka. Pulling up the zipper, she thought about Robert. He was still alive, she knew it, she could feel it. But he was in trouble, she could sense that too. Shouldering her pack with renewed determination, she resumed her climb while cautioning herself to stay alert. The last thing she wanted to do was lose her footing on the unstable ground and go sliding back down the mountain on her backside.

The day drug on. To the west, the dark cloud above Lascar's smoking saddle was growing larger. Cyd scanned the lava-strewn landscape above her looking for the easiest line up. Her eyes roamed the mountain and came to rest on a section of the volcano off to one side that looked less sunburnt than the rest, an area that appeared to have been recently scraped off and exposed. Below that, she saw a ledge of some kind. Was that something behind it? An opening of some sort? She shaded her eyes with both hands and saw what looked like a long, vertical slit or cut in the mountain.

"Alex!" she called excitedly. "I think I see something!"

"What?" he called back. "Where?"

"Up there. Look! Under the landslide. It looks like an opening or an entrance with a ledge below it!"

He strained to see what she was pointing at. "You must have eyes like a hawk. I don't see . . . Wait, you're right! I see it too!"

Chapter Fourteen

REUNION

Hand over hand, foothold after foothold, Cyd, Alex, Carlos and Mateo climbed as quickly as they could. By the middle of the afternoon the ledge that Cyd had seen—the only thing left of an ancient road that had been cut into the mountain thousands of years ago—was still another five hundred feet above them. The going looked steeper and more dangerous from here, the sulphur smell coming from Lascar was making them nauseous, and the forty percent oxygen loss at fourteen thousand feet was making them lightheaded.

***

At the same time, five thousand feet below and twenty miles west back across the desert, a contingent of Chinese soldiers were trying desperately to pull their lead vehicle out of the sinkhole it had driven into. The job of getting the four-wheel drive truck out of the sucking sand was proving impossible. Frantic cries from the men stranded on top of the sinking vehicle filled the air . . . and suddenly stopped.

The remaining nineteen soldiers from the other trucks stood with their stern-faced Lt. Colonel watching helplessly as their lead truck sank into the soft, silty ground. Sand slowly sifted over the heads of the four panicked men clinging to the vehicle's roof. The heads disappeared, the desert closed over them and a hot desert wind moaned over their grave. It was as if they had never existed.

Lt. Colonel Chen Li, looking on indifferently, removed his wire-rimmed glasses, raised his field glasses and watched as four tiny figures scaled the big volcano next to the smoking one. The Lt. Colonel stood five feet tall, had a small, downturned mouth and narrow slits for eyes. His men didn't so much respect him as feared him.

***

Carlos led the way up the last five hundred feet of the steep slope and was the first over the ledge. Moments later Alex and Mateo pulled themselves up and reached back to help Cyd. The four of them stood breathing hard, staring in amazement at a towering lava door that had survived countless earthquakes by remaining closed, but now stood wedged open by a boulder that had fallen onto its track after Robert inadvertently opened it.

"Not there before," Carlos gasped. "Opening new."

Mateo rushed toward the rock jamming the door, scrambled over it and disappeared inside calling out Robert's name. His voice echoed down a cavernous lava tunnel that was partially blocked by a caved-in roof. "Robert, you in here?" he yelled. "Can you hear me? Call out!"

Cyd hurried after him, struggling and failing to scale the boulder. Alex gave her a boost, she made it over and disappeared inside as well. He followed, easily scaled the stone and sat straddling its top. Glancing back, he saw Carlos frozen in place.

"*Pachamama*, she try to trap us!" the Chilean Incan warned. "Don't go!"

Muffled sounds came from inside the cave. Alex turned and saw that Mateo had climbed a pile of rubble and was desperately throwing rocks aside. "He's in here, I can hear him!" he cried, his hands covered with small, red cuts from the razor-sharp lava. "Robert, I'm coming!"

Cyd struggled up onto the rubble beside Mateo, saw the cuts in his hands, pulled gloves from her pack and began helping him clear the debris.

"Carlos," Alex called back over his shoulder as he hurried to help. "Get your ass in here! We need you!"

Carlos made a pitiful groan and reluctantly scaled the boulder.

Thankfully, the others had brought gloves, as well. Pulling them on, they worked together for an hour throwing aside chunks of lava. At last, Robert's face appeared through a hole in the rocks cast in blue light. "I wasn't expecting visitors," he laughed. "You should have called."

Cyd smiled tearfully as she heaved a heavy stone aside. "If this isn't a good time, we can always come back."

"You're here," Robert sighed. "You might as well come in."

Minutes later the trapped geologist scrambled out of his would-be tomb holding a ten-inch diameter blue ball in his arms. "You're not going to believe what I found!" he announced excitedly, handing the ball to Cyd while he gulped the bottle of water he was offered.

Cyd stared in wonder at the dimly glowing orb she was holding. "What . . . what is it?"

Robert was about to answer when he saw Mateo. "What are you doing here?" he demanded. "I thought I told you not to come."

Mateo, overwhelmed with relief, smiled tearfully. "You're not the boss of me."

Robert hugged him. "How did you know where to find me?"

"Carlos guided us," Alex answered when he saw Mateo was too choked up to reply. "Now let's get out of here before the rest of this mountain comes down."

Cyd, cradling the orb in her arms, accidentally touched a spot on its exact south pole. Startled, she almost dropped it as three-dimensional images filled the air accompanied by impossibly complicated symbols.

"Found the 'on' button," she laughed nervously, moving her hands for a better grip. As she did, more characters, diagrams and formulas appeared out of nowhere, each more incomprehensible than the last.

Robert gently took the orb from her. "Best I can tell," he said, "what we have here is a vast collection of information. Depending on where and how you touch it, there seems to be no end to the facts and data it contains. It may even be a Gorgon version of Google for all I know: the accumulated knowledge and science of an advanced civilization all in one place."

"Those symbols look like a tangle of snakes," Alex observed. "They make no sense. How do you read it?"

"You don't," Robert replied sadly. "That's the problem. But wait until you see this!" He enthusiastically spread his fingers and touched the orb in several new places at once.

A towering hologram appeared before them that was an exact duplicate of the glowing reactor tubes in the city. Elaborate scientific formulas populated the air around it accompanied by more chaotic symbols.

"Unless I miss my guess," Robert went on reverently, "we could be looking at an explanation of the kind of fusion that powers the sun. If not, it's a kind of cold fusion. Either way, if these characters and formulas could somehow be deciphered, you might very well have an energy system so advanced it would change the face of civilization forever."

"Sun power," Alex said with a doctor's fascination for science. "Using the thing that powers the sun to power the world. Amazing."

Behind them, Carlos was backing away. "*Inti* make sun," he cried in a trembling voice, staring in fear at the orb and its projections. "*Inti* is sun. Only *Inti* can make it hot!"

"Who's *Inti*?" Cyd asked, watching anxiously as Carlos backed further away.

"The ancient Incan sun god," Mateo replied. "The Incas worship the sun."

"Carlos!" Robert called. "Stay! Don't go! If it weren't for you, they never would have found me and I'd still be buried along with the orb."

They watched helplessly as Carlos, appalled by what he had heard and terrified by what he had seen, fled the cave for the safety of the oasis as fast as he could run. Turning back, they saw that the orb had managed to slip out of Robert's hands and was floating rapidly back down the tunnel in the direction of the city.

"Where's it going?" Mateo cried.

"I think I know," Robert said, starting after it with a sad glance at the pile of rubble outside the chamber entrance where he assumed Lucky was buried. "You didn't see a funny looking motorcycle around any- where when you came in, did you?"

They looked at him in confusion.

"Never mind," Robert went on, his enthusiasm returning. "Come on! I've got so much to show you."

"Robert, no!" Cyd called. "This is a volcano. It could erupt at any minute like the one next door is trying to do."

"Aguas Calientes hasn't erupted in over ten thousand years," Robert called back confidently, his voice trailing off as he followed the orb around a curve in the tunnel and disappeared. "Discoveries like this don't happen every day. Get ready to be amazed . . ."

They looked at one another in hesitation, then one by one reluctantly trailed after him.

***

Robert pursued the orb through the streets of the ancient city and the others followed, aghast at the carnage that had befallen the skeletons they saw, wondering at the odd-looking "vehicles" abandoned in the streets, awed by the ruined pyramids that looked remarkably similar to the pyramids found all over South America that archeologists alleged were built by the Mayans. Passing the park where Robert had set up his camp, they arrived at the city's power plaza. Here, they stood staring in stunned silence, staggered by the sight of the glowing reactor, incredulous at Robert's enthusiastic account of what he knew about it. When he finished, they were speechless.

"I feel faint," Mateo moaned. "I'm weak in the knees."

The orb had arrived ahead of them and was hovering between the reactor's two lofty cylinders, suspended in midair as if by magnets.

"Why is it doing that?" Cyd asked, mesmerized by the orb's blue light that was pulsing off and on like a beating heart.

"My best guess is that the reactor is recharging the orb," Robert said. "After being sealed up in a wall for thousands of years, I imagine even a Gorgon battery can get run down."

Alex stood studying the faintly glowing cylinders. "You say the reactor runs on brine from an underground ocean?"

"An underground sea that's being drained dry as we speak," Robert confirmed.

"I don't get it," Cyd said. "What's brine got to do with fusion?"

"I was a physics major in college before switching to geology, so I know a little about it," Robert smiled, delighted to talk about science. "There may be more than one way, but the sun uses deuterium and tritium to create fusion. Both are heavy isotopes of hydrogen. Some say ordinary seawater contains enough hydrogen to generate fusion, but running a fusion reactor on seawater would be like running a race car on watered-down gas. You want fusion, you need rocket fuel, and that's where lithium-rich brine comes in."

"Robert, honey," Mateo said, taking Robert's hand. "Nobody knows what you're talking about."

"There's no other way to say it."

"Some things are better left unsaid."

"That big pump-looking thing next to the reactor that's stopped working," Alex said. "Is that why the reactor is almost out of fuel?"

"There are only two reasons why a perfectly good power plant stops running," Robert said. "Fuel contamination or fuel starvation. In this case, I'm guessing the reactor is running on empty."

"I've got another question," Cyd said. "If Chile has always had the kind of earthquakes it's having now, how is it possible this reactor is still standing? Why hasn't the shaking completely destroyed it by now?"

"Who knows?" Robert answered. "It could be that it's sitting on some pretty incredible shock absorbers."

"That still doesn't explain the lights that keep shooting out of the volcano every time there's an earthquake," Mateo said testily.

"I've given that a lot of thought," Robert said. "I think what you're seeing is a low fuel warning light like in a car when it's almost out of fuel."

"It's more than that," Cyd said sadly. "It feels like the lights are a cry for help. Like ET is trying to phone home."

It was a sobering thought.

"We've seen it," Mateo said nervously. "Now can we please get out of here before it's too late?"

"You go," Robert instructed. "The rest of you go with him. I'm not leaving without the orb, and it probably won't be recharged until morning."

Mateo was incensed. "You expect me to just leave you here? How can you say that?"

91

"Let them stay if they want," Alex said, taking Cyd's arm. "We're leaving. This place is dangerous."

"Not to mention depressing," Mateo added. "It's a graveyard."

"I didn't come all this way to find Robert only to leave him behind," Cyd said, pulling away. "Spending one night here won't kill me."

"How do you know?" Alex said.

Cyd glared at Robert. "If he won't leave in the morning, I'll drag him."

"We all go or we all stay," Alex sighed.

"Much appreciated," Robert smiled.

Cyd was privately relieved. She couldn't imagine trying to get down off the volcano in the dark. After climbing all day, rescuing Robert from the cave-in and being confronted with mysteries that confounded her senses, she was hungry and exhausted.

Robert led the way to the park. Walking along behind him down a path lined with dead trees, Cyd stopped to admire one of the Gorgon statues. "I've seen statues like this before," she said thoughtfully.

"Where at?" Alex asked.

She paused, thinking. "In photographs of the statues out on Easter Island!"

"You're right!" Robert exclaimed. "I thought they looked familiar."

"That's impossible," Mateo insisted.

"The world is full of impossible things," Robert said happily.

Baffled by all they had seen, they settled in around the little fire pit that Robert had built. Everyone produced something to eat from their pack that would ordinarily have seemed bland and uninteresting, but under the circumstances was delicious.

Alex sat eating his share of the peaches that Cyd brought. "Why do you suppose the Gorgons were so easily slaughtered?" he asked. "You would have thought they would have been better prepared to defend themselves."

"I don't think they knew how to fight," Robert said. "I think they were so evolved that violence was a foreign concept to them."

"That would explain why we didn't see any Gorgon weapons," Alex said thoughtfully.

"Furthermore," Robert added, "I'll bet anything they were taken by surprise, taken off guard, sucker punched by the invasion."

"What a tragedy," Cyd mused.

Robert was too excited over his discoveries to be depressed. "Imagine what mankind will do with fusion if a way can be found to translate the orb."

"Blow himself up?" Alex suggested.

"That's not funny," Cyd said.

"Who's being funny?"

After supper Robert and Mateo exchanged looks, picked up their sleeping bags and wandered off into the trees to be alone. Cyd and Alex, utterly exhausted, made themselves comfortable by the dying fire and were asleep before they knew it.

Early the next morning another earthquake struck. Heavy stones rattled down from the nearby pyramids and the ground in the park began to split and crack. Cyd and Alex sat up out of a sound sleep with pounding hearts. Lava dust was sifting down on their heads from the domed ceiling above. The violent shaking went on for nearly a minute before it stopped and they were able to stand. Looking around, they didn't see Robert or Mateo anywhere. Calling out, they received no answer.

"Robert must have gone back to the reactor to get his orb," Cyd said nervously. "Mateo must have gone with him."

"We need to go find them and get the hell out of here," Alex said.

The words were barely out of his mouth when a gunshot echoed through the cavern.

Cyd cried out in alarm.

"That sounded like it came from the direction of the reactor," Alex said, listening carefully. "Not good."

"Not good," Cyd repeated, running toward the sound with Alex right behind.

Chapter Fifteen

NO EXIT

January 17th

Cyd and Alex rounded the corner of a pyramid that bordered the power plaza and saw twenty Chinese soldiers who had captured Carlos in the desert fleeing the wrath of *Pachamama*. They had forced him to return to the volcano and show them the entrance, then moved through the streets of the city following the light from the fusion reactor while Cyd and Alex were still sleeping in the park. The soldiers were standing beneath the glowing fusion tubes holding Robert and Carlos at gunpoint. The orb was apparently fully charged because it had floated down from the reactor and into Robert's arms. Mateo lay on the ground clutching his leg and writhing in pain.

"You didn't have to shoot him!" Robert cried.

"He try to resist," Lt. Colonel Li replied indifferently, yanking the orb out of Robert's hands.

Alex rushed to the fallen Mateo and knelt to examine his wound.

Robert broke free of the soldiers trying to restrain him and fell to his knees beside them. "You're going to be alright," he promised his injured friend, looking up in desperation at Alex for confirmation. "It's nothing, nothing at all, isn't that right?"

Alex had Mateo's pant leg up and was inspecting a bleeding hole. "Bullet went straight through," he said, tearing off a piece of his shirt to bind the wound. Seeing Robert's frightened expression, he smiled reassuringly. "Bullet wounds are my specialty."

The Chinese Lt. Colonel hovered over them. "It is true what man with mules say about blue ball?" he demanded. "That ball explain how sun power work? Is old fool talking about fusion?"

"I tell them I don't know nothing!" Carlos pleaded desperately.

"But you *did* tell them, didn't you?" Cyd said, staring in horror at the guns that were pointed at her.

"All I say is blue ball make funny pictures in the air," Carlos lamented. "I tell them Robert say it explain what make sun hot, but it not matter what I say because Robert wrong and blue ball wrong. Ball not know how to make sun hot. Only *Inti* can make sun hot."

"Why would you say anything at all?" Cyd demanded, still staring at the guns.

"They threaten to hurt my mules!" Carlos cried, writhing in the pain of his betrayal. "Threaten to shoot them one at a time for every lie I tell."

"Last time ask question," Li warned. "Does blue ball explain fusion?"

"I have no idea what the ball does," Robert said, his attention on Mateo.

Li gestured to his men. "Shoot them both!"

"Alright, alright," Robert cried, falling across Mateo to shield him with his body. "It's true. The blue ball explains fusion. Just don't hurt him anymore!"

"It won't do you any good anyway," Mateo cried defiantly despite his pain. "Nobody can read what the ball says."

"Chinese linguists best in world. You perish and secret safe with us." Li turned to his men. "Shoot them all."

The soldiers pulled the three men to their feet and lined them up with Cyd and Carlos in front of one of the lava crash barrier pillars that circled the reactor. Mateo hung supported between Alex and Robert and Carlos was close to tears for what he had done.

"Carlos, it's okay," Cyd assured him despite her distraction. "We don't blame you."

Robert suddenly grabbed at his head in pain. "Earthquake coming," he warned. "Big one."

The next instant a powerful tremor hit. The reactor flickered and dimmed and the soldiers nearly panicked.

"You have the orb," Alex cried angrily, "why kill us?"

"Important only Chinese government know secret to fusion energy," Li replied, thinking his country would rule the world with what was in the orb, and he would be forever known as the man who made that possible.

Just then the full force of the earthquake struck. Everyone was thrown off balance and the reactor dimmed like it was about to go out.

"Probably broadcasting its warning light," Mateo observed through gritted teeth.

The terrified firing squad scattered as the ground split open before them exposing a rushing river of lava just beneath the surface.

"Lava is coming up from the tectonic plates moving under the whole region," Mateo went on in an effort to distract himself from his throbbing leg. "It's feeding Lascar's eruption a few miles away."

"In God's name," Cyd cried as the violent shaking continued, "let us out of here while there's still time!"

Li, clutching the orb triumphantly to his chest as he backed away, had a better idea. "Bind them and leave them," he ordered. "Let volcano finish the job."

One of the soldiers produced a coil of rope from his rucksack, and the five captives were quickly bound hand and foot. Mateo cried out as his feet were tied together

"You can't just leave us like this!" Alex yelled, struggling against his bonds.

"So sorry," the Lt. Colonel said with a curt bow before hurrying after his men. "We go now."

***

The platoon of Chinese soldiers ran through the ancient city in the direction of the tunnel that led to the volcano's jammed entry door. The Lt. Colonel hurried along with his men awkwardly cradling the orb. A tremendous jolt shook the ground, a stone the size of a house tumbled down from one of the pyramids and narrowly missed him. Ahead, he saw a jagged fissure opening up in the ground between where he stood and the tunnel.

The soldiers stopped short, staring in terror at a moat of raging lava that was growing wider by the second and spreading in both directions. It was still only a foot or two wide at this point. Lt. Colonel Li jumped it easily, then raced up the slope to the ledge and disappeared into the tunnel. The bravest of his men followed him over, but the cautious ones hesitated as the fracture widened further. One by one they made the leap and landed safely on the other side. The last of the soldiers stood staring as the crevasse grew beyond three feet. Terrified and trembling, he made his leap, caught his foot on the far side of the fissure and fell back screaming into the river of molten lava.

***

Back at the power plaza Cyd, Alex, Carlos, Robert and Mateo lay on the ground in front of the fusion reactor struggling desperately with the ropes that bound them. Mateo's wound had opened up again and was bleeding profusely.

"*Pachamama*, she trying to kill us," Carlos wailed, his eyes huge as the nearby volcano grew more active and chunks of lava began raining down on them from the ceiling. The heat from the lava rushing through the newly opened fissure was burning their lungs and making it hard to breathe.

"Alex!" Cyd cried. "Do something!"

"Little tied up at the moment," he grunted, squirming across the ground.

They watched as he struggled to sit up against the nearest crash barrier, then painfully worked his way up its side until he was standing. Moving his hands up and down behind his back, he began sawing at his rope. The razor-sharp lava cut at his wrists and blood ran down his fingers. Working the rope back and forth against the jagged rock, it slowly came apart and he finally broke free.

Cries of relief went up from the others as he hurried to untie the rope from his ankles. Minutes later they all were free. Alex quickly re-bound Mateo's bleeding leg and helped him to his feet. Robert took the injured man's other side and together they fled the plaza, supporting Mateo between them.

Cyd and Carlos led the way through the trembling streets of the city, then came to a terrified halt before a raging torrent of lava that lay between them and the exit tunnel. Since the Chinese soldiers had escaped, the crevasse had widened to thirty feet and spread in both directions to the furthest reaches of the cave. Behind them stones were falling from the crumbling pyramids and the lava in front of them was threatening to overflow its banks. The air was so hot their skin felt like it would blister.

Carlos fell to his knees in frightened prayer before the fissure. Robert, clutching Mateo to him, whispered goodbye.

Alex, staring in horror at the crimson river raging through the burning ditch before them, took Cyd in his arms to give her a few more moments of life. The ground was shaking, the ceiling was falling in and their skin felt like it would blister from the heat. Then Robert shouted. They turned and saw something long and round peeking out from between two pyramids. It streaked toward them, came to a halt beside Robert and hovered a foot off the ground enthusiastically wagged its body.

"Lucky!" Robert cried. "Where did you come from? I thought . . ."

The gravitybike's fusion tubes flickered weakly, and Robert got a sudden mental picture of Lucky fleeing down the lava tunnel as the ceiling came down behind it.

"Good for you," Robert shouted. "Now get out of here quick. Hot lava! Burn you to a crisp." A second scene appeared in his mind: the gravitybike was floating across the river of lava with him and Mateo on its back.

"Lucky, you're a genius!" he cried, grabbing Mateo up under the arms and helping him onto her saddle.

Cyd, Alex and Carlos watched in desperation as Robert climbed on behind Mateo, grabbed him around the waist and urged Lucky forward. It quivered, testing the weight of the two men on its back before rising effortlessly and gliding toward the burning ditch.

"Don't look down!" Robert shouted in Mateo's ear as the boiling lava passed beneath them. They coasted to a halt on the other side, Robert slid off and helped Mateo down. Lucky wheeled and dashed back across the crevasse to the cheers of the others.

Arriving safely, she hesitated, not knowing who to take first. Carlos pointed frantically to Cyd as the burning magma oozed over the lip of the trench.

Lucky flew to Cyd's side, she vaulted onto its back and shouted for Alex to jump on behind her. He swung a long leg over the saddle, grabbed Cyd around the waist and the bike shot forward. Moments later they were safely deposited on the other side of the torrent.

The lava was inches from Carlos's boots by the time Lucky returned to pick him up. He jumped on with a yell, fanned its rear end with his hat, and they shot across the burning ditch. Arriving to a wild celebration on the other side, Carlos jumped off and helped Robert get Mateo up the slope to the ledge.

Robert looked back and saw the gravitybike hovering at the bottom of the slope with lava rising toward it. "Lucky, get up here!" he called. "What are you afraid of?" An image appeared in his mind's eye of a child that was afraid to leave home, afraid of the outside world. "You're with us now," he yelled. "Come on!"

Lucky obediently glided up the slope to joined them, then floated at their heels as they ran for their lives down the tunnel. Behind them, the dying sounds of the burning city grew louder.

Chapter Sixteen

NO SUCH THING AS COINCIDENCE

Night of January 17th

A scrawny scattering of palms was illuminated in the headlights of a truck parked at the oasis below. Off to the west, boiling rivers of black and crimson lava streamed down Lascar's slopes and spilled out across the desert. The burning sky, reflected in the quiet pool of water, made it look like the oasis was on fire, but for the moment it was out of harms way.

"*Alto, alto!* (Stop, stop!)," Carlos cried, rushing down the last of the incline toward a man who was bending to remove the hobble from one of his mules. "I will do that!"

Cyd, nearing the bottom of the volcano with the others, gasped at the site of the truck.

"Chinese?" Alex asked, peering through the dark.

Cyd squinted. "It's a pickup. Civilian not military, I think."

"If the volcano didn't kill us," Alex sighed, resuming his descent, "I don't suppose they will."

A slender young woman wearing horn-rimmed glasses that were too big for her lovely face jumped out of the truck and rushed to help them as they stumbled ragged and exhausted into the headlights. Alex and Robert lowered Mateo carefully to the ground as another object appeared behind them. The young woman made a startled cry as the strange, cylindrical-shaped thing floated into the light and dropped heavily to the ground.

"Lucky!" Robert cried, rushing to its side. "What is it?"

The gravitybike's fading fusion tubes blinked weakly and dimmed.

"Poor thing is dying," the woman observed sadly. "I can feel it."

Robert knelt, stroking Lucky's limp head. "It's almost out of fuel."

Cyd was studying the woman closely. "Where do I know you from?" she asked.

The woman thought a moment and smiled in recognition. "We met in Israel."

"Jerusalem!" Cyd cried. "Last time I saw the two of you we were in the courtyard of a church and you had just started a riot between a bunch of monks."

A tall, broad-shouldered man with sun-bleached hair and a ruddy complexion burned red from the sun came into the light extending his hand with a crooked grin. "Long time, Alex."

Alex was stunned. "Sam Sorini? Nikki Perez? How in God's name . . .?" He turned excitedly to Cyd. "These are the people I told you about that I was trapped with for three weeks in that church in Bethlehem while you were fighting for your life."

"As guests of the Palestinian rebels as I recall," Sam added.

"You look fantastic," Nikki said, hugging Cyd affectionately. "Alex told us you had been badly hurt in a bomb explosion. How are you?"

"Never better," Cyd replied, still in shock at finding them here. "What a coincidence."

"No such thing as coincidence," Nikki smiled. "If it's in your life, you put it there." She glanced up absently at the volcano Cyd had just descended. "I can't believe we're too late."

"Too late for what?" Robert asked, looking up suspiciously from tending to Mateo.

Nikki offered him her hand. "Nikki," she smiled. "Sam and I are treasure hunters."

Robert, in agony over Mateo and now Lucky, ignored the greeting. "If the treasure you're hunting is the orb," he said, "we had it and we lost it. The Chinese stole it."

Nikki was confused. "You mean the Sphere of Knowledge? The Chinese have it?"

Cyd was even more confused. "What are you saying? You know about the orb? That's impossible."

"Not as impossible as you might think," Nikki began as another eruption shook the ground and they struggled to keep their balance.

"Talk later," Sam ordered. "Everyone in the truck before it's too late."

"He's right," Alex said, helping Mateo to his feet. "What's more, I need to get this man to a hospital and get him pumped full of antibiotics before he loses his leg."

"I'll tell you everything on the way," Nikki promised Cyd as they climbed into the back seat of the pickup together. "It's a long story."

Mateo's leg was swollen so badly he couldn't bend it. Robert and Alex lifted him into the bed of the truck and settled him on top of a pile of camping gear. Then just as gently they picked up Lucky's depleted body and loaded it in beside Mateo.

Carlos was tacking up his mules for the journey home. Alex brought him some food and water that Sam handed him from the back of the truck. "You going to be okay alone?" he asked the Incan guide.

"We be along, my mules and me," Carlos grinned. "*No problema.*"

Alex nodded, wished him luck and hurried back to the truck where he jumped in the passenger's seat beside Sam who was already behind the wheel. Robert climbed into the bed to hold Mateo in his lap for the long ride to town. Once he was settled, Lucky lifted its head in exhaustion and rested it on Robert's leg.

Sam navigated the desert in the dark trying desperately not to get stuck in a sand dune while giving the rivers of magma oozing down the erupting volcano a wide berth.

Cyd turned to Nikki. "Okay," she said, "let's have it. What did you mean about a Sphere? You can't possibly mean the orb we found. That's been buried for thousands of years."

"The Gorgons called it the Sphere of Knowledge," Nikki said. "It explains how their technology works, how fusion works."

Cyd was incredulous. "No way."

"The good news," Nikki went on happily, "is we know where there's a library that can translate it."

"A library that can . . .?"

"What library?" Alex challenged from the front seat. "Where?"

"Easter Island."

"Easter Island," Cyd repeated slowly.

Alex was incensed. "Even if what you're saying is true, which I doubt, what good is it? The Chinese probably have the orb or Sphere or whatever you call it halfway to China by now."

Nikki cocked her head as if listening to a distant voice. "I doubt that," she said.

"Alex, I believe her," Cyd insisted gently.

"It's all going to be okay," Nikki assured them. "Trust me."

"Before I trust either of you," Alex said, "I want answers. Sam, what are you two doing here? How is it you know so much about something nobody knows anything about and that we nearly got killed finding?"

"Let her tell it," Sam shrugged. "It's her story."

Nikki pushed her glasses back on her nose and smiled. "It all started in the Bahamas when China laid claim to the treasure we spent the last year salvaging."

Cyd and Alex sat spellbound as Sam drove through the night under a sky full of falling stars and Nikki told her amazing tale.

Chapter Seventeen

NEW PROVIDENCE ISLAND, BAHAMAS

December 17ᵗʰ—One month earlier

Hundreds of white, five-gallon plastic buckets sat out on the tarmac at Nassau's Lynden Pindling International Airport. The buckets weighed a total of seventeen tons which explained why China had sent two cargo planes to pick them up instead of just one. Armed Chinese soldiers were lifting the heavy buckets onto conveyer belts that were loading them into the bellies of the planes.

Sam Sorini stood watching from behind a cyclone security fence between the parking lot and the tarmac, his knuckles white from gripping the wire. The chiseled features in his deeply tanned face showed no expression. His ice blue eyes alone betrayed his anger.

The soldiers worked all morning as the sun moved higher in the sky and the day grew hotter. By noon they were soaked in sweat and still had not loaded all the buckets. Sam had seen enough. He turned on his heel and marched back to his shore truck that was parked in a space behind him. A tall, silent, razor-thin black man with a badly scarred bald head sat erect behind the wheel. Sam got in the passenger side, the black man started the engine and they drove off.

It was a fifteen-minute drive from the airport to Harry's Harbor Bar where crews from the commercial boats that operated out of Nassau liked to drink. Sam's truck pulled up in front of the bar and parked. He got out without a word to his driver and went in.

Harry's was a working-man's bar, not too fancy, not too clean, much loved for its "it-is-what-it-is" atmosphere. Colorful walls rioted in Bahamian headdresses from past Junkanoo festivals, an enormous sailfish hung over the bar, and soft breezes filled the place with the smell of the sea-washed decay that flowed in and out around the pilings that supported the building.

The tavern was crowded now that the workday had ended. Sam sat alone at the end of the bar where he had been all afternoon, staring into a row of empty shot glasses. His efforts to get drunk had failed miserably. No amount of liquor could quell the pain of his loss. He was well known and well liked in this place; this was his bar. It was also well known that when he looked this angry, it was best to leave him alone.

A Scottish skipper named Leslie Fouler walked in with two burly, bearded, weather-beaten crewmen from his salvage ship *Hunter*. Leslie was as ruggedly built and badly maintained as his vessel with the battered, pushed-in face of an ex-prizefighter, although his fighting had all been done in bars. He spotted Sam at the end of the bar, smiled a cruel grin, walked over and stood behind him looking down at the back of his head.

"Looks like the famous Sorini luck has finally run out," the Scottish skipper taunted. "Crying in our beer, are we?"

Sam said nothing.

"Now you know how the rest of us feel coming up empty most of the time. This makes two in a row for you, doesn't it Sammy boy?"

Sam continued to stare into his shot glasses.

"First, he searches all over Israel for clues to a treasure ship that got sunk in Egypt, and in the process gets taken hostage in some crummy church. When he finally gets to Egypt, he finds out somebody beat him to it—by about a hundred years!" Leslie laughed his explosive laugh. Chagrined by Sam's lack of response, he went on. "Then he comes home, he does, and spends all his time and money bringing up half a billion in Chinese gold coin and bars from an ancient Spanish wreck that the courts turn around and hand back to China!" His laugh exploded again. "You must have really pissed somebody off, because I hear you didn't even get your ten percent finder's fee."

Sam motioned to the bartender for another shot and a gorgeous black girl wearing next to nothing poured it out with a friendly smile. "The Chinese bribed everybody connected with the case," he said quietly, nodding his thanks to the girl.

"I'd like to see you prove it," Leslie grinned.

"Me too."

Leslie's inability to get a rise out of Sam made him furious. "Never trust a man drinkin' alone, I say. Means he thinks he's too good to drink with us common folk."

Sam knocked back his shot, then slowly, deliberately, set the glass back down on the bar. "You could be right," he said.

"I know I'm right," Leslie bellowed, loud enough for the whole bar to hear. "Everybody here knows the high opinion you got of yourself!"

Glancing in the bar mirror, Sam saw Leslie reach out to put a hand on his shoulder and spin him around. "You don't want to do that," he threatened.

Just then a cheerful voice called out from the front door. "Sam, there you are!" A striking young woman with shining black hair that hung to her waist crossed the bar and gave him a big kiss on the cheek, then pushed back the horn-rimmed glasses that had slipped down her nose. "I've been looking all over for you."

Sam smiled for the first time that day. "Hello, sweetheart."

"Exciting news," she said in a rush. "We need to talk."

"Later."

"No, now. It can't wait."

"Well, well," the salvage skipper who had been baiting Sam grinned, 'if it ain't the famous treasure hunter's famous girlfriend."

"Hello, Leslie," the girl said guardedly.

"You know, Sam," Leslie went on, "this being your day for giving things up and all, maybe you should give up this sweet young thing here and let a real men have a go at her." He grabbed Nikki by the arm and she squealed in pain. "Better yet, why don't I just take her."

Sam's fist lashed out so quickly nobody saw it coming, not Nikki and certainly not Leslie. His battered face got a facelift as he was lifted a foot off the floor and sent flying across the room backward. Four commercial fishermen were having drinks at a table and he landed in their midst. The fishermen grabbed their glasses and leaned back in time to see their table collapse under Leslie's weight, then stared in dismay at his body lying unconscious at their feet in the middle of a pile of splintered wood.

When Leslie fell, one of his crew members came up behind Sam, threw a meaty arm around his neck and began choking him out. His other crewman hit him in the stomach, knocking the wind out of him.

"Little help here," Sam gasped, struggling for breath.

Nikki picked up a beer bottle from the bar and in rather dainty fashion broke it over the head of the man who was choking him. Fascinated at the result, she watched with absent curiosity as her victim dropped like a stone. Sam staggered back, fighting for breath, as Leslie's second crewman pulled a fish knife and stepped in to finish what his mate could not.

The spear-shaped black man with the scarred head who drove Sam to the bar had been standing stoically against the wall all afternoon keeping a watchful eye on his boss. He stepped forward, broke the knife-wielding man's arm over his knee and lifted him above his head like he was going to slam him to the floor and break the rest of the bones in his body.

"Tashtego, no!" Nikki cried with an anxious smile. "Put him down, please."

Tashtego obediently let the man drop. Hitting the floor with a thud, he clutched at his arm and crawled away in pain. The African took Sam under the arms and helped him to straighten up. Leslie groaned from his resting place in the middle of the broken table and shook himself awake. Sam shook Tashtego off and stepped in to put Leslie back to sleep.

Nikki put a restraining hand on his arm, her voice gentle and sweet. "I really do have something important to tell you, Sam." She motioned to Tashtego to help her, and together they guided him toward the door. "Can we go and get something to eat? I'm simply starved."

***

A few doors further down the waterfront from Harry's Harbor Bar was Bahama Betty's gaily painted eating establishment. The restaurant sat at a slight tilt on sinking pilings and advertised "All Day Fish Fry" in faded letters.

Sam and Nikki sat at a table with a view of the busy harbor and Paradise Island beyond. Tashtego took up a position on the deck outside and stood like an ebony statue watching them through the window seemingly without looking at them.

"Sam," Nikki implored, "tell Tashtego to come in and join us."

"He says he isn't hungry."

"He's never hungry. When does he eat?"

"I have no idea."

Their meal came. Nikki took off her glasses and fell on her fried fish and chips like she hadn't eaten in a week. She was a beautiful woman with the smallest of gaps between her two front teeth that on her looked adorable. Despite her remarkable looks, she rarely gave her appearance any thought. Were it not for Sam, she probably wouldn't have thought about it at all. He was always telling her how pretty she was, so she made an effort to look nice for him, but her efforts were out of love, not vanity. Her indifference to the impression she made on others made ignoring her impossible. Heads turned when she passed even though she looked like an awkward schoolgirl carrying her schoolbooks when she walked. Of all her physical attributes, perhaps the most arresting were her eyes. They were the color of amber, halfway between yellow and orange, and looked to be lit from within. Nikki was twenty-five, ten years younger than Sam, but in many ways was so much older.

Sam hadn't touched his own food. He sat watching Nikki eat, amused and entertained as always by the mere sight of her. How she maintained her slender figure he couldn't imagine; she ate anything that was put in front of her and inhaled it like the suction hose on his dredging rig. When she had cleaned her plate, she glanced enviously at Sam's. He pushed his fish toward her, she took a big drink of beer and carried on.

Of all the people in the world, Nikki was one of the few he liked and trusted. When she wasn't frustrating him with her insights, she was surprising him with their accuracy—and he wasn't easily surprised.

"You want more?" he asked in fascination as the last of the fish disappeared from the plate he had given her.

She shook her head and daintily wiped her mouth. "I'm on a diet," she sighed.

"So, what was it you were so anxious to tell me?"

She hesitated. "I don't know how to say this, Sam. I'm sorry. I'm always so careful about these things."

His smile faded. "Everybody makes mistakes. What's wrong?"

"It's not like I didn't know this could happen. It happens to other girls all the time."

He was starting to get worried. "Other girls?"

"Missing things, missing something."

112

Now he was really worried. "What are you saying? Did you miss your period?" She looked startled and he hurried on. "Nikki, it's alright. I know we never talked about it. I never saw myself as a father, but if this is what you want, if you want to keep it . . ."

"What? No!" she laughed. "I'm not pregnant. Whatever gave you that idea?"

He forced a smile. "I can't imagine."

"Well, I'm not, okay? I'm not ready for kids any more than you are. What I missed in all those months we were diving on the *San Fernando* was the most valuable thing in the whole wreck. The most important treasure on that ship is still down there."

"Gold?" he asked with growing interest. "Silver?"

"Nothing like that."

"Nothing like that," he repeated.

"A box. A trunk of some kind."

"Diamonds, emeralds, jewels then?" Now he was really excited.

She shook her head and looked off, smiling at something only she could see. "More like a seaman's chest."

He let out a long breath. "That ought to bring a tidy sum."

"Sam, you know I know things."

"Let me get this straight. No gold, no silver, no jewels. Something more valuable? Have you finally lost your mind?"

She shrugged and put her glasses back on. "All I know is we have to find it."

"Nikki, I vacuumed every inch of that ocean floor. There isn't anything left down there but sand and rocks."

"It's not *in* the wreck," she said. "It's *under* it."

"Under it," he repeated slowly. "Under what?

"The keel, actually."

"It can't be under the keel."

"Why not?"

"Because ships don't carry things *under* their keel."

She smiled patiently. "I think what happened is when the ship went aground and broke up on that reef a lot of things went overboard. This trunk or chest or whatever it is settled to the bottom and the ship settled on top of it."

He blew out his cheeks. "Do you have any idea how much work it's going to be to move that keel? If they catch us back diving on that ship we could go to jail. Somebody said they're actually trying to make it an archaeological site."

"In a hundred and fifty feet of water?" she scoffed. "That ought to attract a lot of snorkelers. Sam, my intuition tells me there's something down there, something we have to find."

He sighed again. They had an agreement: when she reminded him of her intuition, he had agreed to trust her. And he did; he had never known her to be wrong when she put it that way. It was just that so often the things she came up with made no sense at all.

Nikki went on confidently. "Whatever is in that box is likely more valuable and important than all the treasure the Chinese confiscated from us. The only thing I don't know is how we are going to be able to go after it. Aren't we pretty much broke?"

He smiled in the way that always made her feel safe and secure.

"Are you saying we're not broke?" she asked expectantly.

Sam fished in his pocket, pulled out a canvas bag and dropped it on the table with a heavy clank.

Nikki stared. "You didn't!" She picked up the bag, untied the drawstring, peered inside and gasped. "You did!"

His smile broadened. "I figured the least China could do was pay our expenses. I brought up so much gold from that wreck, they wouldn't know the difference if I'd pocketed half a ton."

"This is more than enough," she cried delightedly, fingering the contents of the bag. "Do we melt them down, or can you cash them in here?

"I know a coin dealer in Miami who will take them off my hands—at a hefty discount."

"So, when do we go? I can't wait to find out what's in the chest."

"I don't know if I can even find it," he sighed.

"You'll find it," she laughed gaily, rescuing her glasses from falling off her nose. "I know you will."

Chapter Eighteen

THE TREASURE OF INAGUA ISLAND

December 20th

Cotton-ball clouds floated in a baby blue sky under a blazing hot sun. The *Fortuna Explorer*, Sam and Nikki's two-hundred-and-forty-foot freighter that he had converted to a deep-sea salvage and recovery vessel, dropped anchor just outside the mile-wide reef that completely encircled Little Inagua Island. The impassable barrier was the reason the island's thirty square miles of low, sandy terrain was inhabited exclusively by herds of feral donkeys and goats living in peaceful harmony with a countless number of brilliantly pink West Indian flamingos.

Five miles south of Little Inagua was Grand Inagua Island where another eighty thousand or so of the long legged, skinny necked flamingos flourished in flocks of pink-hued glory. Fifty-five miles further south from there lay the eastern tip of Cuba, making Grand Inagua the southernmost island in the Bahamian chain. Some would argue that its location inside the Bermuda Triangle explained the many documented treasure-laden ships destroyed on Inaguan reefs over the centuries. Whatever the case, the wreck of the eighteenth century *Galeón San Fernando* was one of them. The Spanish treasure ship, laden with Chinese gold worth nearly half a billion in today's dollars that Sam and Nikki had recovered, lay just off Little Inagua where they now were anchored. It was here, Nikki insisted, they would find the mysterious seaman's chest she had envisioned.

The *Fortuna Explorer* was nothing much to look at unless one had an appreciation for discarded machinery and equipment that had been salvaged from other wrecks and made to work again like new. Sam's one great talent, apart from his tenacious passion for sunken treasure and his boundless love of Nikki, was in being one of those remarkable men who can fix almost anything by doing little more than laying their hands on it.

A huge skeletal dredging rig hung off the stern of his boat, salvaged off another ship that had sat abandoned in a backwater slew for years. The two-man submersible submarine lashed to davits on the foredeck that Tashtego and Sam's two other Bahamian crewmen were just now hooking to the hoist cable on the cargo boom had been bought for scrap at an auction in Miami.

The underwater exploration craft was as dented and beat up as a coffee can that had been kicked down the road. Rust spots showed through where the bright yellow paint had chipped off. A pair of claws extended from the front, round ports for two observers bulged out above the claws, jump seats for two additional passengers were crammed into the back, and a big cage enclosed the hydraulic thruster in the rear. At first glance, the sub looked like a bug-eyed yellow crab. Water tight and certified to a depth of a thousand feet, nobody in their right mind would take it below five hundred feet in its current condition. The autonomy of the "one atmosphere" submersible was rated at eight hours, meaning the interior cabin pressure would stay the same down to a thousand feet, and it could supposedly stay underwater for eight hours without coming up. In reality, its banks of heavy-duty marine batteries went weak after four hours, and its oxygen supply ran out after six. Sam had named the craft *The Crab* and, despite its limitations, regarded it with pride and affection.

Tashtego and one of the crewmen guided *Crab* as it splashed into the water while the other crewman operated the hoist. Sam climbed down a boarding ladder and lowered himself into the hatch. Looking up, he saw Nikki watching expectantly from the deck.

"You coming, or what?" he called.

"You know that thing scares me to death," she called back.

He grinned his crooked grin. "No worries, love."

The grin faded as he closed the hatch and secured the lugs from the inside. He had a bad feeling about this. Settling himself at the controls he radioed Tashtego to release the hoist hook, then flooded the tanks. *Crab* sunk like a lead fishing weight. Crystal clear water rushed past the ports, colorful fish swam by and a green sea turtle looked in before banking away.

Sam had anchored a mile or so from the actual wreck so he could deny he was diving on it, if anyone asked. Once in the water, it took him twenty minutes to get there maneuvering past the steep, ragged cliffs of the reef. Visibility was nearly a hundred feet, but the wreck lay at a hundred and fifty feet so he had no visual reference. Fortunately, the locator beacon he left at the site was still working and it took him straight to it.

Switching on his floods in the semi-darkness, the skeletal remains of the *Galeón San Fernando* came into view resting on the edge of a cliff that fell away into oblivion. After almost three hundred years underwater, the heavy timbers of the ship's hull sat in the sand looking like the ribcage of a dead cow.

He hovered a moment, staring at the site where he had spent countless hours salvaging riches that were going to buy him a new salvage boat equipped with the latest technology and Nikki the home in the islands she had always wanted. That was gone now, the treasure, not the dream. His anger had dissipated as well, leaving only his sadness at being robbed by a judge he was convinced the Chinese had bribed.

He shook himself out of his reverie, extended *Crab's* claws, flexed the pinchers and moved in to go to work. Lifting the heavy keel wasn't going to be easy. The three-decked galleon was one-hundred-and-sixty-feet long with a forty-five-foot beam and had weighed five hundred ton when afloat. Its four masts with their six sails measuring almost eleven thousand square feet had disintegrated, but it's sixty-four bronze cannons still lay scattered in the sand like discarded cigars butts. He had thought about salvaging them, but abandoned the idea when he realized China would only confiscate them too. Records from the time indicated that the *Galeón San Fernando* was weighted down and leaking badly when a hurricane drove it aground on the reef. He tried to imagine what it was like trying to keep a ship with the maneuverability of a dead whale off the rocks.

Working *Crab's* claws under the keel, he began to pull and push and tug. It was like trying to lift the reef itself off the bottom. There was a loud cracking sound and a sudden release. The front fifty feet of keel broke off and tumbled over the cliff taking the first fifty feet of the rib cage with it.

Clouds of silt and sand clouded the water and for several long minutes he couldn't see a thing. The sediment filtered down, the water slowly cleared and he found himself staring into the trench where the front third of the keel had been. There was absolutely nothing in it, just more sand.

He sighed and maneuvered *Crab* into position to start trying to lift the next section. Applying such heavy pressure to the claws put a desperate strain on the batteries. He had been working for an hour when his floodlights flickered and started to dim. The rotten midsection of the ship broke loose and tumbled into the abyss. When the water cleared, he glided along the trench looking for anything that resembled a trunk and again he saw nothing. Continuing on to the stern, he began working on the final third of the keel. If Nikki's seaman's chest wasn't here, he had no idea where else to look.

The back part of the keel was closest to the cliff, and as he shoved and tugged, it inched even closer. This section was heavier than the other two because of the lofty stern that was attached. Struggling to move it, he was startled when it suddenly gave way and fell into the trench, spiraling down and disappearing into the dark. One of *Crab's* claws hung up on a curved elbow that secured the keel to the stern and started to take him with it over the cliff. Jamming the controls frantically back and forth, he managed to free himself just as the final part of the keel went thundering out of sight.

He hovered the sub, waiting impatiently for the dirt and debris to clear. Checking his instruments, he saw his oxygen and battery gauges were dangerously low. He should be on his way to the surface by now. Gradually, his floodlights pierced the murky gloom and there it was, sitting on the cliff, teetering on the edge: a large seaman's trunk with oxidized bronzed straps riveted to its oak planking that were holding it together, and a rusted antique lock securing the lid.

Sam let out an excited whoop and extended *Crab's* claws to snag it. The pinchers eased around either side of the chest, but it skidded away and hung dangling precariously over the edge. Taking a deep breath, he inched closer, extended the arms again and brought them gently into the trunk's sides. As he did, it slipped away, fell off the edge and disappeared.

Without thinking he plunged over the cliff after it and in an instant was plummeting straight down at full throttle. The cliff flew by in a blur and the inky darkness closed in. *Crab's* arms were fully extended in his spotlights, claws open and grasping. Just ahead he could see the trunk tumbling through the dark water. He was closing in on it, but it was taking too long and he was already too deep. He had the feeling he had just jumped out of a plane without a parachute.

His depth gauge spun like an out-of-control clock. Three hundred . . . four hundred . . . approaching five hundred feet. An alarm buzzer sounded, the hull creaked and groaned, water began to seep in through the seams and the lights dimmed further. Five hundred feet flew by with the trunk still a few feet away. Heart pounding, he reached with the arms, yanked at the levers and buried the claws deep into the sides of the oak chest. The weight of the falling object threw *Crab* to one side. Frantically, he reversed the thrust, reversed the bow planes and blew the tanks. It slowed his descent, but not entirely. The sub turned in an agonizing arc, then slowly picked up speed as it began to rise. He stared up into the rushing darkness praying for any sign of light. Out in front, *Crab* held the chest in its claws like a runner with a football.

"Comin' up," Sam radioed casually to Tashtego as his depth gauge spun upward past three hundred feet.

Nikki's anxious voice came over his headphones. "Sam, did you find it? Did you get what we were looking for?"

"Nothing to it," he radioed back.

Her squeal of delight hurt his ears.

Chapter Nineteen

THE JOURNAL OF MAX MARTÍNEZ

December 20th—Little Inagua Island, Bahamas

Tashtego swung *Crab* back aboard the *Fortuna Explorer* at the end of the cargo boom, and the two crewmen guided the submersible into her davits on the foredeck. The chest hung dripping wet in the sub's extended claws.

Nikki was beside herself with excitement as Sam climbed out of the hatch. "Any problems?" she asked happily, running her hands over the bronze-strapped oak and seeing a bronze nameplate on the padlocked lid. "Vicente Maximilian Martínez," she read aloud. "Pleased to meet you, Señor Martínez."

"All I can say is, Señor Martínez better be worth it," Sam remarked.

Tashtego helped Sam carry the heavy chest into the ship's crew mess and lounge and put it down on the linoleum floor. The room looked more like the common area in a fire station than the crew lounge of a ship. Well-worn sofas and chairs sat about, all with a view of a TV and DVD player. Racks of dog-eared books lined iron-bolted walls and a row of small portholes opened to the main deck on either side. At the forward end of the room, separated by an eating bar, was a stainless-steel kitchen. Secured to the floor in the center of the room was a communal dining table littered with papers, old charts and thick research books.

Tashtego knocked the corroded lock off the chest with a hammer and chisel, Sam cleared away the clutter and together they set it up on the table. Nikki opened the lid, peered cautiously inside and recoiled at the strong smell of tar and tobacco. A set of neatly folded formal clothing sat on top. She lifted off an embroidered frock coat, a gold stitched vest, a white lace shirt, rose-colored stockings, knee britches and pointed shoes.

"Wedding clothes!" she announced happily, then sobered as a far-away look came into her eyes.

"Wedding clothes?" Sam asked.

"Just a feeling," she said, looking back down into the trunk. Her face fell. The bottom of the trunk was filled with waterlogged papers, drawings and nautical charts. There was a rusted seaman's knife, an elaborate Spanish clock, a brass compass and a crude version of an early sextant made of mahogany. There was also a soggy book of early sailing directions and another that looked like an early version of a nautical almanac. She carefully lifted the items out one by one and tried to remove the papers, but they started to come apart in her hands.

Sam spread the documents out to dry on the table and saw that they mainly consisted of scientific notes and calculations. Continuing to gently separate the papers, he came upon some rather good drawings of naked, tattooed natives. One of the drawings caught his eye and he stared. It resembled pictures he had seen of the enigmatic statues out on Easter Island—except in this case the big-eared, long faced fellow with the square jaw seemed to be reclining casually and smiling.

Nikki made a little squeal of delight. Sam looked up and saw her pulling a large, rectangular, fabric-wrapped object from a side chamber in the truck that had been thickly waterproofed with tar. She set the heavy article on the table and began removing the wrapping. It had a waxy feel and came away in thick chunks in her hand. When the last of the fabric was peeled away an oversized leather-bound journal was revealed, perfectly intact. The volume had apparently survived nearly three hundred years underwater thanks to its waxed fabric wrapping and the tarred compartment in which it was hidden.

Nikki, her amber eyes bright with anticipation, picked up the weighty book and carried it to one of the sofas where she sat, folded her long legs under her, pushed her glasses back on her nose and gingerly opened the leather cover.

Sam watched her lips moving slowly. "What does it say?" he asked.

"It's in Spanish, my native language, but old Spanish. A little like trying to read Shakespeare in Elizabethan English. I'll figure it out. It's going to take a little time is all." She looked down fondly at the journal. "His name is Vicente Maximilian Martínez, but he says to call him Max." Then concentrating, she fell silent and read on.

Amsterdam—21 August, 1721

It is with boundless enthusiasm and great hope that I embark on this adventure. The purpose of this journal is to record my travels and, with any luck, the discovery of unknown and unstudied cultures and civilizations. I take it as a sign of good fortune that we are departing Holland on this, my twenty-fifth birthday.

Captain Jacob Roggeveen is the leader of our expedition and master of our three ships, the *African Galley*, the *Arend* and our flagship, the *Thienhoven*. The captain and I are aboard the *Thienhoven*, a one hundred and sixty foot, three-masted frigate with three decks and twenty-one gun ports that open on either side of our rounded hull.

The patent that Jacob inherited from his father, Arent Roggeveen, gave him the right to mount an expedition in search of the southern continent of *Terra Australis*, which our party of intrepid explorers is henceforth committed to find. The will contained only one stipulation:

"Should the boy I consider my second son, Vicente Maximilian Martínez, known affectionately to me as Max, choose to join this arduous voyage to unknown regions of the earth, he is to be commissioned as the expedition's lead navigator."

Nikki sat up with growing interest and went on.

I am from Spain, but my mother was Dutch. As a result, I grew up with two native tongues. My father was a much-admired and sought-after pilot of Spanish ships. When he returned from one of his voyages there would always be intense days where his latest discoveries in navigation would be drilled into my head. Sadly, he never came home from his last voyage, and we never learned his fate.

It was from my mother that I inherited my flaxen hair and fair complexion (attributes that I fear will suffer greatly under the tropical sun) and my unbridled passion for antiquities. She sent me to study at Leiden University in the Netherlands where I was fortunate enough to fall under the tutelage of Arent Roggeveen who was himself a mathematician, astronomer, geographer and navigator. For five glorious years I lived in a world of artifacts, archaeology, historical sites, archives and manuscripts, at the end of which I was privileged to call myself an 'Antiquarian.' My life, I decided, would henceforth be dedicated to chronicling the history and evolution of civilizations.

Captain Jacob Roggeveen is Arent Roggeveen's only biological son. Sixty-two years old at our sailing, he is over twice my age, but remains bigger and stronger than most of his crew. His less becoming characteristics include a hairline that recedes to the top of his head where it erupts in a mass of gray curls, and bulging eyes that make him look like a fish brought up too quickly from the depths. In everything he says and does, there is an undercurrent of violence. I have always called him my brother and tried to defend him against those who call him a fat, feckless fool. To make our journey as pleasant as possible I intend to continue to ignore the deep-seated resentment and jealousy he has always harbored toward me.

Nikki looked up from the journal and cleaned her glasses on her shirttail. "Sam, these experiences I'm reading about, they seem so familiar. It's like you are telling me Max's story yourself."

"Me?" he said. "I'd probably have to set that captain straight before we left the dock."

She smiled and delved back into the heavy volume. The antiquated Spanish was getting a little easier to decipher now, and she was able to go a little faster. For the next thirty-six hours Nikki sat transfixed on the sofa reading, pulling a comforter over her when she felt sleepy, returning to the journal when she awoke, eating and drinking whatever Sam handed her while barely tasting it and getting up only for quick trips to the head.

She read how the Dutchmen's trip was sponsored by the West Indian trading company, arch rival of the East Indian company, and how the two companies were actively competing for routes to the "Spice islands". She read how Roggeveen's three ships crossed the Atlantic, touched briefly at the Falkland Islands, then sailed for Le Maire Strait and Cape Horn . . .

Falkland Islands—10 January, 1722

The night before we left Amsterdam, the crew snuck five whores of stout, Scandinavian blood aboard. Captain Roggeveen didn't find out about them until we were well into the South Atlantic. When he did, he was furious. There was little he could do about it until we reached the Falklands at which time the first thing he did was throw the women off the ship. I couldn't imagine the ladies wanting to work their way home in the same manner that had gotten them here; they appeared to be pretty worn out by this time. With no place to spend the money they had earned while aboard, it was a fair assumption that they had enough saved to start new lives.

West of Cape Horn—8 February, 1722

Our three-week passage 'round the Horn to the Pacific was a nightmare beyond description. Roggeveen's ships were caked in ice. Floating icebergs popped up everywhere threatening to rip holes in our hull. The Roaring Forties (gale-force westerly winds and west-to-east currents in the southern latitudes between 40° and 50°) howled straight over the bow forcing us to sail a zig-zag course in monstrous seas. Fortunately, we only lost two men overboard.

Robinson Crusoe Island—4 March, 1722

Escaping the torrents of the Cape, we sailed up the west coast of Chile and put in at the port city of Valdivia to refit, resupply and rest. From there we again set sail and traveled four hundred miles west where we made landfall on the pleasant, inviting shores of Robinson Crusoe Island—one of three isles that make up the Juan Fernandez Islands. It was here in 1704, I recalled, that a lone sailor named Alexander Selkirk was marooned for five years, and later became the inspiration for Daniel Defoe's 1719 novel from which the island took its name. As an aristocrat and an academic, I couldn't imagine living such a life.

By this time, Captain Roggeveen was arguing constantly with me over the strange device I was using to measure the angle between the sun and the horizon at noon to fix our position. Despite the accuracy of my calculations, Roggeveen insisted his own method, based on dead reckoning alone, was superior. Fortunately, he couldn't bring himself to go against his father's wishes that I, and not he, pilot his ship. Had he done so, his stubborn, offhanded way of doing things would have put us aground more than once. My calculations, based on methods devised by my father that supplemented dead reckoning, invariably proved accurate. Each time we arrived safely at a destination Roggeveen fell silent and would not speak to me for days.

The *Thienhoven* carried a crew of two hundred and thirty-three. Most had the faces of men and the hearts of beasts. Death was seemingly of little consequence to them. My guess is they viewed Hell as not all that different from the life they were living. A few of the sailors became my friends. One was the sailmaker, a Swede by the name of Oskar who was so old it was impossible to guess even the decade of his birth. Oskar spent his days passing a heavy needle through thick canvas, and the rest of his waking hours carving whalebone into wonderful images and sculptures with his powerful, restless hands.

He and I would sit for hours while he told me tales of the exotic places he had been—all the while working his jackknife into the hard bone and teeth of gigantic fish and adding the fine detail with his sail needle. He called his carvings "scrimshaw" and they were intricate and beautiful and fine and his stories were brave and true and made me want to visit the places he described and be as brave as he was, but I knew I could never be that brave. Distant planets couldn't possibly be any more enchanting than some of the places he had lived, nor the women any more beautiful than the ones he had known. It never occurred to me to question the veracity of his claims.

One day Oskar noted my interest in his carvings and asked if I would like to learn how to do it. I readily accepted the invitation and from that day forward we sat together for hours on end working our knives and needles into sculptures made of ivory-colored bone. My carvings were, to say the least, extremely crude and poorly made, but Oskar always went out of his way to praise my efforts.

Easter Island—5 April, 1722

From Robinson Crusoe Island Roggeveen sailed his ships west over eighteen hundred miles. On Easter Day, nearly eight months after departing Holland, we spotted what was first thought to be the elusive continent of *Terra Australis*.

There was great rejoicing, but bad weather kept us offshore. Rising smoke from different locations gave enough definition to the land that I suspected we had happened not upon a continent, but an island, and a small one at that.

Roggeveen moved his well-armed ships in closer to look for a suitable place to anchor, but the bad weather continued and by April 7th we still had not found good holding ground. Then out of the driving rain a canoe was sighted slicing through the foaming waves toward us manned by a single islander.

***

December 21st—Little Inagua Island, Bahamas
Aboard the Fortuna Explorer

At this point in her reading Nikki stopped, took off her glasses and stared into space. A shiver went up her spine. The words were too real, too vivid, too familiar to anyone but Sam. This was his story. He was there on that ship seeing it, living it, telling it. She could feel it in her bones, in her heart, in her gut. It was the kind of intuition she was very familiar with, a knowing that came with emotions so powerful, so deep, the truth was inescapable. Sam was Vicente Maximilian Martínez in this life she was reading about. Sam was Max!

Chapter Twenty

SLAUGHTER

Easter Island—7 April, 1722

I stood on the deck with the rest of the crew of the *Thienhoven* watching with a degree of trepidation as the islander paddled alongside, scrambled up the netting we had thrown over the side and landed triumphantly on deck. To my dismay, I saw that he was completely naked and covered in tattoos. He presented a startling figure as he stood looking around in utter amazement. I couldn't help being captivated by his tall, remarkably fit body.

Utterly innocent, dangerous in his exuberance, he moved quickly about the ship examining the rigging and construction and marveling at everything he saw. His running commentary of exclamations and questions were met with silence since they were in a strange tongue, but by his enthusiasm and excitement I could easily imagine he thought the he had boarded a chariot of the gods.

Having made a cursory examination of our vessel, the handsome islander turned his attention to the crew. With a complete lack of inhibition, he began pulling and poking at everyone's clothing. Unable to get over his astonishment at the presence of such strangely dressed men, he yanked the three-corner hat off the head of one of the ship's officers, installed it on his own head and grinning broadly began prancing about in delight. He was a one-man parade and the sailors all laughed.

Captain Roggeveen appeared on deck with a few trinkets in hand and in kingly fashion offered them to the native like he was bestowing articles of great value upon an honored guest. The savage grabbed them out of his hand—two strings of blue beads, a small mirror, a pair of scissors—and was over the side with his treasures before anyone could stop him. The crew laughed and jeered as he paddled away, but I couldn't help admiring his exuberance and athleticism.

The next day the weather was still too bad to attempt a shore landing. Again, however, we had visitors. Dozens of tattooed men arrived this time in a flotilla of canoes. The crews from our ships stood watching, suspicious and wary, as the naked islanders scrambled aboard without invitation, snatched the hats off the stunned crewmen and dove back over the side. The bareheaded Dutchmen were furious and shook their fists at the thieves escaping in their canoes.

I saw no danger in their playful antics. The natives were like exuberant children discovering unimagined delights and reveling in them. Roggeveen saw it quite differently and quickly organized a shore party of a hundred and thirty-four armed men to go after them. I was most anxious to know more about these handsome, gregarious people and took up an oar in one of the shore boats to join them.

As we drew closer to the island the rain turned to drizzle, the steamy mist began to lift and the terrain came into better view. End to end, the remote isle could not have been more than fifteen miles long. Three low-lying, extinct volcanos, surrounded by a number of smaller craters, commanded the highest points on the island. Looking over my shoulder as I rowed, I made out that the land was completely denuded; there was not a single tree in sight. Instead, the rolling terrain was dotted with cultivated fields in a patchwork of random farms. Drawing closer, I turned and stopped rowing to stare. Scattered about were hundreds of enormous statues, some thirty feet tall, carved from what looked like black lava. The silent monoliths had huge humanoid heads with long ears, long noses and wide jaws.

My heart felt like it would come out of my chest. Every antiquarian dreams of a find like this, a discovery of such magnitude that his name will ring in the halls of academia for generations to come. I couldn't wait to start my examination and study of these standing idols, and assigned myself the initial task of taking their exact measurements.

We landed on slippery boulders and had to scramble over the rocks to come ashore. Roggeveen himself led our party as we marched inland. I followed along craning my neck and gawking at the statues. Without trees to make logs for rolling, how could effigies of such immense size and tonnage possibly have been moved and erected?

Almost immediately we were confronted by a large crowd of intensely curious islanders. I smiled at the first one I came across and received an infectious grin in return. The most powerful and aggressive of the young men pressed close to the armed sailors and began grabbing at their clothing. Having lived their lives in humid, subtropical heat, they could not get over these strange people who arrived draped in heavy, cumbersome garments. Lacking any kind of reserve or shyness—I doubted they even knew what embarrassment was—the excited natives grew increasingly aggressive in their fascination with the visitor's dress. The sailors, in turn, grew increasingly cautious, defensive and frightened.

I realized I had arrived in a kind of Eden, a flourishing, thriving garden of innocents untouched by civilization. This was man in his purist form; a people who knew nothing of the outside world and an outside world that knew nothing of them. The island was a miracle of creation and I wanted to leave immediately before we sullied it with our so-called civilized and cultured ways.

Just then I heard loud voices rising from the mob of natives followed by angry warnings shouted in Dutch. Cheers of celebratory glee drowned out the visitor's threats as the islanders grabbed at their hats and coats. I found out afterward that a particularly aggressive boy had tried to snatch a musket out of the hands of one of the sailors and the sailor had knocked him to the ground. The shocked islanders grabbed up rocks in their defense and the shore crew opened fire. A dozen naked, tattooed men fell dead on the ground in pools of blood. Another musket volley followed and the crowd of horrified natives fell back in horror at the lifeless bodies that lay around them.

Sickened and revolted, I watched Roggeveen ordering his men to spread out over the island in search of all the fruits and vegetables they could lay their hands on. The natives ran in fear, and just like that, Eden evaporated into the mist and was no more.

The grief of the wailing islanders was more than I could bear. I turned away and followed aimlessly along behind a group of men from my ship who were headed inland, scarcely aware of my surroundings. The horrific event I had just witnessed played over and over in my head. My stomach turned, I put my hands on my knees and threw up.

When the retching stopped, I looked up through watering eyes and saw that I was in a little valley between two small craters. I sat down heavily on a rock and stared. I had just witnessed the slaughter of a group of innocent people for no reason. My stomach turned again, I convulsed and tasted bile.

My face was damp with sweat. I wiped at it aimlessly as my thoughts began to clear. I had seen a few bare-breasted old women in the crowd that greeted us at the shore, but no young women and no children. Where were the wives and babies of all these virile young men? Surely, they must have families. My eyes came into better focus and I found myself staring at the opening to a large cave not a hundred feet away. The gaping cavity was so obscured by brush I probably wouldn't have noticed it even if I hadn't been so aggrieved and distracted.

As I stared, tiny frightened cries came out of the darkness of the cave. I saw something move and strained to look. As I did, a creature nearly twenty feet tall appeared in the opening. It was a horrifying sight.

The giant had an enormous square-jawed head and a long, slender body. The statues, I thought! He looks exactly like one of those lava statues I saw along the shore. His arms hung loose at his sides with his palms open and his fingers spread as if proclaiming the innocence of those he was protecting. Behind him in the cave, I saw the frightened eyes of women and children huddled in the dark. The giant's posture wasn't aggressive, it was defensive. He was standing guard over the group of small and terrified people behind him.

I stood and imitated his gesture to show I meant no harm. As I did, an angry shout came from behind me. I turned in time to see one of the crewmen from our ship, a second mate with whom I had had a number of unpleasant encounters since leaving Amsterdam. His musket was raised, his eyes wide with fear, and in that instant I realized he was about to fire at the towering figure standing in the mouth of the cave.

The thought of any more senseless killing was unbearable. I grabbed the musket leaning against the rock beside me that had been thrust into my hands when we came ashore. With no thought to the consequence, I wheeled and fired. The second mate fell and to my dismay was dead to the ground.

His two mates coming over the hill behind him saw me fire. Bellowing with rage, they rushed down the hill, grabbed me by the arms and pinned me between them. As they were hauling me away, I glanced back at the cave. The darkened mouth of the cave where the giant had stood was empty.

I was half dragged, half carried to the shore boats. On the way I saw the Island's traumatized old women, their gentle eyes filled with tears, humbly laying baskets of fish, fruits and vegetables at the feet of the sailors. A crowd of naked young men stood a safe distance away staring furiously at the invaders. The Dutchmen, keenly aware that one wrong move would result in a bloody uprising, hurried to load the stolen food on their boats and be gone.

Chapter Twenty-One

MAROONED

Easter Island—8 April, 1722

Captain Jacob Roggeveen's cabin was on the third and highest deck of the *Thienhoven* with a tall array of little square windowpanes that looked out the stern. His suite stretched from port to starboard, served as both bedroom and office, and was decorated with elaborately carved furniture upholstered in red velvet that made it look more like an Amsterdam whorehouse than the nautical quarters of a ship's captain.

Roggeveen sat behind his cluttered desk drumming his fat fingers on the polished surface and glaring at the two sailors who had brought me aboard. He flicked his hand and they immediately withdrew, leaving me to his mercy.

In the eight months I had been his pilot I had learned that Roggeveen's leadership skills were confined mainly to his ability to fly into a deadly rage at the slightest provocation. Since I had given him more than a slight provocation in killing his second mate, I was surprised at his deathly calm.

"Do I hang you or turn you over to the crew and let them tear you to shreds?" he asked politely with bulging eyes.

"I can't say as I am overly fond of either option, sir," I replied with equal civility.

"Then perhaps I should just shoot you like you did my second mate and be done with it."

"I doubt your father would approve."

"Were he still alive, he would say I am perfectly within my rights."

"I didn't mean to kill the man," I protested emotionally. "I was trying to stop the mindless bloodshed. The giant in that cave was harming no one."

"Giant in a cave?" Roggeveen smiled humorlessly.

"He was six meters if he was a foot. He looked like one of those huge statues that are all over the island."

"Max," the captain sighed, "I always suspected you of being delusional. Now that you have proved me correct, I see you are a danger to yourself and others. I'd be doing you a favor by putting you out of your misery."

"I'm telling you, Captain, I saw a monster!"

"Of course you did, my boy. A big green one with horns and a tail I imagine." His laugh sounded like a leaky bagpipe. "If you weren't a murderer, I'd almost feel sorry for you."

"Your crewmen, your sailors, they're the bloody murderers!"

Roggeveen's fat face turned a bright shade of red. "There was only one murder on that island today and you committed it. Those islanders are ignorant savages. They count for nothing!"

"Those islanders are peaceful, indigenous people that your band of barbarous sailors killed for the sin of being overly friendly."

"You being so fond of them and all, perhaps you would like to go and live with them."

For a moment I was speechless. "Who will navigate your ship then?" I asked weakly.

"As I told my father, and as I have repeatedly told you, I am perfectly capable of piloting my own ship."

I took a deep breath. "In that case, sir, I shall leave you to it."

"Indeed, you shall." He raised his voice and shouted. "Guards!"

They hauled me away feeling like a musket ball had been fired at my heart and another had ventilated my stomach.

***

That same afternoon my trunk was unceremoniously deposited on shore and I was unceremoniously deposited on top of it. I sat watching the shore boat row back to the ship feeling helpless without so much as a pistol or musket to aid in my survival. Having just killed a man, I doubt I could have fired another gun at anyone or anything again, but it didn't keep me from wishing I had one. Desolation overtook me. I was no Robinson Crusoe. I certainly possessed none of his survival skills. What was to become of me on this tiny island in the middle of an endless ocean? I felt at my belt and found to my great relief I had at least been allowed to keep my knife.

The storm had passed and the sun was busily heating the moist tropical air to a temperature just slightly below boiling. I hadn't moved from my spot. Determined to watch until my former shipmates set sail taking my last hopes with them, I continued to stare out to sea. But no anchors were hauled and no sails were set. Instead, I saw great clouds of white smoke rising from all three of our ships and the crews abandoning ship. Shore boats filled with men were being quickly lowered and filled as smoke enveloped the three anchored vessels. There had been no attack from hostile forces, no deadly cannon fire. What could possibly make three seaworthy ships spontaneously combust all at once?

The shore boats, in danger of being swamped by the smallest wave due to the weight of so many men aboard, rowed upwind of the smoke, shipped their oars and sat there rocking gently in a glassy calm while waiting for their ships to burn.

But no flames came. How could three ships be set ablaze and not be burning? Then as I watched, the sea between the boats and where I sat on my trunk seemed to blacken with a squirming wave of tiny black objects swimming ashore. Hundreds more were abandoning the ships to join them, tiny black bodies churning the sea in an effort to escape the deadly smoke. The blanket of seething, boiling swimmers churned the water. As it came closer, I was able to make out what it was. Rats! The disgusting black rodents had been smoked out from their cozy berths aboard ship and sent scurrying overboard to avoid the fumes. The shore boats with the crews aboard were returning to their ships now in preparation for departure as the desperate emigrants continued to pull for shore in a mass invasion of unimaginable filth and destruction.

My horror at what I was witnessing was short lived. Behind me I heard the sounds of an angry mob coming my way. I turned in time to see a hundred or more islanders bearing down on me waving rocks and farm implements, apparently determined to rid the island of at least one murderous vermin who sat on his trunk looking out to sea.

I stood to face my judge and jury and my eyes fell on one of the mysterious statues towering nearby. Determined to take my love and fascination with it to the grave, I resolved to make it my last waking image.

To my amazement, I then saw a tall figure loping after my mob of executioners. He passed them with long easy strides and came to a halt in front of them with upheld arms. I stared, unable to believe my eyes. He was the living image of the statue I'd been staring at, the giant I had first seen at the cave.

The crowd ceased its advance and fell silent as the frightening creature addressed them, gesturing with his big hands and long, expressive face. But there was no sound. Clearly, the giant was talking to them, reasoning with them in some fatherly fashion, but I couldn't hear any speech. I watched, scarcely able to believe what I was seeing as the angry crowd seemed to relax and nod in understanding—if not agreement. One by one, they began to disperse and finally, to my infinite relief, the lot of them turned and walked away with their weapons hanging loose at their sides.

The giant put his hands on his hips and turned to look down on me from a great height. I had to tilt my head back to see his face. There is no way to describe the look of sadness I saw in his eyes. His expression of grief and sorrow broke my heart.

I nodded in an effort to show my relief and gratitude.

"You'll be safe now," I heard him say. But he hadn't said anything. His mouth hadn't moved.

"I don't understand," I said.

"Languages are merely constructs of thought and emotion," his silent response. *"I communicate a thought and your brain reconstructs it into your language. Someday the brain of your species will evolve to the point where you will be able to use more of it than the tiny bit you are currently accessing. Then you will be amazed at what you can accomplish."*

I was dazed. "And until then?"

His sadness turned to disgust. *"Until then you are a stupid, violent, nascent race of humanoids that cannot be trusted to do anything but destroy all that is good."*

"I can see how you might think that."

"This is not the first time I have had to watch my friends slaughtered at the hands of barbarians." His sadness returned and he turned to walk away. Then looking back, *"I see in you the possibility of a good man."*

"I'm no different from the rest," I replied. "I just don't happen to believe in senseless killing."

"What is your name?"

"Max. They call me Max. And yours?"

"It translates in your language to something like Boris."

"You saved my life, Boris."

"And you saved mine. I believe that makes us even."

The rats were clamoring over the rocks now, scurrying ashore and disappearing into the underbrush in a frantic rush to safety. I watched as my savior lumbered away with his loping gate, a sad and broken giant.

"Yes," I said to his retreating back. "I suppose it does."

***

Lost and alone, I sat back down on my trunk. Boris had discouraged the islanders from tearing me to shreds, but I didn't dare go into the village for fear of reigniting their hatred of the invaders who had just slaughtered a dozen of their finest young men. Having nowhere else to go, I took up shelter in the mouth of the cave where I had first encountered the giant. It took me some time to carry my heavy trunk there, but it contained everything I owned, or would ever own, until another ship happened by—which might be some time since it had apparently never happened before.

I made myself as comfortable as possible using my ordinary seaman's jacket as a backrest, and in the hot, tropical twilight looked out at what, under any other circumstances, would have been an idyllic sunset. Having lived a full and active life with my studies, my career as an antiquarian, my friends and family in Holland and Spain, I don't believe I had ever known a moment of loneliness. It descended on me now like the weight of dirt on my grave. I felt as trapped as if I had been buried alive.

I would have made a fire, but with nothing to cook and no need to be any warmer than I already was, there was no point. It wasn't such a bad place to die, I thought, although the idea of starving to death didn't exactly appeal to me. And starving I was, I realized. It occurred to me I could go out and raid one of the many gardens and fields I had seen. At least, if I was caught and killed for thievery, I wouldn't die hungry. I was about to get up and go do exactly that when I saw someone coming toward me over the same hill where the second mate had been standing when I shot him.

Silhouetted against the setting sun, I made out the lithe and slender figure of a woman with long black hair shiny as a raven's wing descending the slope toward me. The figure came nearer and I saw it was a young woman with a large basket over her arm. She stopped and stood before me and to my chagrin I saw that she was entirely naked from the waist up. I had never seen a woman naked in broad daylight before. I was mortified and averted my eyes, but not before she caught me staring. It was hard to believe a face that beautiful could look that angry.

She dropped her basket on the ground in front of me with a heavy thud and turned on her heel to leave. The basket, I saw, contained all manner of fruits and vegetables as well as smoked fish wrapped in leaves. Behind me I heard movement, scrambled to my feet and saw Boris towering in the entrance to his cave. Between his alien presence and her shocking beauty, I felt like I was having a heart attack.

The giant seemed to be saying something to the young woman because I heard her answer in a youthful voice that was full of fury. Her words were clearly in the language of the island, and sounded like she wanted to kill someone. I had a sinking feeling that that someone was me.

"Max," I heard Boris think out loud, *"this is Iolana. Iolana, this is Max."*

The lilting, youthful voice—a voice that would have been musical were it not filled with so much hate—came at me in a torrent of words.

"What did she say?" I asked, my eyes still respectfully averted.

"She said why won't you look at her. Are you that ashamed?"

142

I looked up slowly. She took my breath away. A sculptor would have dulled his chisel trying to capture a figure like that. We locked eyes and stared. It saddened me to think that eyes so full of innocence could have seen anything to fill them with so much fury.

As I watched, her eyes grew huge and softened. It was as if she were fighting to keep something back that was fighting to get out. Her eyes widened further and filled with tragedy as tears ran down and flooded her high cheek bones. A choking sob escaped her throat, and with a cry of anguish she turned and ran away.

I watched her bare feet flying under her loose skirt as she ran, then turned desperately to Boris who was looking on in heartbroken silence.

"What . . . what did she want?" I asked. "What was she doing here?"

"She brought you an offering so you would not kill her like you killed the others," Boris intoned in his deep mental voice. *"As to what she was doing, I imagine she wanted to see for herself what one of the devils who killed her husband today looked like."*

I was incensed. "I didn't kill the others and I didn't kill her husband! The only person I shot was the man who was going to shoot you!"

"She's not ready to admit that."

Chapter Twenty-Two

A NEW BEGINNING

December 22nd—Little Inagua Island, Bahamas
Aboard the Fortuna Explorer

Nikki was sitting upright, sound asleep on the sofa in the crew's lounge of the *Fortuna Explorer,* her long legs still curled under her, her big glasses perched precariously on her nose. Open in her lap was Max's age-worn, leather bound journal. The sound of Sam making morning coffee in the galley woke her. She smiled and struggled to stand, but her legs had gone numb.

"Ouch," she said, stretching stiffly.

He brought her a steaming cup. "You've been up all night again reading, I suppose?"

She took the cup gratefully in both hands, sipped gingerly at the hot liquid and looked up in despair. "Sam, things can't go on like this. What's to become of you?"

"Me?" he smiled. "Well, if I have anything to say about it, I'll live a long and happy life of adventure and fortune with you at my side knowing every minute how deeply and extravagantly loved you are by yours truly."

"I already know that," she said impatiently. "I mean you in the journal, in the story I'm reading about you in a former life where you are Max. You are in so much trouble, Sam!"

"Trouble?"

"You just fell in love and you don't even know it."

"Who did I fall in love with?"

"A beautiful young native girl named Iolana."

"Things could be worse," he grinned.

"You have no idea." She sat back down, curled her legs back under her, opened the journal and adjusted her glasses. "Now leave me alone so I can read."

***

22 April, 1722

Boris must have tired of stepping over and around me camped out in the mouth of his cave because after two weeks he invited me inside. We hadn't gone fifty meters when we came upon a large garden of root vegetables flourishing under some kind of mysterious lights that hung down from the cave's lava ceiling and did not appear to burn candles or oil. The plants were thriving like none I had ever seen and included potatoes, yams, turnips, rutabagas, carrots, radishes, beets, parsnips and onions, plus a number of others I didn't recognize that had wide-spread leaves bursting with color.

Further on, the cave widened out and we entered a somewhat cozy cavern with furnishings as big as Boris himself. Looking up at the huge table and chairs and bed, I felt the way a three-year-old must feel looking at an adult-size world. It was cool and pleasant in here, not oppressively hot and humid like it was outside in the sun.

Looking around at the softly lit charcoal-colored walls and ceiling I asked Boris the source of the light. He answered by asking if I knew how to play chess. I admitted that I did and watched his enormous mouth spread into the semblance of a grin. He produced an oversized chess board and carefully set out chess pieces so enormous I was going to have to use both hands to move them.

Seating himself at the table, he motioned me into a chair opposite him. I climbed up into it, speechless with gratitude at his hospitality,

145

then watched as he moved a pawn two spaces forward. I countered with the same move and we played in silence. After losing the first game where I clearly had the advantage, I realized the giant was reading my mind. I leaned back, looked him in the eye and told him if he wanted me as a chess partner, he was going to have to stay the hell out of my head. The sheepish look on his six-foot face told me I was right. We played a second game and he beat me fair and square.

I hadn't eaten all day and realized I was starving when I saw him drinking a strange concoction made from the starchy vegetables in his root garden. He must have read my mind because without saying anything he handed me a cup of his brew. I took a tentative sip, found it to be delicious, and drained the cup in a series of greedy gulps. He smiled and asked if I would like him to arrange a sleeping pallet for me on the floor. Neither of us realized it at the time, but it was the beginning of a beautiful friendship.

Boris was generous to a fault, but remained guarded. I had endless questions: Who was he? Where did he come from? How did he get here? Were there others like him? If so, what happened to them, did they all die?

His response was always the same: *"How about another game of chess?"*

12 October, 1722

Six months passed and no one tried to kill me, so that was a relief. That is not to say I was accepted or even acknowledged by the islanders. For the most part, I was ignored—or I should say shunned. I was a castaway marooned for murder on a speck of lava in the middle of the Pacific Ocean. The fact that I had taken a life to save a life didn't seem to matter. I would likely never leave this prison alive. It was a depressing thought.

At the rear of Boris's cave was a small opening to another cave. Boris cautioned me the day I moved in that he didn't want me going in there, and I had respected his wishes, but its mysterious glow fascinated me, and after seeing the opening every day for six months my curiosity got the better of me. I entered the cave and was about to go exploring when I heard Boris speaking to me:

"I thought I made it clear that cave was out of bounds."

I backed out and asked him why. He told me the lava tunnels beneath the island were endless. *"Were you to get lost,"* he explained testily, *"I would have to go looking for you, and I doubt I could find you with so many of the tunnels being too small and narrow for me to get through."*

That wasn't the truth. I knew it and I could tell he knew I knew it. He didn't want me seeing what was in there for some reason, and he didn't want to discuss it.

Soon after my arrival, I learned from Boris that despite Captain Roggeveen's insistence on naming the island "Easter Island" after the day he arrived, its proper name was *Rapa Nui*, meaning Big Island. He went on to say that he understood what it was like to come here as an outsider. He himself was from another star system an unimaginable distance away, and that he and his companions were explorers and researchers.

"Anthropologists, I believe you would call us."

I was astonished. We were alike, he and I. Scientists who studied cultures and societies of civilizations past and present, researchers of archeology, biology and linguistics, chroniclers of the ever-evolving miracle of existence.

"I might also add that we are itinerate missionaries tasked with seeding the stars."

"With what?"

"Enlightenment," he said. *"Our directive is not to interfere with the people we encounter, but to give them a boost, a leg up in evolution and understanding by splicing a bit of our DNA into theirs. Unfortunately, the species we encountered on the mainland would have none of it."*

"Why didn't you just go home then?"

He sighed. *"It's complicated. I doubt you'd understand. Suffice to say the city we had built in the volcano and come to love was discovered and viciously attacked by the very tribes we had been trying to help. After all we had done for them, their hatred of us caught us off guard. Our losses were catastrophic. Only a few of us managed to escape and come here."*

I wanted to know so much more, but he fell silent and I didn't press him. I knew him well enough by now to know that when he was ready, he would speak—and not before.

As time went on, Boris and I grew more accustomed to one another, more familiar with the impossible differences in our appearances and origins. I can't say exactly when it happened, only that our differences eventually disappeared and we rarely thought of them again. We became two men sharing a rather comfortable cave together. He was three times my size with a head that was too large; I was three times smaller with a head the size of one of his fists, but somehow that no longer mattered.

Boris was loved and admired by everyone on the island. He would go out each day and teach the children who sat cross-legged on the ground paying rapt attention to his mental lectures. The kindly giant, or others like him, had apparently been educating the people of Rapa Nui for hundreds of years, which might explain why the islanders appeared more evolved and civilized than the primitive, isolated tribes around the world that I had studied.

Iolana was older, eighteen or nineteen I guessed, but she was still his student. She came often to Boris's cave and would sit at his feet while he gave her private instruction. She never took notes—the island did not appear to have a written language—but she had a quick mind and a remarkable memory. While I never knew what it was he was teaching her, she would begin each session by repeating back what sounded like the things she had learned from her previous visit. Clearly, she was very intelligent.

I was usually there when she came for her lessons. She would see me and look right through me. As cool as the cave was, things definitely got chillier the minute she walked in. I didn't exist in her eyes, although she certainly existed in mine.

17 April, 1723

I had been living in Boris's cave a year when Iolana arrived one day terribly upset. The distress in her voice as she spoke to Boris was extraordinary. He came immediately to his feet and followed her outside. I trailed behind, curious to learn what was so distressing and to help if I could.

Iolana led us out into the fields, and with an anguished cry pointed to swarms of rats going up and down the rows of flourishing crops eating the leaves and seeds. Farmers were out with rakes and hoes trying to beat them back, but there were too many and they were too hungry to be intimidated with weapons they could easily avoid.

Boris was as horrified as I was at the seriousness of the situation. If left unchecked, the rats would destroy the agriculture on the island and create a famine. The lumbering giant made a few long strides and arrived at the summit of a small hill overlooking the field. Here, he put his hands on his hips, tilted back his head, opened his huge mouth and let out an inaudible scream. The high-pitched sound must have been unbearable to the rats because they immediately stopped eating and looked up in excruciating pain. Boris's scream was driving them wild with agony and they ran. Waves of them bolted for the sea cliff and in their panic they didn't stop. Sheets of the sprawling, crawling creatures poured over the edge of the bluff and into the sea until the water boiled black with their drowning bodies.

The crowd of farmers shouted for joy and followed the towering giant to the next field a short distance away where he raised his head, opened his great mouth and again let out the torturous scream. If the centuries-old legends of the Pied Piper of Hamelin town were true, he must have been a popular fellow because our villagers came running from all over the island to follow Boris from field to field and watch him drive the rats into the sea. By day's end, the land had been purged of the menace and the crops were safe.

A huge bonfire was lit that night in Boris's honor and everyone celebrated. Their alien resident had saved their food supply and saved them from mass starvation. I was as thrilled as anyone for their salvation and joined in the festivities. Their joy was my joy even though I was obligated to stand some distance apart so as not to offend them with my presence.

Sometime in the distant past the people of Rapa Nui had discovered the secret of distilling spirits. Boris's throat must have been extremely raw from screaming because I saw him down copious amounts of their intoxicating beverage in an apparent effort to ease the soreness.

I managed to secure a shell full of the local brew for myself and stood sipping the bittersweet drink as I watched Iolana dancing all but naked in the firelight. The sparks were like fireflies dancing around her body in a kind of frenzied burning glow. I'm sure the sight of her wild and graceful figure whirling in and out of the shadows to the sound of flutes and drums would have been intoxicating enough without the alcohol. As it was, I thoughtlessly drained and refilled my shell over and over, unable to avert my eyes, until finally I had to sit down to keep from falling down.

18 April, 1723

Boris and I both had splitting headaches the next day and stayed secluded in our cave. For once, neither of us felt like playing chess. To pass the time I asked him to teach me a few words of the local language. He mentally transmitted the Rapanui equivalent of several simple phrases like 'please' and 'thank you' and 'you're welcome.' Having grown up in a bilingual home I had a natural talent for languages, and as a result was able to easily commit the words to memory.

19 April, 1723

The following day Iolana came for her regular lesson, eager as always to learn something new. It was a drizzling wet day with fog and rain and she came into the cave soaked and shivering from the steamy heat outside. Fearing she might catch a cold, I fetched a wool seaman's sweater out of my trunk that I had worn when we rounded Cape Horn in freezing weather and offered it to her.

She refused it at first, but Boris must have said something because she spitefully snatched it from my hand, then hesitated, not knowing what to do with it. I made a motion of slipping it over my head and she cautiously imitated my movements. The garment hung half way to her knees and made her look adorable. The added benefit was it allowed me to look at her for once without expending considerable effort to keep my eyes off her chest.

She hugged the sweater to her and I could tell she was enjoying its warmth, but angrily ceased her appreciation when she saw me witnessing her pleasure. Boris must have said something more at this point because she turned to me grudgingly and said *"Māuru-uru."*

I recognized the words and said "*Ô te aha no,*" the appropriate response to 'Thank you.'

She looked startled and addressed me angrily. Boris translated:

"She says you are so stupid you cannot even pronounce the simplest words correctly."

"If I'm so stupid," I responded with equal fervor, "then why don't you teach me?"

She looked at Boris and his translation really made her mad. She tried to stomp away, but he stopped her with a communication that turned her red in the face. More words were directed at me and I looked to Boris.

"She says Max is not a real name. Nobody is called Max."

"Vicente Maximilian Martínez," I said with a small bow. "Friends call me Max."

Her response sounded unpleasant.

"'I am not your friend,' she claims. She says she will call you Maximilian."

I smiled in approval and heard an irritated retort.

"She says after her lesson each day, if you are still interested, she will try and make you not so stupid." He paused. *"She says she doubts such a thing is possible."*

My smile broadened. "She may be right."

20 April, 1723

My language lessons began the next day. Iolana's lack of patience made her instructions awkward at first, but as time went on and we grew more familiar with one another she came to realize that I didn't have horns and a tail after all. Her indeterminate hatred turned to indeterminate indifference and tensions slowly eased. For my part, I was desperately in love with her and did everything I could to drag out our lessons and make them last as long as possible. The Rapanui language had a small vocabulary that I picked up rather quickly, but pretended to learn slowly so she would have to spend more time drumming the words into my head. I have a good ear for pronunciation, but acted tone deaf so she would have to keep correcting my pronunciation. She had no interest in learning Spanish, but by way of our constant association she was rapidly picking it up anyway. Her presence was so intoxicating I couldn't help smiling when we were together, which never failed to infuriate her.

13 October, 1723

A year and a half had passed since Iolana's husband was killed. My hope was that her sorrow over his death would gradually diminish until she could move the pain of her loss into a compartment in her heart rather than letting it rule her whole heart. I had been her student for about six months when this began to happen. During one of our language lessons, I heard her laugh for the first time without bitterness or irony. The tragedy still haunted her, but there was happiness in her voice as if her heart had been washed clean by the rain, and to my great relief I realized that death had not killed her joy. Her temper remained fierce, but passed as quickly now as storm clouds in a gale. It was around this time that I began to live again as well.

14 November, 1723

One day a month later Iolana came into the cave in tears and announced that the rats were back. Boris had apparently not been able to scream them all off the cliffs and they had been busy multiplying ever since. Nearly everyone on the island showed up this time to participate in the screaming. While Boris stood on the knolls and hillsides silently making the painful sound that drove the rodents into the sea, the islanders joined in and screamed themselves hoarse.

That night there was another festival around another raging bonfire and to my infinite delight I was invited to join in. No longer a complete outsider, I celebrated with the islanders and we danced and laughed ourselves into a drunken frenzy. In my wild abandon, I stripped to the waist, a daring and risqué move for a European of my stature, and at some point found myself dancing with Iolana.

"You are so white!" she cried gaily as she whirled away to dance with someone else. "You look like you fell in a bag of flour!"

I went outside the circle of dancers and sat down in the dark. Staring out at the festivities in a drunken haze I realized she was right; I did look like I had just emerged from a flour sack. Then and there, I resolved that I would henceforth leave my shirt off in all weathers and let the sun do its worst.

That night was also the beginning of a new tradition on Rapa Nui. "The Screaming of the Rats" became an annual ritual with everyone following Boris around the island screaming their heads off and then partying all night to celebrate the driving out of evil spirits.

Chapter Twenty-Three

FOREVER ONLY TAKES A SECOND

2 April, 1724

After living with Boris for nearly two years I had so many unanswered questions that desperately needed answering I didn't know where to start. What was the source of the mysterious lighting in his cave? What was he hiding down that tunnel at the back of his cave that he didn't want me to see? Tempting as it was to go exploring on my own, he had been too good of a friend for me to go against his wishes. His goodwill had saved my life and the least I could do was show him the respect of not violating his trust. My curiosity was killing me and there was nothing I could do about it. I was thinking this as we sat absorbed in one of our endless games of chess when I looked up, saw him watching me and realized he was reading my mind. "We agreed you wouldn't do that," I said angrily.

"Forgive me for taking so long to trust you," Boris replied, coming to his feet. *"I want to show you something. Will you come with me?"*

He led the way into the forbidden tunnel at the back of his cave, and I followed excitedly. The passageway was large enough for a horse and carriage to go down and looked as if it had been chewed out of the lava by some enormous creature with big teeth. An endless maze of twists and turns and forks and junctions led deeper into the bowels of the island growing smaller and narrower the further we went until I lost all sense of direction. I feared if I were to lose sight of his figure hurrying ahead me, I would never find my way out.

"I put a map in your head," Boris replied in response to my thoughts, and suddenly I knew all the lefts and rights to wherever we were going as if I had come this way my whole life.

It should have gotten colder and darker the further we went, but instead it got brighter and warmer. The tunnel I was following turned down and I descended a gentle slope. At the bottom I emerged into a chamber as big as the inside of a cathedral with ragged lava walls and a high domed ceiling. Stunned, I stopped and stared. In the center of the chamber was one of the most startling things I had ever seen.

Hovering in midair a foot off the ground was a cylinder about thirty feet long and five feet in diameter that gleamed with a dull metallic sheen and looked like a giant cigar. It had a solid bullet nose behind which was a compartment about twenty feet long with a transparent lid. Behind the compartment it was solid again and ended in a blunt back end where a single glassy tube was sticking out and glowing dimly. In the center of the tube was a rotating black hole that was drawing tiny lights like fireflies into its center. I approached it cautiously, looked inside the compartment and a shiver went up my spine. Beneath the lid was a narrow, coffin-shaped bed of white satin with a white satin pillow.

A circular shaft of light was shining down on the cylinder from above. I followed it up and saw that the light was coming from a hole in the center of the ceiling that was slightly bigger around than the cylinder. The hole went straight up in what I assumed was a vertical lava pipe and ended in a tiny pinpoint of light far above.

I looked around in dismay. Near the back wall was a round pool of shimmering water roughly fifty feet in diameter. Its mirrored surface reflected the lava walls and ceiling that surrounded it.

Boris appeared amused at my consternation. *"Ask your questions and I will try and answer them as best I can,"* he offered.

"What . . . what is it?" I stammered, pointing at the cylinder.

"A solar gravity ship."

"Gravity?"

"Gravity is the most omnipotent, omnipresent force in the galaxies. It is the force by which all things with mass and energy—molecules, planets, stars, even light—are pulled toward each other. The greater the mass, the greater the gravity. It's what keeps us anchored to this planet, what makes the tides rise and fall as the moon circles the earth, what keeps the planets in orbit around your sun from flying off into space. Gravity is the glue that holds it all together."

"What has that got to do with . . .?"

"A solar gravity ship? Its power plant, the thing that propels it and makes it go, is a gravity generator that attaches to the gravity of the stars and amplifies it. It allows us to slingshot across the vast reaches of space in virtually no time at all."

"Cuts down on trips to the commode as well, I imagine." It was a stupid remark, but I felt stupid trying to make sense of what he was saying.

"The gravity generator magnifies the gravity in front of the ship to pull it forward and simultaneously voids the gravity in back to create a vacuum that pushes it forward."

The image of a solid black cube, smooth on all sides, appeared in my mind. I had no idea what it was, but assumed it had to do with the thing Boris was trying to describe.

"Small gravity generators are what propelled the vehicles we drove and rode back in our city on the mainland," he went on. *"Full-size gravity generators are what allow our gravity ships to achieve the speed of light."*

"Light has a speed?" I was dumfounded.

"Time and distance are relative to speed and gravity. The greater the speed and gravity, the more time slows down. With enough speed

and gravity, time ceases to exist. Gravity curves spacetime. The greater the gravity, the greater the curvature of spacetime, and the closer two points in space can be brought together. Simple, really."

"Simple?" I snorted. "Really?"

"Relatively speaking, time and distance are an illusion. By controlling speed and gravity, we control time and distance. With enough speed and gravity, we can fold time and space and make a quantum leap to anywhere in spacetime we want to go." He paused. *"Close your mouth, Max."*

"Is that how your people got here in the first place?"

"By folding time and space, yes. Forever only takes a second that way."

"And saves in travel expenses," I added, feeling stupider by the second.

He gave me an indulgent smile. *"The gravity generator is only capable of holding two distant points in spacetime together for an instant. The timing has to be perfect. You leap a second too soon or a second too late and there is no telling where you might end up."*

"No telling," I repeated, numb with confusion.

"What else would you like to know, Max?" he asked impatiently.

"That black hole in the center of that tube there, what does it do?"

"A black hole creates gravity of unimaginable force. It crushes the atoms that are drawn into it and fuses their nuclei together. The energy that is left over from the fusion is what powers our gravity generators. It's called 'gravity fusion'."

My astonishment turned to wonder. "I'd love to see the formulas and drawings that explain how it all works."

"Not that you could read them. The science for gravity fusion, along with the rest of our technology, was contained in the Sphere of Knowledge."

"Sphere of Knowledge?"

"A big round blue ball that looked like your planet earth. You could hold it in your hands and call up anything you wanted to know."

"You talk as if it no longer exists."

"The Sphere of Knowledge was lost when our city was sacked by the barbarians."

"How do you mean by lost? Did you see it destroyed?"

"I was escaping in my gravity ship when I heard that the chamber where our most valuable artifacts were hidden had been overrun by the savages and everything in it stolen or smashed."

"The miracles that ball must have contained," I mused. "Wouldn't it be something if it still existed."

"Little possibility of that," he said.

I fell silent thinking about what he had said when something occurred to me. "If this solar gravity ship of yours is so fast," I said, "why don't you just get in it and go home? Why are you still here?"

"Not that simple, I'm afraid. Time is relative to the traveler. In terms of space travel, while it seems like only moments since you left home, in reality eons have passed in the place you left. In the time it took us to travel from our solar system to yours, generations came and went back on our home planet. Everybody and everything I knew is gone.

"The other inhibiting factor," he sighed, *"for me to return home before I died would be a great humiliation. Seeding the stars is a noble calling and a time-honored profession. For a Gorgon to forsake or abandon his mission for any reason would bring great shame not only on himself, but on his descendants. Those who returned home alive in the past suffered a sixty percent suicide rate."*

I heard him sometimes in Spanish, sometimes in Dutch, but it made no difference. My mind was awash in information. "If you can travel forward in time so fast, why can't you travel back in time just as quickly?" I asked.

"That's the romantic notion," he answered, *"but I'm afraid it's not possible. The past, present and future exist simultaneously on the spacetime continuum in theory only. In reality we have found that you can only go forward, not back. You can't go home again, Max."*

It was a sobering thought. Another idea struck me and I brightened. "If you have no use for this gravity ship of yours, how about if I borrow it to get the hell off this island?"

He shook his head sadly. *"It has great purpose, for me at least. A final promise, although I fear it will never be fulfilled. That tube you see sticking out the back of the ship is called a 'Portable Fusion Reactor'. It takes two to power a gravity ship—they work in pairs—and I have only one. Without its mate, and with only seawater to power the one I've got, it can barely generate enough energy to run my cave."*

"What happened to the other tube?"

"I gave it to a friend who was the last Gorgon to die here on the island. His second tube was damaged when we escaped the city on the mainland. He was dead, you see, and it was the only way he could go home."

"I'm confused. I thought you said . . ."

"It is possible for the soul of a Gorgon to be reborn into a new life, but only under the influence of the forces that surround our home planet."

"Advanced beings like yourself believe in superstitious nonsense like reincarnation?"

"Every Gorgon has past life memories," he replied with a wistful look. *"Not all are pleasant, but they are all quite vivid and quite real."*

"So that means, without a pair of these portable fusion things when you die, you're stuck here on this island, you can never go home and never get reincarnated?"

His features fell. *"It is the greatest sorrow of my life. I would make the same sacrifice for my friend again—and he would have done the same for me if the situation were reversed—but you cannot know the pain I live with every day knowing I am nearing the end of my final lifetime."*

"And you say this one power tube full of seawater isn't enough to get you there?"

"In the underground sea below the desert on the mainland where we lived, there is a substance found in abundance on only a few planets in the known galaxies. It is a type of salt that contains metallic elements which are highly conductive and produce great energy. We call it lithonium *and it's the only fuel capable of bending gravity, contracting time and allowing a gravity ship to leap across the vast distances of space."*

"And this lithonium, I take it you're fresh out?"

"There was such panicked confusion in escaping the massacre that many important things were left behind."

His depression was oppressive and I quickly changed the subject. "What's this big pool of water doing in here?" I asked. "Does it have some mystifying purpose as well?"

"The Moon Pool? No, it was here when we got here. It's the other end of a flooded lava tunnel that leads to the open sea and comes out in a place the natives call 'Ana Kai Tangata'."

"Ana Kai . . ."

"Rapanui for 'Man Eating Cave'."

"Ever feel like you can't absorb another piece of information?"

"No."

I turned to leave and walked past the hovering solar gravity ship that Boris claimed was capable of transporting him to the stars. On the side of it, beneath the glass canopy, I saw what looked like frantic scratch marks laid out in a small rectangle. The scrambled mess of frenetic lines curved around one another in a knot of wavy lines with abrupt breaks and direction changes. I ran my hand over the dull metallic surface and found the markings to be smooth as glass.

Boris watched me studying the characters. *"Our names are mono-gramed on our ships,"* he explained. *"That is my name written out in Gorgonese."*

The strange characters were fascinating. I wished I could read them.

Chapter Twenty-Four

WHEN WHALES WALKED THE LAND

8 April, 1724

It was two years since I arrived on the island, and one year since I began my Rapanui lessons with Iolana. I could no longer pretend that I wasn't fluent in the language. Nor could I go on mispronouncing words as an excuse to get her to spend more time with me correcting my pronunciation. She had heard me speak enough at this point to know that my accent was almost perfect. Coincidentally, in teaching me her language, she had learned mine. Her Spanish was remarkably good and our conversations were peppered with a mixture of both languages to the extent that no one but us knew what we were talking about.

She had a quick and agile mind, and her curiosity about the world beyond the sea was insatiable. Europe in particular fascinated her. She never tired of hearing about the different countries and their people, but could never understand how civilizations so advanced, so rich in history and culture, could be in a perpetual state of war. Some things are difficult to explain.

Through almost daily contact I had grown less strange, less foreign, less frightening to her. By the simple act of association, I was less of a threat and more of a pupil, a teacher, and I hoped, a friend. I doubt she would admit it, but I think she was actually beginning to like me. That is not to say that I wasn't often an irritant and sometimes an enemy. I walked a fine line. Iolana was feral in the sense that she was about half wild, and you can never expect to get all of the wild out of any creature that started that way—which is another way of saying a man could lose a hand trying to pet her. Her resistance to any kind of intimacy on my part was assuaged by her unbridled joy in almost anything that came her way. It was impossible for me to be around her without being happy.

I think she came to look forward to our daily walks almost as much as I did because she would often be waiting for me at our appointed meeting place beside a particular group of Gorgon statues that stood on a cliff with their backs to the sea. From there we must have hiked every inch of that island engrossed in conversation and trading stories about the vastly different worlds we came from.

As for myself, I was no longer pale and anemic looking. My hair hung down to my shoulders and was bleached from the sun. My light skin had turned the color of burnt and buttered toast from constant exposure to the elements. If any of my friends back home were to see me now, they likely would think me mad. I certainly must have looked a bit savage, but in truth I had never been more comfortable in my own skin. That is not to say I was willing to go around entirely naked like my fellow islanders. Such indecency was unthinkable given my European sensibilities. My daily attire consisted entirely of a pair of wool pants cut off above the knee. I tried a feathered hat like the ones the men wore on festival nights, but Iolana laughed it off my head. After that I wore a cap of woven ferns to shade my sunburnt face. Despite my odd eccentricities, the good people of Rapa Nui had come to accept me as part of their community and went out of their way to be kind and friendly.

Almost all the young women on Rapa Nui were tall and statuesque, but none were as beautiful and stunning as Iolana. She carried herself like a queen which only made her more exotic in my eyes. Much to my relief, she had taken to wearing a loin cloth on our hikes. Sensing my continued discomfort, she added one of the feathered tops she wore for festivals. At least now I could look at her without blushing.

10 May, 1724

Today we took our walk to *Anakena* beach. The secluded, crescent-shaped cove had the island's only true sandy beach and was one of our favorite places, but it was a long hike to get there. We left early that morning and along the way passed many *moai* (statues) that had been erected near the water. At one point we were walking and I was telling her about the canals of Amsterdam and the men who poled the barges there when she stopped and confronted me.

"So much talk about what your people do and where they come from. Do you think my people just dropped out of the sky like Boris?"

"Did you?"

"We wear feathers, so now you think we have wings?"

"I don't know, let me check . . ."

She pointed impatiently out to sea. "We come from there."

"The northwest? There's nothing out there but open ocean."

"The stories passed from generation to generation say that our ancestors, led by Hoto-Matua, paddled in their canoes for nearly ninety days to get here, bringing with them seeds and plants and animals. Eventually for water to drink they had only the rain that fell. The folklore says that when they arrived, they came ashore at *Anakena* beach."

I couldn't imagine a journey of that kind across open ocean. Then again, how else would these people have gotten here? "How long ago?" I asked.

"Many lifetimes. Some say fifty."

"How long have the Gorgons been here?"

"It is said they were here when our people from the distant islands first came. There were many of them then and the people called them 'Long Ears'. Legend says they came like birds in things that flew."

"Solar gravity ships."

"Solar what?"

"Nothing. Isn't that our cove up there?"

We climbed up on an altar made of gigantic stones that the natives called an *ahu*. The joints between the stones were so tight that I could not get my knife blade between them. Iolana laid out our picnic lunch and we sat eating while watching the seabirds wheel above the water. Behind us on the *ahu* stood seven enormous *moai* wearing red lava hats called *pukao* and staring out at the dark blue, white-capping sea. Waves lapped gently at the sand before us, and above the waves where the sand was dry there were skeletons of four enormous whales that had beached themselves in some distant past. Their bleached bones lay like the curved ribs of big-bellied ships run aground in a storm.

"Why do you suppose those whales committed suicide like that?" I asked absently.

Iolana didn't reply and instead sat staring at the skeletons. "There was a time when whales walked the land," she said at last. "Maybe these whales were trying to remind themselves so when it came time for them to be reborn, they would remember."

"Maybe," I said. Did everybody but me believe in reincarnation?

We looked on as sand fleas danced in and around the see-through bodies of the leviathans. Curious, I jumped off the stone altar and walked the short distance to the beach to examine them more closely. When I was at the university in the Netherlands, I saw a human skeleton for the first time. It was fascinating and I learned what I could about it including the names they had given the bones, but I had never seen anything like this.

The skeletons were at least fifty feet long and the bones of each one must have weighed tons. I tried lifting one of the long jawbones and could not budge it. The bowed ribs towered over my head and attached to a line of what I assumed were vertebrae that stretched from head to tail. A slab of white bone similar to a human knuckle stuck straight up from each vertebra and marched down the ridge of the backbone looking like a row of bleached white tablets. *Tablets,* I thought, tugging on one of the ribs. It was firmly attached to the spine and wouldn't budge. I braced my feet, leaned my weight against it and pulled with all my might. There was a loud cracking sound and I fell backward in the sand with the huge bone on top of me. Behind me on the altar I could hear Iolana laughing.

I picked myself up and made an elaborate show of brushing myself off, much to her amusement. Then, shouldering the great curved rib with the vertebra attached, I staggered back to the altar. Iolana sat watching me like I was crazy. I leaned my prize against the stone near where her brown legs were dangling down.

"What are you going to do with that thing," she giggled, "pick your teeth?"

"Thought I might try my hand at ship building," I said. "Bone would be sturdier than wood."

"Why a ship?"

"I might want to go home someday."

Her face fell. "You are home, Maximilian. Didn't you know that?"

A chill went up my spine. She was right, I was home in a way I had never been home before. Smiling to myself, I picked up the rib, swung it in a wide circle and broke the vertebra off against the stone.

"You don't have to get mad about it." She sounded hurt. "I thought you were happy here."

"I am." I picked up the vertebra with its white knuckle attached and brushed it off. "This is the piece I wanted."

"I think the sun, it has affected your brain."

"My brain is fine." I sat the piece down and scrambled back up onto the altar beside her.

"What are you going to do with that ugly thing?"

"I need to talk to Boris first before I tell you."

"You men and your secrets. Why not take those ribs and build us a house?"

"Us?" I was stunned.

She turned suddenly and kissed me. I nearly fell off the altar. If one of those whales had gotten up off the beach and swam off, I couldn't have been more stunned.

"You . . . you just kissed me," I stammered.

"I would be old and gray if I waited for you to do it," she announced indignantly, then sobered when she saw my startled expression. "It is not okay?"

"Do it again and I'll let you know."

I had been dying of longing, drowning in loneliness, and didn't even know it. Rousing myself, I saw she had climbed down off the wall and was smiling back up at me. I climbed down after her, she took my hand and silently led me around behind a sandy knoll a short distance away.

Afterward, we lay together in the warm sand. Iolana was silent a long time staring up at the sky. I was afraid she was having regrets and asked her what was wrong.

She laughed gaily. "I was just making our wedding plans is all."

"I didn't know we were engaged."

Her eyes filled with anger. "What do you think it was that we just did?"

My heart beat wildly. I was so filled with happiness I couldn't speak.

"It was all a lie, then?" she demanded. "You didn't propose?"

I took her in my arms. "If it's all the same to you, I would like to 'propose' again so I can make sure you heard me this time."

She blushed. "I was hoping you would."

My life rushed back into me, and for the first time since arriving on the island, I began to live again. We were very late that night getting home, and after that we went to our secluded cove at *Anakena* beach as often as possible so I could repeat my 'proposal'.

Chapter Twenty-Five

CARVED IN BONE

December 23rd—Little Inagua Island, Bahamas
Aboard the Fortuna Explorer, 3 a.m.

The sea was calm and the salvage ship was motionless in the water. Everyone aboard was asleep except Nikki who sat on her sofa in the common room with a blanket around her shoulders absorbed in the leather bound journal in her lap. The only sound was the low, electrical hum of the ship's motors and pumps. She loved that sound. To her, it sounded like the pulse of a great, benevolent beast that was holding her safe and protected in its arms. Nobody had to tell her she wasn't the domestic type. The ship was her home, and she loved that it floated and went exciting places. And she loved this time of night. Her intuition was so much clearer without the noise and distraction of other people's energy and emotions.

She looked up from the journal and sighed. *Sam would like this*, she thought. *Sam* did *like this in his former life when he was Max.* She smiled thinking of them both. They were different in so many ways, and yet they both loved her—which was all that mattered, really. She felt twice blessed.

Exhausted as she was, she couldn't stop reading, and turned the page.

***

11 May, 1724

The day after Iolana and I made love for the first time, I returned to *Anakena* beach without her to retrieve my piece of whale bone. Shouldering the big vertebra I had broken off from the whale's rib, I lugged it back to our cave and set it at Boris's feet. He looked down, then up at me in disgust, waiting for an explanation.

I cleared my throat. "You said that when your people had to flee the barbarians and escape to Rapa Nui that some things got left behind. Most important of these, you said, was 'The Sphere of Knowledge' that explained how your amazing science works including how to make light in a bottle."

"Tubes, not bottles."

"You also said that it was written in Gorgonese."

"In our language, yes."

"You may recall that by education and nature, I am an antiquarian like you, a student and chronicler of history and civilizations."

"Do you have a point, Max, because I'm hungry?"

"My point is this: I have a strong feeling your Sphere of Knowledge may still exist. Whether it does or not, I would still like to make a record of your language. A translation for future generations to discover and read. Does that sound crazy?"

"Impossible, but not crazy."

"Why impossible?"

"Gorgonian is far too complicated. A translation would take years, a lifetime, and I doubt you could complete it even then."

"You got anything better to do, because I sure don't?"

"I assume this has something to do with this disgusting piece of bone you just brought into my cave?"

"Before arriving on this island," I explained, "I spent many months aboard ship. To occupy my time, I learned a new skill. Something that could prove very useful to us now. An old sailor taught it to me. It's called 'scrimshaw'."

"Scrimshaw," he repeated. *"What is this 'scrimshaw'?"*

"A way of making beautiful carvings on whale bone."

He made a thoughtful sound deep in his throat while studying the vertebra that lay on the ground between us. *"You want to carve my language into that?"* he asked.

"I'd like to try. Science like you described would make this a better world in so many ways."

"In the right hands, it would. In the wrong hands it would bring nothing but chaos and disaster. Your species is not ready for such knowledge."

"I'm not talking now. I'm talking generations from now when some-one finally finds what we've done and tries to make use of it."

And then what?"

"Then maybe you will have fulfilled your mission of seeding the stars to aid evolution after all. Leaving a key to your language behind could be your greatest accomplishment. A legacy that would assure your science does not die with you."

He walked a short distance away, rubbed his massive chin and came back. *"You're going to need a lot more bone than this."*

"There's an unlimited supply back on *Anakena* beach. See this knuckle sticking out of this piece of the backbone? It would make the perfect scrimshaw tablet. All I need is a way of cutting it off. My knife is good for carving, but as a saw it's useless."

Boris reached behind his back, drew something from his waistband and shook it out as if to free what was inside. A thin, slender beam of red light shot out. He made a swift movement, drew the burning light across the base of the slab of bone I wanted, and my tablet fell free.

"What . . . what is that thing?" I stammered in amazement.

"A knife like the one you carry on your belt," he answered. *"I use mine for all the same things you do. A Gorgon is given one at birth and it stays with him even after death."*

"After death?"

"He might need it to cross over, but the main reason is to keep it out of the hands of primitive people like you."

"I see." I couldn't tell if he was making a joke or not.

"Do you?" he went on. *"Miracles like a laser knife are a double-edged sword. Humans at your stage of evolution would spend all their time cutting each other in half with it if they had one."*

"Laser knife," I marveled, picking up the piece of bone he had cut off for me and turning it over in my hands. It was roughly the size of the big leather-bound journal I wrote in every day, the perfect size and shape for a scrimshaw tablet. All I needed now was a way to smooth the surface so I could carve on it with my knife and sail needles that Oskar had given me for detail.

I sometimes forget that Boris can read my mind. He took the bone fragment from me, made an adjustment to his laser knife and passed a wide beam of red light over its surface. Brushing away the residue, he handed it back. The piece of bone was smooth as glass.

"We begin!" he announced abruptly.

"Now?"

"Of course, now."

"Okay," I said, thrilled that he was willing to participate. "Let's start with your alphabet. How many letters?"

"We don't have letters per se, we have characters. A character generally represents one syllable in spoken Gorgonese and may be a word on its own or a part of a polysyllabic word."

"Characters," I repeated slowly. "How many?"

"Over fifty thousand, although you only really need about twenty thousand to get by."

I was overwhelmed. This really was going to take a lifetime. "Okay," I said, "let's start with something simple. How about the word 'the'?"

"That's easy," he said, *"there are only five characters for that."*

"Easy," I repeated weakly as five characters appeared in my mind looking like five different plates of spaghetti.

"Here are how they are used." He proceeded to make several high-pitched, unintelligible sounds to demonstrate that hurt my ears.

I went to my corner of the cave and retrieved the packet of sail needles from my trunk. Returning, I selected the sharpest one and etched the Spanish words for 'the' into the bone: *la-las-lo-los-el.* After *la* I etched the feminine singular Gorgon character for 'the', then showed it to Boris for his approval. He studied the character a moment, made a couple of small corrections and remarked that I had lousy handwriting—an unfortunate handicap acquired from years of scribbling notes in academic lectures. Undeterred, I took out my knife, and with the promise and excitement that comes with the beginning of a new endeavor, I began to carve.

***

18 May, 1724

My first attempt at a scrimshaw tablet took a week and ended up a mess; my characters were too large and I soon ran out of space. The next day Boris went with me to *Anakena* beach to help me harvest a supply of whalebone tablets. Using his light knife, he went down the spine of the whale I had taken my first tablet from slicing off squares of bone like pats of butter. On the way back I struggled to carry four of them in my arms while he carried a pile of the bleached rectangles under one arm like a stack of schoolbooks. I now had enough writing material to carve on for a few years, and there were still three more skeletons I hadn't touched yet.

Walking home laden down with whalebone, we passed a number of random *moai* scattered along the barren coast. Boris stopped at each one, gazing up at the gigantic, square jawed face so like his own as a sorrow settled over him.

"I'm sorry about your friends," I said, watching him mutter a silent prayer. "For your loss, I mean."

He nodded and walked on without looking back. The trail wound inland over rolling, denuded hills. Eventually he brightened and I heard him say, *"Congratulations on your engagement, Max."*

"You know about that?" I was shocked.

"The whole island knows. We've known for over a year."

"Iolana and I have only been engaged eight days. How could you possibly . . .?"

"Apparently, the only people who didn't know you were in love were the two of you."

My cheeks flushed red. "Since I'm the last to know," I said irritably, "can I ask you something?"

He shifted his load of my bone tablets to the other arm. *"Certainly."*

"Will you be my best man?"

"I'm not a man, Max."

"My best Gorgon, then."

A smile spread across his immense face. *"It would be an honor."*

Chapter Twenty-Six

WHALE HOUSE

20 May, 1724

Iolana made it clear from the beginning she had no intention of living in a dark cave; she needed to live in the sun. I couldn't say that I disagreed; Boris's cave had become oppressive now that I could see a way forward with my life. Once we realized our engagement was public knowledge, we started making plans for our new home.

Iolana was thrilled. "Shall I start collecting straw to make the mud bricks you told me about?" she asked excitedly.

"I've got a better idea."

In the days that followed I made so many trips to *Anakena* beach I thought my arms and feet would fall off from dragging back the heavy ribs from the whale that had provided me with my initial supply of tablets.

Iolana chose a plot of land on a sunny knoll she had always loved about half way between the village and Boris's cave, and we went to work leveling the ground as best we could. Working side by side, our joy in building our first home together was intoxicating and our energy was boundless.

Boris used his light knife to help me square the ends of the towering whale ribs, then cut blocks of lava for foundation stones and put a big hole in the center of each one. I sunk the stones in the ground about a foot apart and used them to secure the bottom ends of the ribs. The top ends of the bones I leaned together so that they supported each other at the peak, and Boris reached out with his long arms and tied them together for me. With the framework complete, the ribs curved out to form a wide circular base that was as solid as a stone church. Standing back and studying it, I thought it looked vaguely familiar and realized it reminded me of drawings I'd seen of teepees used by indigenous tribes dating back thousands of years.

With the help of some women from the village, Iolana set about weaving heavy matting from palm fronds to cover the walls and floor. I installed the panels, sealed the seams with a kind of glue the natives made from fish stock, then discovered to my delight that they allowed the light and the cooling tropical breezes to pass through while keeping the worst of the elements out.

We built a small interior fire pit and a larger one outside, then fashioned a whalebone door covered in the skin of a wayward seal that had somehow found its way to Rapa Nui and eventually died of old age.

30 August, 1724

Three months after we started the house, it was finished. Everyone from the village came to see what we had built. Most agreed it was the most beautiful and amazing dwelling on Rapa Nui. Those that didn't like it I could tell were jealous. When our visitors had gone Iolana and I stood hand in hand on our knoll, our backs to the sparkling sea, admiring our new home.

"I'm going to live in a whale!" she cried excitedly. "I feel like that fellow Jonah you told me about."

"The whale kicked Jonah out after three days."

"He better not try it with me, I'll kick him in the ribs. Whale House is our house now, mine and yours!"

"Whale House," I repeated. "I like it."

"Maximillian, when we have a family, we're going to need to add on. I want lots of children."

"I've got three more whales," I said. "Plenty of ribs for a house full of kids."

***

13 November, 1724

Six months after I first 'proposed', Iolana and I were married on *Anakena* beach before the altar of the seven *moai*. The ceremony was performed by the high priest of the island who wore a painted cape, an elaborately feathered headdress and brandished a tall feathered staff as a symbol of his mystical authority. The wedding guests numbered a thousand or more and represented nearly half the population of the island. Food and decorations were brought, driftwood was piled high on the beach for a bonfire and excitement ran high in anticipation of the feast and celebration that was to follow.

Gasps of admiration went up when Iolana appeared wearing a white feathered skirt, a white feathered top to match and a garland of white flowers atop her black flowing hair. The gasps were of a different sort when I appeared. My wedding attire, carefully folded in my trunk since leaving Holland, consisted of an embroidered frock coat that hung to my knees, a gold stitched vest, white lace that billowed at my throat, rose-colored stockings, knee britches and an elegant pair of pointed shoes.

It had always been my intention to dress in this fashion if I were to marry. Seeing the shock on everyone's face, I realized I might be a little overdressed for the occasion. Poor Iolana looked like she was going to die of embarrassment. Her day would be ruined if I couldn't fix it. The situation called for drastic action.

I stuck out my chest and began to strut about like a toy soldier, marching around with my head held high while proudly holding out my lapels with both hands. If the islanders were going to accept me, I was

178

going to have to accept myself. If I was uncomfortable, ashamed, embarrassed to be me, I would be an embarrassment to my bride forever. At first, no one knew what to make of my antics. I continued to parade getting more and more worried that I was making an even bigger fool of myself when I began to see smiles, then heard laughter and finally wild cheers of approval going up from the crowd. The world loves a clown apparently, even on Rapa Nui.

My performance that day earned me not only the wholehearted approval of my differences, but the wholehearted approval of my marriage to the most beautiful woman on the island. My bride's chagrin over my costume turned to relief when she saw that everyone was loving it, and then she loved it, too.

We stood in the sand before the high priest with our backs to a setting sun as it boiled into the sea. Boris towered over us looking especially elegant with flowers wound around his gigantic head. Iolana's sisters and cousins stood in a row beside her, her twelve brothers stood beside me in rather menacing postures and our many guests crowded around. I won't try to describe the shouts and grunts and incantations of the priest in performing our ancient ceremony, but I will record that as it went on the left sides of our faces were painted in streaks of brown, and our hands were painted in red. With the paint still wet on our palms we pressed them to a square of papyrus-like paper made from the pressed stems of reeds. The paper with our red handprints on it was then laid at our feet as our binding wedding contract. I realized then that in the distant past the red on our hands had not always been paint, and was relieved to think that the bloodletting portion of the ceremony had been eliminated.

At some point the traditional roasted bird appeared, and we both ate from it before it was passed around to the relatives to have a bite. As for the rest of that day, it is all a blur of ritual chants and the gentle swaying rhythms of island music with Iolana's magnificent face smiling up at me bright and joyful as the day.

That night, beneath the looming presence of the seven *moai* that seemed to come alive in the sparks of the fire, we danced and feasted with our friends and relatives in a wild, frenetic celebration of our union. I remember Iolana's mother showering me with tearful kisses, her father promising to make a farmer out of me and her brothers, all twelve of them, promising to teach me how to fish unless it was necessary to kill me for wronging their sister. I remember Iolana telling me how excited she was that I could start getting my *"tataus"* now. I swallowed hard. As much as I admired the elaborate skin drawings that decorated the bodies of the island's men, I didn't have the heart to tell her that tattoos were definitely not for me.

And in the gray dawn, when it was just the two of us laying together warm and close in Whale House, Iolana moved into my heart and into my soul, and I was no longer from Spain or Holland, I was from Rapa Nui and I was truly home.

Chapter Twenty-Seven

THE LIBRARY

December 23rd—Inagua Island, Bahamas
Aboard the Fortuna Explorer, 10 a.m.

Nikki sat on her sofa sound asleep with the blanket still wrapped around her shoulders. Max's journal lay open in her lap and her big glasses were in her hand. Sam came in covered in grease from servicing the big dredging rig on the stern of his ship, saw that she was still sleeping and stood smiling down at her. His presence woke her up. She stretched, sat up straight and wiped dried tears from her eyes.

"Honey, what is it?" he asked in alarm.

"I'm so happy, is all! We just got married, Sam! Isn't that wonderful?"

He looked confused. "Did I miss something?"

"No! You told me all about it in your journal. You were so cute. I just adored you."

"Nikki, what the hell are you talking about?"

"Us, silly. Our wedding on Rapa Nui. We made the most beautiful couple."

"Wish I could have been there."

"But you were! That's the point, don't you see? I'm reading about *us*!"

"Us," he repeated. "You sure this isn't just your overactive imagination talking again?"

"I've never been surer of anything in my life. I loved your wedding outfit, by the way."

"I've always been a snappy dresser. What were you wearing?"

"More than my usual, from the sound of it. I can't wait for us to get there."

"Easter Island? No way."

"We don't call it that."

"Whatever you call it, it's thousands of miles from here. Why would we want to make a trip like that?"

Nikki took a sip of her coffee, set the journal aside on the sofa, and got up to take a shower before continuing her reading. "I don't know why. Soon as I do, I'll let you know. All I know for sure is we're going."

***

Max's Journal
December 1, 1724

With our wedding behind us, we settled comfortably into Whale House, and I got back to work on my scrimshaw dictionary. My progress was slower than I hoped not because I was a slow carver, but because I was no artist. It took me a long time to scratch my sloppy characters into the bone.

I was sitting cross legged in Whale House carving one of my bone tablets when Iolana walked in. She watched me for a few minutes before shaking her head and telling me I was doing it all wrong.

"You can do better, I suppose?"

"I can show you a better way, yes."

"Please," I said irritably. "By all means."

"Boris can put the images in my head just as easily as he can put them in yours," she began. "I can use them to make little pinpricks in the bone using one of your sail needles and *tataus* dye. The black color will fade over time just like it does on skin, but at least it will give you a pattern to work from. You won't have to make the designs yourself or worry about their size or accuracy. Working together we can make it go a lot faster."

"You really want to spend your time doing this?" It made me mad that she was right, so naturally I wanted to discourage her. "It's tedious work."

"If I make the words in Spanish to go with Boris's strange characters, I learn to write your language as well as speak it," she went on brightly. "A good thing, no? I don't know how it is in this Kingdom of Spain where you are from, but here on Rapa Nui, Boris has taught us that a husband and wife are equal partners who help each other every way they can."

"How do you expect me to be in charge if we're equal partners?"

She smiled and didn't say anything.

Iolana's method worked perfectly. Boris put the Gorgon characters in her mind, she dipped the sail needle I gave her in black die and rapidly tattooed the image into a bone tablet with tiny dots. I was then able to follow her design with my knife and carve the characters twice as fast. An added benefit was that she was an artist. Her drawings were delicate, precise and beautiful where mine were awkward and ugly.

22 March, 1725

We had been working on the scrimshaw tablets together for several months. One day we were in Boris's cave working because he had given Iolana a complicated character and she wanted to make sure she was translating it correctly before going home to complete the work. Boris walked in, looked over Iolana's shoulder and complimented her on her needlework. He said it was as good as any Gorgon scholar could do. He then disappeared into the tunnel at the back of his cave and we didn't see him again for hours. We were about to leave and go home when he reappeared.

"You are going to want to see this," he said, ducking back into the cave and motioning for us to follow.

Curious to find out what he was being so mysterious about, we got up and trailed after him. He quickly disappeared ahead, but he had let me show Iolana his "Cave of the Moon Pool", as he called it, so we both knew the way. She had pretty much recovered from her incredulity over seeing his gravity ship, but she was still asking endless questions. Boris's explanations seemed to make more sense to her than they did to me.

A lot of twists and turns later we arrived at his cave. The pond of seawater lay shimmering in soft light as before, his Solar Gravity Ship still hovered a foot or so off the ground, and the shaft of daylight from the long, narrow well above it was shining down. Protruding from the back of his ship, the single Portable Fusion Reactor still glowed in its tube like a candle flickering in the wind.

Boris was waiting for us when we entered. *"What do you think of that?"* he announced, pointing the beam of his light knife at a wall.

I searched the area where a red light was dancing over the black lava, but could see nothing unusual.

"Shelves!" he announced proudly.

"Shelves?"

"That is what you call them, isn't it? A place to keep books?"

I looked again. Boris had indeed been busy with his knife. The walls of the cave were carved out in rows of perfectly shaped rectangles tall and deep enough to accommodate our scrimshaw tablets.

"A library for the dictionary!" I exclaimed. "What a terrific idea!"

Iolana was relieved. "I was wondering where we were going to put all the carvings. They're piling up all over my house until we can barely move."

And that was the beginning of how a record of the language of a great and advanced civilization came to be hidden in a lava cave deep beneath an island in the middle of the Pacific Ocean.

Chapter Twenty-Eight

THE LAST MOAI

18 December, 1727

Three years passed and Iolana still wasn't pregnant. She wanted to keep trying and I certainly had no objection to that, but I already knew it was hopeless. She kept wanting to blame herself. I told her it wasn't her, it was me. She refused to believe it, but I knew, don't ask me how, that we would never have children of our own.

Sadness overwhelmed her. Before now, I had never seen Iolana desolate and miserable. It was hard to watch. Then one day after weeks of grieving, the light came back into her eyes, warm and healing as the sun after a storm. And in the way happy people always manage to be happy no matter what, we found another way.

She started inviting the children of her brothers and cousins to come and visit us. Some days we had a dozen or more boys and girls of all ages in and about the house squealing and making noise. They came to love us as much as we loved them and it was often hard to get them to go home. We were usually grateful for the peace and quiet after one of their chaotic visits, but always looked forward to them coming back again. I enjoyed the children and they enjoyed me, but Iolana was their favorite. They considered her their second mother. I was glad of it because they clearly filled a place in her heart that needed young and helpless things to love.

I fished and farmed and together we worked on the whalebone dictionary, and over time we became "grandparents" to half the children on the island. Parents were continually dropping their kids off for us to watch while they went about their daily business. It seemed to me that they were taking advantage of us, and I suggested to Iolana that we should start charging a nanny fee.

She looked at me like I had suggested we start roasting the children and having them for supper. "Are all Spaniards as greedy as you?" she demanded.

"Probably a little," I said, wondering what she would think of the Spaniards who I assumed were still engaged in the African slave trade.

21 August, 1764

Our life on Rapa Nui for the most part was as gentle and fragrant as the South Pacific breezes. We lived and loved with all our hearts and somehow forty years slipped away. One day we were young, and then we were old. Neither of us knew how it happened so quickly, it just did.

I was sixty-eight years old and my hands were gnarled and painful from years of carving. Iolana's long black hair was short and gray now, but to me she was as beautiful as ever. I asked her one day if she was sad about never having children of our own. She shook her head. "Sadness is a language of the heart," she smiled. "It only has words if we give it words. It only has a memory if we give it one. I sometimes visit my sadness, but it is like returning to a place I used to live and seeing it through a stranger's eyes. I don't live there anymore."

***

1 November, 1764

We stood with Boris in the Cave of the Moon Pool while he removed the light tube from the back of his gravity ship and filled its holding tank with seawater from the shimmering pond. I had retrieved my last candle from my sea chest and held it high so he could see what he was doing.

He grunted and straightened painfully after closing the lid to the reservoir in the rear of the tube and plugging it back into the ship.

"You alright?" I asked as the soft glow that lit the cave flickered back on.

"Just age," he replied. *"My centuries are catching up with me. My time is almost done."*

"Don't say that!" Iolana cried. "I don't know what we'd do without you."

"Miserable excuse for fuel, this sea water," he complained, looking down at his inoperative gravity ship. *"My deepest regret is that I don't have the second power tube with the right fuel to take me home."*

Iolana gathered his massive hand in both of hers and held it gently. He looked down at her with a sad and gentle smile.

After all the many years of carving scrimshaw tablets, the library had morphed into a somewhat abridged version of a Gorgon dictionary. I walked over and slipped one of the last tablets into the shelves. All around us now the walls were lined with the outside edges of the bone-white slabs. I marveled at how we could have drawn and carved so many. The Cave of the Moon Pool was packed with so many "books" it looked like one of the rooms in the great library at Leiden University in the Netherlands where I had gone to school so many years ago. It was a magnificent sight and a magnificent accomplishment, the work of a lifetime, and I was glad to have shared it with the two people I loved most in the world.

We were about to leave when I heard Boris cough. He sounded like a sea lion with a toothache. Iolana helped him to rest his weight against the slender cylinder of his gravity ship. His coughing fit got worse and he was having trouble catching his breath.

I reached up to try and pat his back, but he waved me away. *"I'll be alright,"* he gasped. *"Just give me a minute."*

He recovered and stood up, wavering slightly. Then taking out his "light knife", he walked over to the central wall and above the highest row of tablets proceeded to carve a large round circle in the lava that was nearly twice the depth of the book shelves. The gaping hole was clearly the place of honor in the library and it stood stark empty.

"We've already recorded practically every character in the Gorgon language," Iolana said. "What would you like us to put in there?"

"Nothing," he sighed. *"It is only a symbol for the thing your dictionary was meant to translate and never will."*

"You don't know that." I was angry that he would think we had done all this work for nothing. "The Sphere of Knowledge could still exist."

"Even if it did, how would it ever find its way here?"

***

7 November, 1764

Boris disappeared after that and we didn't see him again for several days. Iolana and I were on one of our walks to one of the more remote parts of the island when we saw our giant friend up on the side of the hill that had been the lava quarry where most of the *moai* on Rapa Nui were carved.

We climbed the hill to join him. When we got there, he was breathing hard and leaning against a partially carved *moai* that was laying on its back beneath a wall of lava. The statue was over seventy feet long, twice the size of any *moai* on the island.

"It's beautiful," Iolana said, admiring his handiwork. "Why is it so big?"

He mopped at his brow with the hand that held the "knife" he had been using to make his sculpture. *"I am the last Gorgon,"* he replied. *"I want my* moai *to be a fitting tribute."*

"It's certainly that," I observed.

"How are you going to stand it up and move it?" Iolana asked. "It must weigh twice what any of the other ones weigh."

"More than twice," he said, coughing into his hand. *"If I had a pair of properly charged fusion tubes, I could take the gravity generator from my solar ship and use it to transport my statue as easily as a mother carries her baby. As it is, I do not believe my* moai *will ever stand in my honor."* His eyes roamed over the partially completed statue. *"Another sorrow I must bear."*

Iolana, feeling his sadness without really understanding what he had just said, smiled and nodded, her eyes moist with tears.

***

14 November, 1764

It came time for the annual Screaming of the Rats. Iolana and I joined in with the rest of the islanders to follow Boris around joyfully yelling our heads off as he drove thousands of the disgusting rodents over the cliffs and into the sea with his own horrible silent scream.

This year the jolly giant wasn't moving as rapidly from hilltop to hilltop and crop to crop as usual. Each time he stopped to drive another hoard of rats to their doom with his god-awful noise, he broke out in a coughing fit and had to sit down. We were concerned, but he pressed on and managed to complete the task for what was to be the last time. At the celebration that night around the festival fire in the village with everyone singing and dancing and getting drunk as usual, Boris was conspicuously absent.

The next day, somewhat hungover, Iolana and I made our way to Boris's cave to add our final scrimshaw tablet to the library. He wasn't in his chamber when we got there. We passed through, entered the cave at the back and followed the labyrinth of lava tunnels to the Cave of the Moon Pool. The cave was lit as usual with pale light. Boris's Solar Gravity Ship hovered as it always had under the shaft of sunlight from the vertical lava pipe above, and our scrimshaw tablets filled the shelves.

I was slipping my last "book" into a bottom shelve with a great sense of satisfaction and relief when I heard Iolana make a stifled cry. I turned to see her staring down through the gravity ship's canopy cover. I hurried to her, followed her gaze and my mouth went dry.

Boris lay dead in his ship stretched out on his back in the white satin bed. His huge head rested on the satin pillow and a sad smile lingered on his enormous lips. Iolana bent and kissed the canopy above his head and her tears fell on the lid. She straightened and I put my arm around her and we stood a long time looking down at the still body of our friend. His sadness at not being able to return home in his ship hung about him like smoke from a dying fire and made the heaviness in our hearts even worse.

For as long as anyone on Rapa Nui could remember, Boris had walked among them. His disappearance was quickly felt, and as the days went by their concern grew to the point that they knew something terrible had happened.

Iolana and I could not reveal what we knew about Boris's death without revealing the whereabouts of his body in the Cave of the Moon Pool, the library we had spent our lives creating, and the inevitably terrifying sight of the "solar gravity ship" where he lay at rest. To expose these things would risk their eventual destruction. The islander's anxiety and despair over Boris's disappearance made our agony over not being able to reveal what we knew difficult to bear. It was Iolana who came up with a way to bring closure to the situation.

She announced to the village that we would likely never know what had happened to Boris, but that he was surely gone, and we should hold a memorial service in his honor. She went on to suggest that the most fitting place for his memorial would be out at the *moai* he had carved for himself that was still lying on in its back unfinished at the base of the lava cliff.

There wasn't a person on the island who didn't consider Boris a beloved friend, and they all attended the service. Around his *moai's* head the women wound a garland of flowers that looked exactly like the flowers he had worn on the day of our wedding. Iolana saw the wreath and tears streamed down her cheeks.

No one at the gathering that day could think of a thing to say. Rapa Nui had lost a son and his eulogy was written in the tears of those who loved him. After a time, the people who had gathered at his wake began to trail away in twos and threes as an unusually cold wind blew in off the ocean.

Iolana and I were the last to leave. "Sorrows are a language of the heart," she reminded me. "Some have words, and some are buried so deep there are no words."

***

14 November, 1765

Over the next year Iolana and I only visited the Cave of the Moon Pool once. Seeing Boris in his coffin perfectly preserved—he looked like he was sleeping and could easily rise up again at any moment and walk away—was too hard to bear. As proud as we were of the work we had done to memorialize his language, Boris was gone and so was the spirit with which he infused our work. He was the librarian of his own library now, and we left him to his silent vigil.

The black rats came again, as usual. There were more of them this year than I remembered. The villagers eagerly joined in for the annual ritual of screaming them into the sea. The noise they made could be heard all over the island. For their part, the rats ignored it. Without the sound of Boris's horrific scream in their ears to drive them mad, I doubt they even heard the racket everyone was making.

The celebration that night in the village around the traditional bonfire was a subdued affair, muted and muddled. No one knew what to do about the rats until someone suggested burning them out. It was agreed that this was indeed an excellent solution, and the following day much of the island's food supply went up in smoke. The rats, driven from feasting on the tasty fruits of the farmer's labor, grudgingly ran for cover. Few if any of the nasty creatures were lost in the conflagrations, but the heat from the flames did succeed in ridding them of most of their troublesome fleas. The tiny vermin, forced to abandon their hosts, quickly found refuge on the two-legged creatures of the island. People everywhere were seen itching and scratching at their arms and legs and torsos. And the unintended consequence didn't stop there. The burning of the crops started a famine.

Iolana and I saw it all happening and could do nothing about it. To our horror, people began coming down with a sudden fever. Nobody at the time thought they were going to die, but often within a day they became alarmed when swelling appeared in their groin and armpits that quickly turned to large, purulent abscesses. There was no change in their body color until black spots appeared on their skin and began to spread.

The Black Plague, the Black Death, the Pestilence—I'd read about it in my studies. People in Europe were acutely aware of its fatal effects. In the sixth century it was said that up to ten thousand people a day were dying from it. Between 1347 and 1350 the Plague killed over twenty-five million people in Europe alone, the equivalent of a quarter of the population. In the Great Plague of London, 1665-1666, a fifth of the population, some one hundred thousand Londoners, died. Nobody knew what caused it, nobody knew how to cure it, nobody knew why some came down with it and others were immune. All anyone knew was that when an individual died, the mass of fleas that inhabited the corpse jumped onto the nearest living person and they too began to itch and scratch.

Bodies were accumulating faster than we could bury them. Each night funeral pyres lit the sky. Iolana was everywhere at once trying to minister to the sick and dying. The Pestilence that arrived aboard the three Dutch ships that brought me here forty years ago was finally decimating the island's small population. Deadly fever burned through our midst the way the fires had burned our crops. A pall of fear and panic settled over what, only days before, was a peaceful paradise. We were living a nightmare, and overnight everything changed.

With so many dying of the Black Plague, food became a little more plentiful, but was still in short supply. Iolana brought the sick and dying what we could spare from our garden and any fish we could spare from what I caught. She would put it to their lips, they would smile weakly up at her and shake their heads.

Chapter Twenty-Nine

SEE YOU SOON

1 May, 1766

We thought for the longest time that we were among the lucky few who were immune to the Black Death. Tragically, it was only me. Iolana died on a spring day in 1766. It was the kind of day she loved the most, the kind when nobody dies, with the flowers in bloom, the sun shining brightly and the tropical breezes blowing gently through Whale House.

She lay propped up on our sleeping pallet. I sat on the floor mat beside her wiping her fevered head with a moist cloth and trying to keep a brave expression on my face. Two days ago, she had been as vital and healthy as ever, going about her chores with encouraging words for everyone. Like so many on the island, the Plague struck her suddenly and without warning. One minute she was fine, the next the life was ebbing out of her and taking my life with it. She knew as well as I did that the dying didn't take long.

She looked up at me and smiled bravely. I tried to smile back, but my tears got in the way.

"Thinking about it only makes it worse," she said, her voice barely above a whisper.

I nodded, unable to speak.

Her lips moved again and I leaned in closer to hear.

"One last kiss?" she repeated.

My lips brushed hers and her eyes fluttered closed.

"Iolana!"

Her eyes fluttered open again and I gasped in relief. She smiled the same way she had smiled at me on our wedding day and I thought my heart would explode.

"See you soon," she murmured, and her eyes closed for the last time.

I buried my wife on our knoll next to Whale House where we had lived and loved for forty-six years. Blindly, robotically, I carved her headstone out of a blank whalebone tablet. When it was finished, I sunk it in the ground at the head of her grave. It read:

Iolana Martínez / Beloved wife of Vicente Maximilian Martínez / 1705-1766.

Tears blurred my vision and wetted the bone. It needed one thing at the bottom, an inscription or sentiment of some kind, but I couldn't carve it. It seemed too final.

In the days that followed, I fell into an abyss of loneliness, bleak and afraid. I was gutted. My only hope was that the dead did not feel the pain of the living for their loss. My only wish was that the Plague would take me too . . . but I was not that fortunate.

***

2 November, 1766

Six months passed. I was a lost and broken man, going through the motions and thinking of Iolana all day every day. She was gone from my life, but not my heart. I saw her in the meadows and the hills where we had walked. At night when I slept I lay beside her, buried alive.

The island's population by now had been reduced from nearly three thousand to under four hundred, and some of them were deathly ill. I haunted the cliffs of Rapa Nui on long walks, an old man of seventy hoping to fall off into the pounding surf like one of Boris's rats. I no longer had a reason to live or a reason to even be here. Boris was gone,

Iolana was gone, my hold on the island was gone, and so was the island's hold on me. A desire rose in me to see my homeland of Spain again, one last time before I died. Once it took hold, the desire became a longing, and the longing became an obsession.

One day I was out walking along the western shore past the towering *moai* where Iolana and I had walked so often before. I felt her presence beside me, but when I looked, she wasn't there. My eyes fell on the horizon and at first, I thought I was seeing things. A tiny white cloud where the gentle curve of dark blue of the ocean met with the light blue curve of the sky. A billowing white bird, growing larger as it flew toward me. Then I saw, and my heart nearly stopped. Sails! The sails of a tall-masted galleon bearing down on Rapa Nui!

It had been forty-four years since a ship had called on the island. I used to dream of it, then as the island became my home and my life, the dream faded away. I was suddenly frightened. I couldn't let this ship land and bring the havoc and ruin that the last one had. Then a greater fear went through me. I couldn't let this ship land under any circumstances because the island was infected with Plague!

The galleon was close enough now that I could make out some detail. She was enormous, bigger than any ship I had ever seen, with a tall mast in the center, a shorter one and a bowsprit forward, and three descending shorter masts aft. Her bulging sides had too many cannon ports to count, but she was riding so low in the water I doubted a cannon ball would get too far before plowing into a wave. Her problem, I saw to my dismay, was that she was overloaded.

As fast as my old legs would carry me, I ran toward the landing place where the fishing canoes were just coming in. One was manned by fishermen I knew well and I hailed them with waving arms. They looked confused as I approached. I pointed to the billowing sails of the galleon wallowing toward us and they became frantic with excitement.

I had no problem persuading them to take me out to greet the galleon. They were bitterly disappointed, however, when I told them they could not mob the ship and swarm its decks as their fathers and grandfathers had done. I asked them if they wanted to take the chance of infecting the ship with the same black death that had killed so many of our friends and relatives, and that seemed to settle them down. It was finally agreed that a single man would paddle me out, and a fearless lad of seventeen volunteered. Before we left shore, I made him promise to stay in the canoe unless I called him aboard. He reluctantly agreed, but I had no confidence that he would keep his promise.

The ship was just dropping anchor when the young islander deftly paddled me alongside. To my great relief I saw that the ship was flying a Spanish flag. They threw a rope ladder over the side, I scrambled up, landed on the crowded deck and was shocked to see the crew pull back in alarm at the sight of me.

I couldn't understand what they were pointing and laughing at, then realized that my long scraggly hair, wrinkled, sun-blackened skin and scrawny, almost-naked body probably was not making a very good first impression. In the best Spanish I could muster, I demanded to see the captain. The crowd of crewmen appeared shocked that I spoke their language, although I imagine it was heavily accented with the Rapanui tongue after all this time.

The captain received me with a look of revulsion and disgust at having a wild man suddenly appear before him in his cabin. I had the distinct impression he thought I was going to slit his throat. As quickly as I could, I explained that I was a castaway, marooned on Rapa Nui in 1722, and had boarded his ship to request passage home.

His face hardened. Why was I marooned? I told him I had shot and killed a member of my crew. He raised his bushy eyebrows and waited for me to go on. I explained that when we first arrived here, Captain

Roggeveen's men were slaughtering the natives for no reason at all and I was desperate to stop the senseless killing.

Captain Don Felipe Gonzalez nodded thoughtfully, but did not respond. He was a tall and muscular man with a brooding face, a booming voice and, as I would soon learn, a violent temper. There was about him an air of command and authority that demanded obedience. Later on, as I got to know him, I learned that he was as quick witted as he was quick tempered, as skilled at seamanship as he was at knocking heads, as good humored and funny as only a fearless man can be.

Captain Gonzalez assured me that he had no intention of harming the natives. His crew had spotted the island quite by accident and they were stopping only long enough to take on fresh food and water.

When I told him everyone on his ship would die if he sent men ashore, he exploded with laughter. When I told him why, he sobered and quickly backed away.

"Have you then taken it upon yourself to infect my ship with the Plague, sir?" he demanded.

"Unfortunately, I am immune to the disease," I assured him. "Were I not, I most certainly would not be here speaking with you."

He let out a long breath. They had just crossed twenty-five hundred miles of open ocean and were in desperate need of fruits and vegetables. I explained about the famine the island was experiencing and told him the closest place to resupply his ship was going to be the mainland some twenty-three hundred miles east of here. He slammed the top of his desk so hard with his fists it shook the cabin.

This probably wasn't the best time to bring it up, but I reminded him I was seeking passage home for myself and several tons of 'books' that I had assembled.

His explosive laugh sounded like a cannon going off. "A *single* ton of books would send us to the bottom! The extra weight of even one more man might sink us!" His fury subsided and in a less agitated state he went on to explain that they had been three years plundering China's coastal cities for gold. He had lost his two other ships, one on a reef and the other in a typhoon. The survivors and treasure from both of the other boats had been transferred to Captain Gonzalez's ship. "There isn't a bunk or a square foot of deck space left on this vessel. If you have your heart set on departing this rock, you will just have to wait for another ship to come along."

I explained that I didn't have another forty or fifty years to wait, and he said that was not his problem. Nothing I could say would convince him, and in the end, I could only take my leave. I was heading for the door trying not to show my distress when an object on his chart table caught my eye. It was a remarkable device, made of mahogany and far more delicate and sophisticated than the one my father invented and that I had used to safely navigate Roggeveen's ships as far as Rapa Nui.

I picked it up to examine it and heard Gonzalez telling me if I broke his sextant, he would break every bone in my body. I continued my examination, sighting through and aligning the lenses, working the curved, metal, one-sixth circle at the bottom that was marked off in degrees, expressing my amazement at the advances that had been made in navigational equipment in my fifty-year absence.

"How could a madman living alone on an island for fifty years possibly know anything about navigation?" he thundered.

"I have been anything but alone," I assured him, carefully setting the wonderful sextant back on the chart table and continuing on toward the door.

"I asked you a question!" the captain demanded.

"I am a pilot," I answered without turning. "My father was the best in his day. I was the best in mine. Neither of us ever lost a ship nor once ever came close to putting one in danger."

He asked who my father was. When I told him he knew the name immediately. "Come back here," he ordered. "I lost my navigator. Fool got drunk and fell overboard on a perfectly calm night. Wasn't until the next day when he didn't show up to take his noon sighting that we realized he was missing. I'm a terrible navigator myself. Never could get the hang of that thing. Think you might still be up to the task?"

"I'm a bit rusty," I replied. "I'd have to refresh my memory, but I think I can handle it."

"It's settled then," he declared.

I paused, fingering the pieces of a beautiful chess set he had sitting out, amazed that I could hold a bishop in my palm instead of having to use both hands to move it. "Where would I bunk?"

"You can use my sitting room, but not before you get a haircut and put some clothes on."

"I don't have any clothes."

"We'll find you some."

The thought of rounding Cape Horn half naked sent a chill up my spine. "I'll need to go ashore and get my trunk."

"What's your name?" Gonzalez asked, noting my fascination with his chess set.

"Vicente Maximilian Martínez. My wife called me Maximilian."

His demeanor softened. "You play, Maximilian?"

"I had a chess partner on the island for many years," I admitted. "He taught me a little about the game before he died."

Captain Gonzalez leaned back in his chair and laced his hands behind his head. "Me, I like to place a friendly wager on a game now and then. Are you a gambling man, sir?"

"I have nothing to wager."

"We'll keep an accounting then."

My knees were weak with gratitude, but I wasn't going to let him see it. "In that case, I wouldn't mind a game to pass the time," I said as I went out.

***

Once ashore I packed my trunk with everything it would hold, then slipped my journal into the waterproof compartment in the side. When that was done, I sat down to say goodbye to Whale House and found myself in tears. It was like parting with a piece of myself. I dried my eyes and went outside to say goodbye to Iolana. Standing over her grave with a lump in my throat, I explained that I was leaving and why.

I shivered in a breeze that no longer smelled sweet, and in the silence that used to ring with Iolana's laughter and the laughter of the children, I realized this wasn't really goodbye. We take the life we lived with us wherever we go. Feelings, like storm clouds, fly on, but memories, good or bad, remain. We would always be together, Iolana and I, no matter the time and distance that seemingly separated us. I bent to kiss her head-stone and fell to my knees. Fumbling blindly for the knife in my belt, I pulled it from its sheath and began to carve the rest of her inscription. *Death is merely an intermission*, I heard her say as clearly as if she were standing there, *a time out, a pause in eternity*. Brushing away the bone dust, I stood and smiled down at her final promise to me that read . . .

See You Soon

***

The only other person I really needed to say farewell to was Boris. Heaving my heavy trunk onto my shoulder, I walked to his cave, dropped the trunk at the entrance and followed the now-familiar twists and turns of the lava tunnels to the Cave of the Moon Pool.

Looking down through the transparent canopy of his gravity ship, I thanked him for all he had done for me and all he had taught me. I told him what he had meant to me. I said that I was going home now, and understood how badly he had wanted to go home once his life here was done. I said I was sorry he didn't have a ship like mine to take him there. His suggestion of a smile told me he wasn't that concerned. He wouldn't say why.

Looking around, I admired the library Iolana and I had created together. The edges of our scrimshaw translations lined every shelf on every wall. No longer the spines of whales, they were now the spines of books. Above the central stack of crowded shelves was a large circle that was conspicuously empty. The dark hole felt like the hole in my soul, longing to be filled. I would never again be without a heavy heart over all I had lost, but as I left the cave that last time, I made a resolution to try and at least live until I died, to carry on as bravely as possible until the end, however long it took.

Chapter Thirty

THE WRECK OF THE GALEÓN SAN FERNANDO
Loudly came the savage wind
and on its breath did devils swim

1 December, 1766

Standing on the quarter deck of the *Galeón San Fernando,* I watched Rapa Nui grow smaller until it faded into the distance and finally disappeared over the horizon. Leaving the island wasn't as hard as I thought. Rapa Nui was no longer mine to lose.

The closest place to resupply, closer than the South American continent itself, was the Juan Fernandez Islands some eighteen hundred miles southeast of Rapa Nui. With good weather, favorable winds and the use of my wonderful new sextant, I managed to navigate us there in two weeks. Supplies were plentiful and the locals were generous in helping us to fill our hold. From there it was another seventeen hundred miles to Cape Horn. The weather held and we rounded the cape in fairly calm seas with the Roaring Forties at our backs. Were it not for the freezing temperatures, the floating icebergs passing dangerously close by our wooden hull, and the wallowing motion of our overloaded ship scudding along before the howling wind at a breathtaking ten knots, it might have been fun.

Our course from the Cape to Spain took us northeast in almost a straight line along the eastern shore of South America. Stopping at the Falkland Islands, we once again resupplied. During our brief stay, I was pleasantly surprised to learn that the sons and daughters of the prostitutes Captain Roggeveen marooned here fifty years ago had grown up to be prosperous and respected members of the community with the next generation following in their footsteps.

Setting sail again, I plotted a course for the eastern most tip of South America where we would leave the continent behind and head northeast across the Atlantic to Spain. It was here, off the tip of Vera Cruz, that our luck ran out. The winds no longer favored us and we were pounded by a series of gales that drove us to the west instead of the east.

Galeón San Fernando was square rigged, but with recent advances in sail design she also had sails that ran fore and aft that allowed her to run at a ninety-degree angle to the wind instead of just straight before it. As a result, we were able to sail on a broad reach up the northern coast of South America to the Caribbean Sea where I hoped the storms would abate and we could change course for Spain.

The heavy weather added many weeks to our journey which in turn prolonged the ongoing chess competition between the captain and myself. It didn't take long for me to realize that Señor Don Felipe Gonzalez was a degenerate gambler. And like most degenerate gamblers, he was not as good at his game as he thought he was. The more he lost, the more he bet. Fortunately, his supply of gems that he had plundered from the Chinese was almost endless. The diamonds, rubies and emeralds themselves meant nothing to me, but I enjoyed watching Gonzalez thunder about the cabin throwing things after he lost a few to me. If Iolana were alive, I would have given the stones to her. She liked shiny, colorful rocks.

By design, I did not win every time. After each of my big wins I would allow him to win as series of games in a row where the wager was small. Once he was puffed back up with confidence, I would suggest doubling, tripling, quadrupling the bet so that the wager for the final game was far greater than my losses on the preceding games. The technique, which I learned the hard way from Boris, never failed to draw him in. Boris seemed to enjoy letting me win games until I thought I was good enough to beat him. He would then trounce me in the next game so quickly and easily it would take my breath away. My gentle giant friend thought it was funny. I told him his mean streak was going to get him killed one day. Certainly, the captain wanted to kill me each time he was forced to hand over another of his priceless gems. For my part, I began to understand the perverse pleasure Boris took in watching me suffer. It was a pleasant way to pass the time, I must admit.

The storms drove us well north of South America until I was forced to chart a course between the islands of Cubanascam and Hispaniola. From there I hoped the winds would shift and allow us to sail east to Spain. When we arrived, conditions had only grown worse. Unseen forces had driven a westward-bound hurricane south of its course. The forces then abated and turned it north again. It was now chasing us from behind.

***

December 24th—Little Inagua Island, Bahamas
Aboard the Fortuna Explorer

"The last entry in the journal is dated *15 August, 1767,*" Nikki told Sam. "It reads, 'Inagua Island lies somewhere dead ahead. We are caught in the violence of a most fearsome storm, and if we cannot change course, I fear the worst.'"

"Adios *Galeón San Fernando,*" Sam said. "Hello sunken treasure."

"How can you be so callous?" Nikki cried. "Max died. *You* died!"

"Seems like only yesterday."

"You know, Sam, sometimes you can be a real blockhead."

"There could be some truth in that," he grinned.

Nikki spent the rest of the morning recounting to Sam all she had read in Max's journal. When she finished, he sat thinking.

"Some story," he said.

"Isn't it though."

"What do you suppose happened to those gems I won for you? I didn't see them anywhere in the wreck when I was diving on it."

Nikki had an inspiration. Bounding to her feet, she went over to Max's trunk that was still sitting on the table and began rummaging through it. Her arm disappeared up to the shoulder. Feeling around deep inside the tarred compartment where she had found the journal, her fingers closed on something soft and lumpy. She withdrew her hand, opened it and saw she was holding a leather pouch. Untying the draw-string, she peered inside.

"What?" Sam asked impatiently.

Nikki, eyes wide with excitement behind her glasses, dumped the contents of the pouch out on the table. Diamonds, rubies and emeralds rattled across the varnished surface. She gathered the sparkling gems gleefully up in her hands. "Sam, thank you!" she cried. "Thank you for my gift!"

He picked one up—a blood-red ruby that was at least five carats—and held it up to the light and whistled softly in admiration. "We can get a fortune for these."

She was horrified. "I wouldn't dream of selling them!"

"Nikki, the money from these gems will buy us a new boat."

"You won them for me," she insisted. "And you were right, I do love shiny, colorful rocks."

The look on her face melted his resistance. He wouldn't dream of depriving her of something she truly loved and wanted. "Don't know what I was thinking," he said, putting the ruby back on the table.

Heaving a sigh, she put the stones back in their bag. "I can't wait to get to Chile," she said, retying the drawstring.

"As in over-four-thousand-miles-from-here Chile? To do what, exactly?"

"Recover the Sphere of Knowledge from Gorgon city, then go on to Easter Island and find Max and Iolana's library so we can translate it."

"Nikki, that's crazy. What makes you think this Sphere even still exists?"

She raised her eyebrows and looked at him over the top of her glasses with an expression that said, "*What part of* I know things *don't you understand?*"

"Okay, so it exists," he conceded. "It's not like gold and gems that you can turn into ready cash."

"Star power, Sam! Fusion energy to make fossil fuel obsolete forever! Can you imagine giving something like that to the world?"

"I can imagine a company called 'Fusion Power and Electric' with you and me as principal shareholders."

She shook her head in exasperation. "Before you get too involved in starting your own utility company, we need to find the Sphere first."

"In a city inside a volcano," he said doubtfully.

"Dormant volcano," she corrected. "Boris told Max how to find the entrance. He put it in his journal. I could find it in my sleep."

"So now you want to go sleepwalking on a volcano. I'm a diver, Nikki, not a mountain climber."

"How hard can it be? We have to do this, Sam. It could be the find of the century."

"Or the biggest wild goose chase of our lives."

"I'm so excited. When can we leave?"

"For Chile?"

"And then for Easter Island to find the Cave of the Moon Pool!"

He blew out his cheeks. "How do you propose we pay for this little expedition of yours? If we spend the money we have left from the gold coins I lifted off the Chinese, we'll be truly broke."

Nikki untied the drawstring on her bag of gems, took a last lingering look inside, and carefully placed the bag of beautifully colored stones back on the table. "We're not going to pay for it," she smiled. "Max is."

***

December 27th—Aboard the Fortuna Explorer

Sam, Nikki, their first mate Tashtego and Sam's two Bahamian crewmen departed Little Inagua Island aboard the salvage ship *Fortuna* on a southerly course to the Panama Canal. Three days later they crossed the canal from the Caribbean to the Pacific and on December 30th dropped anchor among a cluster of cargo ships waiting at Panama City to cross the canal.

Sam went ashore with the gems from Max's chest that Nikki had given up to pay for the trip, but he could not find a buyer who would give him a fair price. Leaving Nikki aboard the *Fortuna* with Tashtego, he flew to Miami where he had a contact who bought treasure from sunken ships and didn't ask questions. As it turned out, the gems were worth more than he thought, and a week later he returned to Panama with enough money to finance two expeditions.

From Panama they charted a course to the Chilian coastal city of Antofagasta twenty-three hundred miles south. Six days later they arrived at Antofagasta's long shipping pier where they tied up the *Fortuna* behind a Chinese freighter that was loading lithium for shipment to China. Sam went into town and rented a red, four door, four-wheel drive Mitsubishi pickup. Returning to the ship in the truck, he threw camping gear and food supplies in the back, left Tashtego in charge of the boat and he and

Nikki departed on the two-hundred-mile drive to the high desert town of San Pedro de Atacama. In all, the trip from the Bahamas to Chile, with the side trip to Miami to sell the gems, had taken nearly three weeks.

January 16th—San Pedro de Atacama

That evening they checked into the same luxury hotel in San Pedro where Cyd and Alex had stayed. The next morning, January 17th, they were preparing to set out across the desert when Lascar began to erupt. The ground shook as great plumes of gray and black smoke exploded from the saddle between the volcano's east and west cones, filling the clear blue sky above with hot volcanic ash.

Nikki sat with Sam in their rental truck staring out at the eruption.

"If that city isn't toast by now," Sam lamented, "it's about to be."

Nikki referred to the map she had in her lap that detailed Atacama's topography and named the various volcanos. "The volcano that's erupting is called Lascar," she announced happily, looking up and pointing. "The Gorgon city is in Aguas Calientes. That's the bigger volcano just to the east that's sleeping like a baby."

"I don't know how any baby can sleep with all this racket going on," Sam remarked, putting the truck in drive and setting out across the desert.

By midday, rivers of lava had begun streaming down Lascar's slopes. Sam detoured to the north to avoid any chance of being stopped by a lava flow. They were nearing the sinkhole when they saw a Chinese military caravan racing back toward San Pedro and making a wide berth around the quicksand that had earlier claimed one of their vehicles. Sam assumed they had gone out of their way for a reason and followed the same roundabout route in the opposite direction. His detours were adding a lot of travel time to their journey, but what they were doing was dangerous enough without taking unnecessary chances.

Darkness had fallen by the time they arrived at the oasis at the base of Aguas Calientes. Nearby, beneath a burning sky, heaving, boiling magma was streaming down the sides of Lascar and oozing out across the desert floor in red-glowing rivers. Shadows from the eruption danced and flickered over the water and palms in front of them.

"That volcano could blow and cut us off at any minute," Sam said. "We need to get out of here before it's too late."

Nikki was peering through the darkness at something she saw moving just outside the lights of the truck. "What are all those mules doing here?" she cried. "They look like they're hobbled!"

Sam threw the shift lever in park and jumped out. "I'll turn them loose so at least they can run if they have to."

"Hurry! I'll get the truck turned around."

He was bending to unbuckle the padded leather shackle around the first mule's front feet when behind him he heard someone shouting in Spanish.

"*Alto, alto!*" came the voice. "I will do that!"

Chapter Thirty-One

VOLCÁN LASCAR

January 18ᵗʰ—San Pedro de Atacama

The sun was just coming up over the Andes behind the billowing clouds of blackened smoke rising from Lascar's saddle when a red pickup with four people inside and two more in the bed in back pulled up in front of the new medical clinic in San Pedro. The small, gleaming facility was owned, operated and staffed by China Mining and Energy Co, LTD for the use of its employees out at the lithium mine and, as a gesture of good will, for the employees of the American mine and the local citizens as well. This clinic had replaced the old one that for years had buzzed with flies and stunk of decay.

Out at the *Aeropuerto de San Pedro de Atacama* less than two miles away, a small jet had just touched down. The dull gray aircraft had a red and yellow Chinese flag emblazoned on its tail and a red and yellow star on either side of its fuselage.

The Chinese convoy returning from the volcano had radioed ahead that they had discovered a valuable artifact that needed to be airlifted to China immediately. Lt. Colonel Li was patched through to his superiors in Santiago and an intense conversation followed in which the Lt. Colonel explained the magnitude and importance of the large blue alien ball he had just recovered at great personal risk to himself and his men. He rushed on to explain that the ball contained scientific knowledge that would speed the process of China's worldwide domination by a decade or less.

A jet with two pilots aboard was dispatched from Santiago to San Pedro in the middle of the night. Their orders were to take possession of the artifact the Lt. Colonel had found and fly it to Santiago where a military transport would fly it directly to Beijing.

The military jet from Santiago sat waiting on the runway. Through its windshield the pilots could see Lascar's cones and smoking saddle forty miles south outlined sharply against the morning sky. The jet's engines were running, but its pilots could still feel the tremors shaking the plane beneath its tires.

***

Back at the clinic, Alex helped Robert carry Mateo into the clinic through the urgent care door. Sam, Nikki and Cyd followed and were told by the medical staff to wait in the lobby. Alex accompanied Mateo into the examination room so he could advise the Chinese physician on duty of the patient's condition, then stood by to make sure Mateo was treated properly.

Robert sat with Cyd, Sam and Nikki in the cold, impersonal waiting room beside himself with concern over his partner. To distract him, Nikki gave him the highlights of what she had told Cyd and Alex on their all-night trip through the desert about the Sphere of Knowledge and the scrimshaw library out on Easter Island.

"We could steal the Sphere back if we knew where the Chinese were hiding it," Sam fumed.

Robert was overwhelmed with all he had just heard. "They'll have it under such heavy guard we couldn't even get close," he said, finding his voice. "If it's not already on its way to China, I'm guessing it's about to be."

"There must be something we can do," Nikki insisted.

Robert shook his head in despair as a sudden tremor made them grab the armrests on their chairs and hold on.

***

A military vehicle arrived at the airport and drove directly out onto the tarmac where the Chinese jet sat waiting with its engines running. Lt. Colonel Li jumped out of the lead vehicle and hurried toward the aircraft clutching the Sphere to his chest as carefully as he had when he fled the volcano. The aircraft door opened, the copilot appeared in the doorway and reached to take the big blue ball from the Lt. Colonel.

Clipped, angry words were exchanged in Chinese with Li jerking the ball away, boarding the plane himself and securing it in one of the plush leather seats of the deserted cabin using two seatbelts. He then gave instructions that neither the copilot nor the pilot were to touch it. Another officer, he said, would board the plane in Santiago and take charge of it from there.

The Lt. Colonel exited the plane, the copilot closed the door and climbed back into the righthand seat of the cockpit. The jet's engines wound up with a high-pitched whine and the aircraft taxied away for takeoff.

***

Alex came out of the clinic's operating room and they all looked up expectantly. "Doctor on duty drained his wound," he informed them. "Mateo is in stable condition and in good hands medically."

Robert lifted his eyes to heaven, clasped his hands and exhaled in relief.

"The staph infection in his leg has turned septic and he might lose it," Alex went on in an objectively somber tone. "We'll know in the next forty-eight hours if the antibiotics are working or not."

Robert's lips quivered and he came to his feet wiping awkwardly at his eyes. "I want to see him," he said.

"They've given him something to sleep," Alex replied gently. "You can visit him this evening."

***

At the same time Alex was giving Robert an update on Mateo at the clinic, halfway back across the desert, Carlos was approaching the sinkhole leading his string of mules. Behind him, Lascar's smoking eruption was clouding the sky and dimming the morning light. He had been thinking all night about causing his friends to lose the strange blue ball they had found and then nearly getting them killed. Guilt and anger consumed him. The Chinese had kidnapped him and threatened to shoot his mules one at time if he didn't tell them where the others had gone, what they had found and everything he had overheard them saying about it. His forced betrayal had violated his personal code of ethics to the core. No matter that he couldn't let them kill his beloved mules. Everything that had happened was his fault.

He was so furious he nearly led his mules straight into the sinkhole before pulling up short at the rim. Sitting on his mule, he felt the ground shake violently, then heard a violent explosion. It sounded like *Pachamama* was as mad as he was and had blown herself up over it. He wheeled in the saddle in time to see the top 1,300 feet of the volcano twenty miles away detonate and disappear entirely.

Expanding magma from inside the volcano was sending thousands of tons of scorching rock and super-heated gas into the atmosphere at speeds of up to 400 miles per hour. A dense plume of dirty gray ash billowed into the sky turning the day dark as it expanded. Carlos's mules screamed and reared as a storm of choking ash fell like snow over the desert making breathing almost impossible.

***

The wind had backed into the south forcing the Chinese jet with the Sphere strapped into a seat to take off in a southeasterly direction. It thundered down the runway, achieved flying speed and rotated. As it did, the asphalt it left behind began to buck and roll in heaving waves.

The volcanic eruption was so loud even the two pilots aboard the thundering aircraft could hear it. Thinking something had gone wrong, they quickly checked their instruments and found everything in perfect working order. Glancing back up, they saw an enormous cloud of billowing black smoke fill their windshield. The captain executed a steep, desperate turn, but the wind blew the cloud directly in his path. The plane flew straight into the cloud and was completely consumed.

Scalding hot volcanic ash entered the engines, melted and stuck together in clumps of molten material, then quickly cooled, solidified and destroyed both power plants. The aircraft was still in takeoff power, but had not yet gained sufficient speed and altitude to glide. The engines quit and the jet fell out of the sky like one of the rocks that were being launched from the exploding volcano.

***

Cyd, Alex, Sam, Nikki and Robert were just coming out of the clinic and getting in the rental truck when the volcano blew. The deafening explosion shook the ground with terrifying force. Holding onto each other, they stared in horror as a mushroom cloud of boiling smoke and scalding bits of debris rose miles into the air.

"What do you suppose that did to the Gorgon's city?" Cyd asked in alarm.

"Just glad we're not there to find out," Alex said.

They heard a small jet taking off from the airport. Looking up, they saw it disappear into the cloud of volcanic debris.

Chapter Thirty-Two

RECOVERY

Carlos was fighting to control his frightened mules when he saw something falling from the sky and coming straight at him. Terrified, he quickly crossed himself. The crippled jet hit the desert floor in an explosion of sand, bounced once and careened toward him. The muleskinner closed his eyes, waiting for the end. When it didn't come, he reopened them. The plane had disappeared! He looked again and to his amazement saw that it had fallen into the sinkhole right in front of him.

Confused, he peered into the hole, saw the plane start to sink into the quicksand and jumped back. The wings found firm ground on either side of the pit and the jet shuddered and stopped. Supported by its wingtips, the crumpled jet hung suspended over its would-be grave.

It took Carlos several moments to regain his wits. When he did, all he could think was there might be survivors. He jumped from his mule and ran stumbling down the steep side of the sinkhole, then stopped in fear when the downed plane groaned and settled another foot. The wings were like bridges over the devouring sand. Extending his arms for balance, he forced himself to wing-walk along one of them. Reaching the badly damaged cabin door, he found it slightly ajar and tried to open it, but it wouldn't budge. He tried again, gave a mighty heave and it creaked open. Writhing in indecision, he gathered his courage and plunged inside.

The interior of the plane looked like a bomb had gone off. Seats were torn from their floor bolts and debris was thrown everywhere. He clawed his way forward, felt the plane settle again and froze in terror. The movement stopped, he climbed over an overturned sofa, reached the cockpit and saw that it was crushed like a beer can. Anybody in there was dead. He turned and made a quick final search of the cabin for more bodies on his way out.

Half way to the exit, something in one of the overturned seats caught his eye. Thinking it might be a child wrapped in a blue blanket, he heaved aside pieces of wreckage and righted a plush leather chair. Strapped into the seat was something familiar. He stared, then saw what it was. The orb! He'd lost it for them, and now he'd found it again. His heart raced as he fumbled to unbuckle the seatbelt, grabbed up the shimmering ball, and rushed to escape with it before the plane sank completely into the sucking sand.

***

But the Chinese jet didn't sink. The downed aircraft was still in the same position two hours after Carlos had disappeared over the distant sand dunes leading his string of mules back to San Pedro de Atacama. Twenty miles away, the horrifying eruption had died down, but smoke was still blocking the sun and raining ash on the desert floor when the Chinese convoy of emergency vehicles and military trucks arrived.

Lt. Colonel Li climbed down from the lead truck, rushed to the edge of the sinkhole and looked down at the precariously suspended wreckage. An aftershock shook the ground and he jumped back as the plane slipped a bit further. He had already lost a truck and four men to this evil sand devil and was well aware of the danger. He was also aware that the orb was aboard that plane. His reputation and his very career depended on him recovering it. Preferring to die rather than lose face, he ordered his men to keep their distance and walked alone along the wing. If it had been a cable strung between two high-rise buildings, he couldn't have been more frightened, yet his features remained blank.

The Lt. Colonel was such a zealot, such a fanatic in his loyalty and dedication to China and its leaders, that even his own soldiers didn't much care for him. Watching him now from a safe distance, the men under his command changed their opinion. The Lt. Colonel was a very brave man indeed, to try and rescue pilots who were obviously already dead.

The jet's cabin door was hanging open and Li entered cautiously. Once inside he ignored the cockpit. Two pilots more or less were unimportant. What was important was the orb. He started overturning debris, shoving things aside and searching under the seats. The seat where he had secured the alien ball was sitting at an angle. He righted it and saw it was empty, its seatbelt intact but dangling open. How could that be? He desperately searched the area around the chair, then searched the cabin again front to back thinking the orb might have gotten wedged under something. It had to be here! It couldn't walk away on its own!

Or could it? He racked his brain. Someone must have gotten here first; someone must have beaten him to it, that was the only possibility! But how? Who would even know what the orb was, let alone want to steal it? There were the people he left duct taped inside the volcano, but they were most certainly dead, burned up in the lava. They did burn up, didn't they? Had they escaped somehow? Fled the volcano, made their way here, saw the plane go down and found the orb in the wreckage? Impossible as it seemed, that had to be the answer. So where had they gone? They couldn't have gotten far on foot. He scrambled out of the plane and ordered his men back to the trucks to begin a search. The thieves were somewhere between here and San Pedro de Atacama and he would find them.

***

That evening Cyd, Alex, Sam, Nikki and Robert went back to the clinic to visit Mateo. When they walked in, they found him sitting up in bed, a little hyper from the pain pills he'd been given, but otherwise alert and in good spirits. His Chinese doctor had been in to see him. It looked like he was responding well to the antibiotics and hopefully would not lose his leg after all. His visitors celebrated the news, and Robert hugged him in relief.

Their enthusiasm quickly faded and an awkward silence fell over the room. They had risked their lives to recover the Sphere only to have it stolen by the Chinese. The thought that the miracle of fusion energy might now be used to create the ultimate weapon of mass destruction was both devastating and horrifying. They didn't want to tire Mateo any further and were saying their goodnights when the door burst open and Carlos walked in with something in his arms.

Their shouts of greeting and surprise could be heard all over the hospital. Everyone was talking at once and making a big fuss over his safe return when Cyd's voice rose above the rest.

"Carlos, what is that you're holding?"

The muleskinner grinned sheepishly and held out a big blue ball. "You looking for *theese*?"

Nikki's hands flew to her mouth. "Oh, my god!"

Alex was incredulous. "Where did you find it? How did you . . .?"

Carlos squirmed in embarrassment at being the center of attention. "Crashed airplane was sinking in the sand, you know. I walk along the wing and . . ."

"Carlos, you're amazing!" Robert cried, gently taking the Sphere from him and cradling it protectively in his own arms. "This changes everything!"

"Did anyone see you?" Alex asked anxiously. "We're you spotted?"

Carlos adamantly shook his head. "Oh *nooo* . . ."

"Are you sure?" Sam persisted. "Not the Chinese?"

"I don't *theenk* so."

"You still can't read it," Mateo remarked bitterly from his hospital bed. "What good is it?"

They'd forgotten that Mateo was in the bed of the truck on the drive back to town when Nikki told Cyd and Alex what she'd learned from Max's journal. Robert remembered that he was in the waiting room distraught over Mateo's condition when Nikki told him about the scrimshaw library. He turned to Mateo and gave him an excited summary of everything Nikki had said.

"So, we're going to Easter Island after all!" Mateo proclaimed, his incredulity turning to happiness as he struggled to get out of bed. Pain shot up his leg and he cried out.

Alex eased him back down onto the pillows. "*We* may be going to Easter Island. *You,* my friend, are staying right here until your leg is better."

"I can help," Mateo protested, struggling again to sit up.

"You're not going to be of any help to anyone if you lose that leg," Alex cautioned, gently restraining him. "Your job is to stay here, heal up and get well."

Mateo's face fell. "Go on then," he pouted. "See if I care."

Robert squeezed his hand affectionately. "Back before you know it," he promised.

They left to let him get some rest. Before following the others out, Robert stuffed the Sphere under his shirt to hide it from view.

Once outside, Carlos stood in embarrassment as they thanked him profusely for his courage and for all he had done for them. As far as he was concerned, he had been responsible for the loss of their funny looking blue ball and the very least he could do was return it to them. He mounted his mule with a humble smile and waved as he rode away.

Robert, looking nine months pregnant with the Sphere protruding under his shirt, waved back.

Cyd grew concerned watching him go. "How do we get to Easter Island without the Chinese finding out?" she pondered. "We buy airplane tickets and they're sure to know."

"She's right," Alex said. "They'll know we're alive, know we survived the volcano, know we wouldn't be going half way across the Pacific unless we had the Sphere."

"They couldn't possibly have any knowledge of the scrimshaw library that translates it," Nikki reminded them.

"Doesn't matter," Alex argued. "They'd still know there was a connection. Otherwise, why would we bother going?"

"I might have a solution," Sam grinned. "Our ship is docked at Antofagasta only two hundred miles from here."

Nikki clapped her hands in delight. "It's true," she assured them. "We can leave tonight and be on our way in the morning!"

"Nikki, wait," Robert said. "I need you and Sam to do something for me first."

"Me and Sam?"

"The Chinese know who the rest of us are, am I right? We have to stay out of sight until we leave."

"How can we help?" Sam asked.

"In the morning, I need you and Nikki to join one of the tours from the hotel that take people out to see the lithium mines."

"You want us to go sightseeing at a time like this?" Sam was incensed.

"Take two of those one gallon water jugs from the back of your truck," Robert went on. "If anyone says anything, tell them you're worried about being in the middle of a desert and getting dehydrated."

"Okay," Sam said slowly.

"To be safe, make sure you join the group that's going to the American mine, not the Chinese one. When they take you out to see the drying beds, hang back. While everyone is listening to the guide's lecture about the mining process, dump the water out of your jugs and fill them with brine from one of the beds. Think you can do that?"

Nikki laughed, excited to be part of a conspiracy.

"Mind if I ask why?" Sam said skeptically.

Robert saddened. "Lucky is in the back of the truck nearly expired. It saved our lives and it's desperately in need of refueling. With ponds full of lithium rich brine just down the road, I'm not going to let it perish if I can help it."

Chapter Thirty-Three

THE HUNTER AND THE HUNTED

January 19th

The tour bus ride the next morning from San Pedro de Atacama to the American owned lithium mine located three miles from the Chinese mine took forty minutes. Sam and Nikki got off the coach with the rest of their group and were escorted inside a complex of metal buildings for a tour of a busy laboratory and a lecture on the benefits of the company's mining operations throughout the world. Outside, they were taken for an up-close inspection of the vast checkerboard of holding ponds laid out on the desert floor. The volcano was still smoking moodily in the distance; there were still a few aftershocks and everything was covered in ash, but the fireworks were over.

Sam and Nikki stood at the rear of the group listening along with the others as their guide talked about how lithium-rich brine is pumped from a vast underground sea and left to dry in the ponds until it turns to a pure, white powder that is then refined to make lithium.

They held their plastic gallon jugs at their sides and let the water drain out in the sand. Then backing away, Sam stood watch as Nikki knelt beside the nearest pond and submerged first one jug and then the other in the brine, filling them to the brim.

An elderly woman from England who Nikki had been chatting amicably with on the bus saw what she was doing and became concerned. "I wouldn't drink that if I were you, love," the friendly lady advised. "I don't think it's good for you."

"Doctor advised us to increase our salt intake," Nikki explained, coming to her feet and capping the jugs. "Not only that, lithium is nature's own antidepressant, didn't you know? It's all the rage back home."

The English woman nodded in vague confusion and turned back to listen to the guide.

***

Cyd, Alex and Robert were packed and waiting in the rental truck back at the hotel when Sam and Nikki returned from their tour of the lithium mine. Nikki proudly handed Robert their two jugs of brine and he nodded in relief.

Lucky lay in the back of the truck with its two fusion tubes flickering with barely a trace of light. Robert climbed in beside it, released the safety latch on one of the tubes, took a firm grip and worked it free from its socket. It came away in his hand and Lucky made a faint gasp. Opening the fill cap at one end, he dumped one of the jugs of brine into the tank, reinserted it in its socket, refastened the latch and did the same with the other one. The tubes came immediately to life with a blinding glow. Lucky stirred and lifted its head as if it were waking from a drugged sleep.

Robert smiled down gently. "Just lie still," he said, making it as comfortable as possible on top of the camping gear. "You need to get your strength back." He closed the tailgate, hurried around and got in the back seat with Cyd and Nikki.

Sam quickly started the engine and they headed out of town.

***

Lt. Colonel Chen Li, having searched a five-mile radius of desert around the sinkhole and finding no survivors, arrived back at the military compound adjacent to the Chinese lithium mine. Bursting into his office shouting orders, word was quickly put out to all Chinese employees in the area that he was looking for a group of three Americans, one of them a Native American, who would have recently returned with a wounded Chilian mine employee named Mateo Rojas.

Mateo's doctor had been on duty for forty-eight hours straight and had gone home to sleep. The next day when he came into work, he learned that the military was looking for a group of three American fugitives who were with a wounded Chilean. He immediately called the Lt. Colonel. The Americans, five of them, not three, had been at his clinic since yesterday. Mateo Rojas was among them and was still at the clinic recovering from an infected bullet wound in his leg.

Half an hour later, Lt. Colonel Li arrived at the medical clinic in San Pedro de Atacama, jumped out of the truck and told his driver to keep the motor running. The doctor was waiting when he walked in and took him back to see the patient.

Mateo's blood pressure spiked when he saw the Lt. Colonel enter his room with his Chinese doctor. Li proceeded to question him, first gently, then sternly, but learned nothing. The wounded Chilean absolutely refused to talk. The Lt. Colonel started shouting in Chinese.

Mateo couldn't understand a word he was saying, but he got the gist of it. "*Vete a la mierda* (Go shit yourself)," he smiled.

The Lt. Colonel stormed out of the room, found the doctor and asked what drugs he had on hand that could be used to loosen a patient's tongue. The doctor returned to Mateo's room minutes later, told him that everything was going to be alright and that he wouldn't be troubled by any more questions. As he was calming his patient, a Chinese nurse came in and administered a heavy dose of sodium pentothal through his IV.

The rapid-onset, short-acting barbiturate coursed through Mateo's veins, and he fell into a troubled dream. The Chinese Lt. Colonel reappeared at his bedside and Mateo gave himself a fierce reminder to keep any information about his friends secret. At the same time another part of him suddenly loved everyone and everything including the Lt. Colonel who he now rationalized was a kind and caring man. Li's face swam before him. He looked like someone who was mean to him a short while ago, but he must be mistaken. With him was the loveliest Chinese nurse he'd ever seen who he desperately wanted to please.

The truth serum fought with his rational mind. A part of him couldn't help answering the Lt. Colonel's questions truthfully while the sane and terrified part of him fought to alter and fabricate the information he was giving them as best he could. Over and over, he reminded himself of all the things he wasn't supposed to tell them until he could no longer remember exactly what they were.

How did he get here? He didn't remember, but he'd had a lovely trip across the desert.

Did his friends bring him? Oh, yes. He had many friends. Especially one that he loved very much. "His name is Robert," Mateo lisped. "Have you met him? Dear, dear man."

The Chinese doctor, nurse and Lt. Colonel gathered around his hospital bed exchanged disgusted glances.

Where are they now? How should he know, they're gone, gone, gone. "And never to return," he laughed.

Where did they go?

"Oh, they flew away," Mateo replied, happily flapping his hands and arms. "Just like that, they fly away."

"Fly?" the Lt. Colonel demanded. "Where they fly to?"

"Far, far away," the tortured patient replied, flapping desperately. "To Easter Island, yes indeed. Isn't that a funny name for an island, Easter?"

"You are certain? How they get there?"

Mateo looked up at the Lt. Colonel with a sloppy grin. "I told you. They fly-y-y!"

"Think hard. In airplane? Take commercial flight from Santiago?"

"You think they swim?" he giggled. "Robert is a fish. He is a trout! Rainbow, I think." This struck him as particularly funny and he laughed loudly.

"Concentrate now," the Lt. Colonel instructed. "The big blue ball. Did they have it with them?"

"Ball full of wonderful, amazing secrets," Mateo chuckled. "Big, round, beautiful ball."

"Why would they take it to Easter Island?"

No answer.

"What's so important about Easter Island?" Li shouted.

"Not supposed to say," Mateo replied sheepishly, looking up and seeing his mother in a nurse's cap smiling down at him.

"You can tell me anything, darling," the Chinese nurse assured him. "What on Easter Island that is so important?"

In a moment of fear, he thought he had told them about the library, then remembered he hadn't. He put a hushed finger to his lips and motioned her closer. "Don't tell anyone," he whispered. "Secret."

"Not tell a soul," the Chinese nurse promised with his mother's smile.

Mateo's eyelids grew heavy and he felt himself drifting off to sleep thinking of the amazing things Nikki had told him. "There's this wonderful library there. Bone books in an underground cave, of all places.

Books that translate the ball . . ." His voice began to fade. "Strange place for a library, don't you think, under an island . . ."

***

Lt. Colonel Li used the hospital phone to call Colonel Zhāng, his superior officer in Santiago. Zhāng was the official in charge of Chilian operations. The colonel listened impassively to Li's frantic ravings. He had captured an ancient alien artifact containing the most important scientific secrets of all time. The plane that was transporting it to Santiago flew into a volcanic cloud and crashed.

Zhāng said nothing as Li rushed on. He needed another plane, one with long range capabilities. He needed authorization to take a squad of men to Easter Island. "Yes, sir, that's Easter Island, E-a-s-t-e-r . . . In the middle of the Pacific, that's right, sir . . . Why? So I can pursue thieves who stole artifact, get it back and find underground library of books that translate it." Li couldn't understand why his superior officer was being so skeptical. This was a matter of life and death! The future of the Republic of China (not to mention his own future) depended on it!

Colonel Zhāng was smart enough not to authorize Li's request immediately. The man sounded mad and he wasn't going to risk his career on the word of a madman. He told Li he would have to contact Beijing to get permission. Yes, he would hurry. Yes, he would get back to him as soon as he heard anything.

Zhāng hung up, cursed under his breath, and called Beijing. It was 2 p.m. in Santiago which made it 1 a.m. the next day in Beijing. He left a message for his superior officer to call him after he'd had his breakfast. The next evening his call was returned and Colonel Zhāng apologetically explained the bizarre call he had received from his Lt. Colonel. The superior officer was as cagy as Zhāng and said he would take the matter under consideration. It took three more days for Li's request to go up the chain of command and reach Major General Wu, the official overseeing all operations in South America. The story triggered Major General Wu's imagination. Something about it rang true. Without a moment's hesitation, he authorized the mission.

Lt. Colonel Li had barely slept or eaten for four days when he received word that Beijing had approved his request. Li had a lot to prove and not a lot of talent or ability with which to prove it. His father and his father before him had both been major generals. He had lost the thing that was going to make him a major general, and he would get it back if it killed him.

By the time the Chinese military transport finally arrived at the San Pedro de Atacama airport to pick him and his men up and take them to Easter Island, his state of nervous exhaustion had escalated to blind rage. All he could think of was the pleasure he was going to take in personally executing the fugitives who had tried to rob him of his dignity and his career.

Chapter Thirty-Four

EASTER ISLAND

January 21ˢᵗ

Sam's salvage ship the *Fortuna Explorer* was two days out of Antofagasta on its 2,300-mile journey to Easter Island. The seas were calm, it was a beautiful sunny afternoon at sea and the Sphere was securely locked in the ship's safe. Cyd, Alex, Nikki, Sam and Robert were in the common room talking when they heard something that sounded like a sonic boom outside the ship.

Sam sat up in alarm. "What the hell . . .?" The passing explosion came again in a rush of air and he bolted outside.

Robert followed him out onto the deck to find a cylindrical object doing loops and barrel rolls in the vast blue sky. "It's never had a chance to play outside before," he observed in amusement.

Lucky made a sudden dive and skimmed the water, heading for the ship to make another low-level pass. Robert could mentally hear it shouting and whooping for joy.

"Well, tell it to knock it the hell off," Sam said, stomping back inside. "It's making too damn much noise."

The next day the seas were calm again and the Fortuna was making good time doing twenty knots on another cloudless sky. Cyd and Alex were out strolling hand-in-hand along the deck. The tropical breeze and relentless sunshine were helping them put the stress and strain of escaping the volcano and the Chinese behind them. Up ahead on the bow they saw Sam's tall, razor-thin African first mate making strange movements. Sensing it was some kind of ritual, they stopped and watched from a distance.

Tashtego stood at the bow in a trance-like state stripped to the waist with a red cloth wound around his narrow hips. His scarred head glistened in the sun as he jumped stiff-legged three feet in the air. Time and again the slender Maasai flew skyward seemingly without effort and without bending his knees.

Nikki came out of the common room to stand with Cyd and Alex. The part of her that was African started nodding to the drums that only she and Tashtego could hear.

"What is he doing?" Cyd whispered in fascination.

"I doubt even he knows," Nikki shrugged, moving her lithe body to the rhythm. "He goes on that way for hours sometimes. Some things are only remembered in the blood."

Their days and nights at sea passed peacefully and melded into one. As a sailor, Alex was fascinated with the ship and explored it from bow to stern asking Sam no end of questions. It was almost evening on their fifth day at sea when the tiny dot of a denuded island finally rose out of the sea. Dormant cones of low-lying volcanos came slowly visible in the fading light. They dropped anchor in the dark off *Hanga Roa*, Easter Island's only town, and decided to wait until morning before going ashore.

The sun was just coming up the next day when they left Tashtego and Lucky aboard with the Sphere and excitedly launched the inflatable. The rubber boat, weighted down with Cyd, Alex, Sam, Nikki and Robert aboard, motored ashore and landed at the small, rocky harbor of *Hanga Piko*.

Nikki, anxious to start the search for the cave, jumped from the dingy onto a small, weathered dock that rocked under her weight. From the pocket of her shorts, she pulled the handwritten directions she had copied down from Max's journal that told how to find Boris's cave, and how to navigate the labyrinth of lava tunnels that led to the Cave of the

Moon Pool. Striking off in the direction of *Rano Kau*, the small volcano with the collapsed cone that formed the southwestern headland of the island, she led them out of town.

The village of *Hanga Roa* where Max and Iolana had celebrated the Screaming of the Rats around the giant festival bonfire for so many years had doubled in size and now played host to nearly a hundred thousand travelers a year. Tourists flew the five and a half hours from Santiago and landed at the new airport just outside of town. Souvenir shops sold t-shirts and little *moai* statues, and tall, striking girls of Polynesian descent, some nearly as beautiful as Iolana, delighted the guests at night with frenetic, tiki-lit, grass-skirted dances performed to the sound of pounding drums. The rest of the ugly little island in the middle of the Pacific remained denuded and little changed from centuries ago. The only reason anyone came here at all was to see the towering, long-eared *moai* that ringed its shores. The silent, lava-carved sentinels spoke to every heart, young and old, with the mystery and magic of their origin and meaning.

It was late morning by the time they found the entrance to Boris's cave. Were it not for Nikki's intuitive radar, plus the fact that she had been emotionally engaged with Max and his journal ever since Sam brought it up from the depths back on Inagua Island, they likely would never have found it. Standing below the hill where centuries before Max had shot and killed a sailor to keep him from shooting the giant guarding the cave entrance, they struggled to pull aside the thick branches and undergrowth that hid the mouth of the cave from the world. Once inside, they replaced the vegetation so that the entrance was once again hidden from view, then turned and peered into the gloom. It felt like they were entering a sealed tomb. Their eyes adjusted to the dark and they saw to their amazement that the walls of the cave were lit with a faint glow that seemed to have no source.

Chapter Thirty-Five

FINDING BORIS

The more the Chinese general in Beijing thought about Lt. Colonel Li's odd rantings about a stolen artifact that contained unimaginable technological secrets, the more enthralled he became with the possibility of its importance. In support of Li's mission, he dispatched a frigate to Easter Island. The iron gray warship, cruising the Coral Sea at the time, began steaming toward Easter Island at thirty knots.

***

Nikki took her time leading them through the cave assuming any threat the Chinese posed had been left behind in the Atacama Desert. The *Fortuna Explorer* laying at anchor off *Hanga Roa* didn't bother her either since the Chinese had no knowledge of Sam's ship.

Walking past Boris's dead root garden, Cyd marveled at what looked like grow lights hanging over putrefied, rotted plants. They reminded her of the lights Otis used in the attic of his funeral home back in Montana to grow his first crop of Cannastar. So far as she knew, the *Grows* of the miracle plant that cured viral disease were still flourishing in New Mexico and in Israel.

Further on, they entered Boris's cavern and stood looking around in disbelief at his oversized furniture. Nikki pulled the directions from her pocket and confidently led the way into the tunnel at the back of the cave.

The dimly lit passageway glowed with the same light as the other walls and they put their flashlights back in their packs. Following closely behind Nikki, Cyd hoped the enigmatic Dominican girl knew where the hell she was going. After all the lefts and rights and hiking down one ragged lava tunnel after another, everyone but Nikki was totally lost.

They came out in the Cave of the Moon Pool. The pool of seawater shimmered like glass and mirrored the lava walls as it always had. Staring in awe, they turned in circles admiring the scrimshaw tablets that filled the walls. Sam saw it all in terms of dollar signs. Nikki, thrilled to finally be looking at the thing Max had described so vividly in his journal, marveled at his life's work.

Alex was pointing at something in the center of the cave. Cyd looked and gasped. Hovering inches above the cave floor under a narrow well of light from above was Boris's long, tubular solar gravity ship. A single Portable Fusion Reactor stuck out the back of it flickering like a dying lightbulb. They approached and stood staring down reverently through the transparent canopy. Inside, Boris lay perfectly preserved, the corners of his giant mouth turned up in the suggestion of a smile.

"Look at those long ears," Cyd whispered.

"He looks like he could sit up and talk," Alex whispered back.

Robert was overjoyed. "Wait until Lucky sees this!" he cried.

Sam, more interested in what the scrimshaw library was worth, walked over to inspect the walls. A big, empty hole was carved in the central wall above the rows of books. "What do you suppose this was for?" he asked, running his hand inside it and finding to his surprise that the interior was smooth as glass.

"You can't guess?" Nikki said ironically.

Sam shrugged and took one of the bone tablets down from its shelf, feeling its weight and turning it over in his hands. The strange, complicated letters with their Spanish translation that Max had so painstakingly carved made no sense to him. "How the hell do we get all these tablets back to the ship without tipping off the local authorities?" he agonized. "Nikki, can you read any of this?"

She took the tablet from him, adjusted her glasses and studied it. The archaic Spanish with its stilted phrasing was familiar to her now after spending so much time immersed in Max's journal, but she had to sound out the scientific words. "This character here I think means 'hydrogen'," she said triumphantly. "This one, I'm pretty sure, means 'lithium'. Wow!"

She handed the tablet back to him and he returned it to its place on the shelf. "That doesn't solve the problem," he said. "How do we make trips back and forth across the island carrying armloads of these things without getting busted for carting off the island's archaeological treasures? Not that the locals would know what to do with these things even if they had them. Nikki, did Max say where this pool of water comes out?"

"He said Boris told him it connects to a convoluted tunnel that emerges at an opening in a cliff just south of town called the Man-Eating Cave."

"Maybe if we used *Crab* . . ." Sam speculated.

"The way he described it," Nikki went on, "the tunnel didn't sound wide enough or deep enough for *Crab* to get through. You could get stuck."

"*Crab*?" Cyd asked.

"*Crab* is my underwater submersible," Sam explained. "That big yellow thing you saw sitting in davits on the foredeck of my ship."

"How about this?" Alex said. "I saw two or three car rental places when we passed through town. Cyd and I can play tourist and try to rent a van or a truck. If we can get one big enough that's four-wheel drive, we can haul the whole library in one load."

"What about ferrying it out to the ship?" Robert questioned. "Won't that look suspicious?"

Cyd brightened. "We pick the truck up tomorrow morning, come back here and spend the day carting the library out to the entrance of the cave. Tomorrow night after dark we load the "books" in the truck, drive them to the harbor and make however many trips in the dingy we need to ferry them out to the ship in the dark."

"What if someone sees us?" Robert persisted.

"Ships come and go from islands like this all the time bringing stuff ashore and taking other stuff aboard," Sam said.

"We do it after midnight," Cyd added. "If anybody is up at that time of night in a place like this, they're probably too drunk to notice or care."

"Moving the library is going to be risky business any way you cut it," Alex surmised.

They agreed that renting a truck and moving the library at night was probably their best option.

"What about that coffin-looking thing with the creature in it?" Sam asked. "It has to be worth something."

Nikki was mortified. "That's Boris's tomb, Sam! We can't disturb that."

Sam shrugged and Nikki led them back through the tunnels to the cave entrance. Sam was the last to follow. Looking back eagerly, he tried to calculate the value of the scrimshaw treasure.

It was the middle of the afternoon by the time they emerged from the cave into the heat of the day. They carefully replaced the vines and brush over the opening, then sat on the rocks outside the cave entrance eating the sandwiches they had brought with them. The tropical sun felt good after the dark cave and they let it bake away the smell of antiquity.

Sitting on the rocks, they looked like any other group of tourists out hiking the island to admire the strange statues. When they were done eating, Cyd and Alex went into town to try and find a truck to transport the library. Robert headed back to the ship to get Lucky and bring it ashore so it could see for itself the magnificent Gorgon lying in his cylinder.

Sam and Nikki, with nothing to do for the rest of the day, followed Cyd and Alex into town. On a narrow street surfaced in pavers and lined with small, stunted palms, they found Insular Car Rental. Cyd and Alex went in while Sam and Nikki waited outside. A number of modern ATV rentals were parked in front, crowding the entrance to the store.

Nikki went over and sat on one. "Sam," she said gaily, pretending to twist the throttle, "you ever ridden one of these things?"

"All Terrain Vehicles are dangerous," he told her. "People are always getting hurt on them."

"It can't be that bad if you're careful," she argued. "Let's rent a couple. I like this blue one here."

"And do what?"

"Try to find Anakena Beach," she declared happily. "I'd love to see the place where Max and Iolana were married, wouldn't you?"

"That's got to be miles from here."

"It'll be fun, come on. Don't you want to tour the island and see the *moai*?"

"From what I can tell, you've seen one *moai*, you've seen them all."

"Please?" she pleaded. "It's important to me."

He sighed and smiled, thinking she looked adorable astride the stubby, four-wheeled motorcycle.

Chapter Thirty-Six

ANAKENA BEACH

January 26th

The same afternoon Sam and Nikki went to find *Anakena Beach* on their ATVs, Lt. Colonel Chen Li and a squad of six soldiers landed at Easter Island's Mataveri International Airport aboard a Chinese cargo plane. Since the island was a Chilean territory, they didn't need anyone's permission to be here.

While the plane was unloading a standardized 6x6 military truck with cross-country mobility, Li marched his men up and down the tarmac to limber them up after the long flight. The Lt. Colonel then signed for the truck, ordered his troops onto the benches in back, climbed in front with his driver and they set off to make a methodical search of the island.

***

It was about ten miles across the island from *Hanga Roa* to *Anakena Beach* on a narrow, winding, one-lane asphalt track that followed the rolling terrain like a drunken snake. A few miles off to the north, rising 1,665 feet in the air, was *Ma'unga Terevaka,* the largest, tallest and youngest of the three main extinct volcanos on the Island. Nikki rode ahead on her blue ATV having so much fun she couldn't stop grinning. Even Sam, keeping a close eye on her careless riding, was enjoying the sun and wind-swept solitude of a volcanic island steeped in the romance of so much unfathomable history.

They reached the beach and parked next to the *ahu* with its seven weathered *moai* staring pensively out at the sandy cove where long ago Max had harvested the whalebone "knuckles" for his scrimshaw library. They climbed up on the altar and sat side-by-side beneath the statues with their legs dangling over the side as Max and Iolana had done. In the far distance, the sky met the sea in a gently curving horizon that hid mainland Chile over two thousand miles to the east. Before them on the sun-dried, wind-swept beach, waves lapped gently where Gorgons once walked and the bleached and weathered bones of four great whales once rested.

They didn't talk, they didn't say a thing. Nikki's sense of a mysterious past here was overwhelming. It filled her with wonder, with being and belonging, with a strange and powerful connection to all she was seeing.

Sam turned and was alarmed to see tears in her eyes. "Honey, what's wrong?" he asked.

She smiled through her tears. "Sam, let's make love."

"Here?"

"In the same place Max and Iolana first made love. It's that knoll, I think, right back over there."

"Sometimes you are so hard to get along with," he grinned, helping her down off the *ahu*.

Hand in hand they walked to the little spot behind the secluded knoll that had once been Max and Iolana's secret place. Sam spread out the beach towels he had brought with them.

Sometime later they lay naked under the baking sun. Peacefully content, Nikki put her glasses back on and sat up on one elbow. "Sam," she said enthusiastically, "let's get a couple of ATVs for the boat."

"The boat?"

"That way, whatever island we're on, we'll always have a way to sneak off and be alone."

"Now why didn't I think of that . . ." A distant sound distracted him and he listened closely. She started to say something and he put a finger to his lips to silence her. The approaching noise of a diesel engine grew louder and they scrambled to peer over the knoll.

A Chinese military truck with two men in front and five soldiers holding onto the wooden slats in back was slowly cruising the beach between the highwater line and the row of statues on the *ahu*. Lt. Colonel Li, frustrated at finding only another deserted stretch of shore, pointed inland and the three-axled vehicle veered away from the sand to continue its cross-country search of the island.

"How did they even know where . . .?" Nikki began in distress.

Sam jumped to his feet. "We have to warn the others!"

They threw on their clothes, mounted their ATVs and moments later were flying down the winding asphalt track that led back to town.

Chapter Thirty-Seven

LUCKY

Robert brought Lucky ashore in the rubber dingy, tied it to the little dock in the harbor, and it floated up out of the boat. They headed off in the direction of the cave with Lucky following along at his heels close to the ground so it would look like a faithful dog should anyone notice. At the outskirts of the village, they quickened their pace and were nearing the cave entrance when Robert saw a large truck cresting a distant hill. It was too far away to make out any detail, but as it made its way toward him over the grassy slopes, he saw the red and yellow Chinese flags fluttering from its fenders.

"Lucky, hurry!" he rasped, his stomach in knots as they rushed away.

Lt. Colonel Li, bouncing around in the front seat of the military transport as it crossed the lava-strewn terrain, raised his field glasses and tried to focus on a man he saw moving rapidly along with a long, slender creature at his side.

"Go, go, go!" Li shouted to his driver in Chinese. "It's one of them!"

Robert entered the small gully that hid the cave and was momentarily shielded from view. Tearing at the vegetation around the entrance, he made a hole and motioned Lucky inside. Behind him he could hear the truck getting closer and climbed in behind it, then rapidly covered the hole back up with vines. Peering back out from behind a wall of shrubbery, he watched as the Chinese truck rumbled slowly past the gully. He held his breath and waited. After a few minutes he saw the truck pass by the gully again.

Falling back against the wall of the cave, he exhaled in relief. He'd lost them. Lucky was already halfway down the passageway. He gathered himself and followed, taking a copy of Nikki's cave directions from his pocket as he went. They passed through the main cave and entered the cave at the back with Lucky leading the way like it knew where it was going.

A series of twisting, turning tunnels brought them to the Cave of the Moon Pool. Lucky hesitated at the entrance, quivering in excitement. Robert watched as it rushed across the cave and hovered beside the gravity ship that held Boris's body like it was celebrating a homecoming.

"Happy now?" Robert called.

"*I always wanted to fly one of these things,*" he heard it say. "*Attach me.*"

"What?"

"*Plug me in!*"

Robert was stunned. He was hearing it, but there was no sound. "When did you learn to speak?" he stammered.

"*The Gorgon capacity for telepathic communication is part of my programming,*" it explained impatiently. "*I have been reading your data base to teach myself English ever since we met. Now hurry. Remove my fusion reactors and insert them in the gravity ship.*"

"Are you crazy?" Robert cried in alarm. "You'll die!"

"*I can transfer my programming and memory into my reactor tubes long enough for you to make the switch. Just be quick about it.*"

He sighed and shook his head. "Tell me what to do then."

Lucky settled to the ground and lay very still. "*Unplug the exhausted power unit from the back of the gravity ship. Then unplug mine one at a time and install them in the ship. You must do it quickly.*"

Robert nodded and fumbled to remove the fusion unit from the rear of Boris's coffin. The glow in the walls suddenly dimmed and went out, but instead of the cave being plunged into darkness, Lucky's fusion tubes burned brighter and lit the dark. He removed one of its tubes and held it in his hands. It was like holding a brilliantly lit torch. Working as rapidly as he could—his fingers felt stiff and clumsy—he plugged it into one of the round receptacles in the back of the gravity ship, refastened the safety latch and repeated the process with its second tube.

The cave was suddenly flooded with light. Boris's coffin floated lightly off the ground and seemed to come alive. Lucky shook itself awake like a dog waking from a nap.

Robert stared down at the limp gravitybike that had saved his life and the lives of his friends with a lump in his throat.

"Thank you, Robert, thank you!" Lucky cried.

"Now that you've had your fun," he admonished, "we need you to get back in your body and back to the ship without getting spotted."

"You don't understand. I'm home. I'm back with my own people now."

"Meaning what exactly? That you're going to stay here for thousands of years until you run out of fuel again?"

"Shh . . ." it said. *"I'm learning the ship's operating systems. You wouldn't believe what this gravity generator can do."*

"I'm sure I wouldn't. So, I'm just supposed to leave you here, is that it?"

"Don't worry. You go on, I'll be fine. This is where I belong."

He turned reluctantly to walk away. Behind him he heard it say, *"You were a good friend, Robert. I'll always remember you."*

Swiping at his eyes, he made his way back through the tunnels to the mouth of the cave. Peering out through the brambles at the sunlit gully, he saw no sign of the Chinese truck. Fearing they might still be around, he decided to wait until after dark before trying to make it back to the boat.

It was nearly midnight by the time he returned to *Hanga Roa*. The town was sound asleep and the streets were deathly quiet. He made his way toward the harbor. When he got there the rubber dingy was gone.

Everyone must be back aboard the ship but me, he thought, desperately searching the harbor for a boat he could borrow. A row of colorful, crudely made native canoes were pulled up on the rocks. Picking one a random, he was slipping it into the water when he heard the sounds of a large ship arriving offshore. Looking out through the inky darkness his heart nearly stopped. An enormous warship the length of four football fields, brilliantly lit with red stars on its armored plated sides, was dropping anchor near where the *Fortuna* lay at anchor.

The approaching tramp of feet and the unintelligible sounds of Chinese being spoken made him duck behind one of the shacks near the water's edge. Peering out and breathing hard, he saw a shore boat being launched from the frigate. As it drew closer, he saw it was empty except for a man at the helm. Six Chinese soldiers and their commander appeared and assembled on the floating dock. The launch pulled alongside and the soldiers climbed in.

Chapter Thirty-Eight

EARTHQUAKE

Earlier that afternoon, while Sam and Nikki were at *Anakena Beach* and Lt. Colonel Li was searching the island with his squad of soldiers, Cyd and Alex were busy trying to locate a rental truck. They found an agency that rented big vans and arranged to pick one up the next morning, then strolled around the little town enjoying the warm breezes and quaint island atmosphere. In one of the shops, Cyd bought colorful sarongs for herself and Nikki. Afterward, they stopped for iced drinks at an outdoor café and sat in the shade of an undersized palm watching the tourists go by. They were returning to the harbor when they spotted Sam and Nikki arriving back at the rental agency on their ATVs.

They waited while they returned their quads and joined them as they were coming out of the store. When they learned that the Chinese had followed them to the island they were horrified.

"How did they know we were even here?" Cyd demanded.

"Mateo was the only person who knew where we'd gone," Sam recalled.

"Poor man, I hate to think what they must have done to him to make him talk," Nikki lamented.

They hurried back to the rubber dingy and returned to the ship to find Robert and Lucky missing. By midnight there still was no sign of them and they feared the worst. They were gathered in the common room worrying over what to do next when they saw the Chinese warship pulling in and dropping anchor a few hundred yards away.

Sam tried to calm their panic. "The Chinese have never seen or heard of the *Fortuna*," he assured them, looking out one of the portholes and watching the ship through his binoculars. "Mateo didn't know we had a boat, so he couldn't have told them. I think we're safe for now."

It was of little comfort.

The ship's clock was striking 2 a.m. when they heard something bump against the hull and hurried outside in the dark to see what it was. Robert was tying a native canoe alongside the ship. He scrambled up the boarding ladder and they greeted him with muffled cries of relief.

Back inside, Tashtego heated Robert some supper. Wolfing his food, he relayed how he and Lucky had narrowly escaped the Chinese at the cave, then told them of Lucky's decision to stay behind.

Nikki smiled knowingly and said nothing.

Sam was furious. "How the hell do we bring that library onboard now with the Chinese watching?"

"We don't," Cyd said. "We leave it and go."

Robert shook his head. "Who's to say the Chinese won't see us hauling anchor and get suspicious?"

"They board us and find the Sphere," Alex said, equally concerned, "and we'll never get it back."

"We're better off sitting tight and hiding in plain sight," Nikki said.

"Maybe when they can't find us, they'll just leave," Alex speculated.

"Fat chance," Robert said, clutching his temples and bending over in pain. "They've already spotted me. They know we're here."

"Robert, what is it?" Cyd cried.

"Earthquake migraine," he grimaced. "Big one. Help me to my bunk."

Cyd and Nikki took him by the arms and guided him toward his cabin.

"When and where?" Sam called after them.

"Don't know," Robert groaned, leaning heavily on the two women as they went down the companionway. "But it's coming, and it's a whopper."

Cyd and Nikki put Robert to bed. He eased back onto his pillow assuring them that he just needed to lie quietly for a while and let it pass. They left him alone and returned to the common room where Sam and Alex were waiting. The Chinese presence on the island weighed heavily on them and they talked until nearly morning about what to do about it without arriving at a solution.

Sam and Alex eventually wandered off to bed to get a few hours' sleep. Cyd and Nikki, too keyed up to sleep, exchanged glances and lingered behind.

***

At 4:33 a.m. that same morning, January 27th, the NEIC (National Earthquake Information Center) issued a world-wide alert that a 9.4 earthquake had just struck along a previously unknown undersea fault that ran north and south between Pitcairn Island and Easter Island. The two islands were nearly thirteen hundred miles apart, it said, and the epicenter was approximately half way in between. Both islands had been sent urgent warnings that a major tsunami could be headed their way.

***

4:33 a.m.

Aboard the *Fortuna*, Cyd and Nikki sat alone in the common room.

"Are you thinking what I'm thinking?" Cyd asked.

"We take the Sphere ashore in Robert's canoe and hide it in the cave with the library where the Chinese will never find it," Nikki said.

Cyd hesitated. "Unless they see us and follow us."

"We both have dark hair," Nikki maintained. "From a distance in the dark, we'll look like two native girls out doing some early morning fishing."

"Or a couple of party girls returning from an all-nighter on a visiting yacht," Cyd smiled, then sobered. "When Alex and Sam find out, they'll be furious."

"And if we wake them and tell them what we're up to, they'll insist on coming with us. Then we're not two native girls in a fishing canoe, we're four suspicious-looking people going ashore in the middle of the night." Seeing Cyd's hesitation Nikki added, "We'll be back before they know it."

Cyd, anxious as Nikki was to get the Sphere to safety, nodded in agreement.

"I'll get the Sphere." Nikki jumped up, crossed the room, opened Sam's big safe and removed the shining blue ball. Cyd helped her put it in one of Sam's large mesh dive bags for easy transport, then produced the flowered, form-fitting sarongs she had bought for them in town. They put them on, shook out their hair and stood looking like two of the loveliest Polynesian girls ever to inhabit an island. Minutes later they were silently climbing down the ship's ladder, struggling into the canoe in their tight fitting dresses, and quietly paddling to shore with the Sphere in the bottom of the boat between them.

***

5:00 a.m.

Fortuna was bathed in early morning light by the time Sam and Alex got up to find the two women missing. Tashtego was in the ship's navigation station, headphones clamped to his head, listening to the

NEIC alert on the crackling radio that was being repeated in a constant loop.

"Earthquake approximately six hundred to the west," he called to Sam who hurried in to listen.

"How large?" Sam asked, putting on the headphones Tashtego handed him.

"Nine point four or five. Equal to biggest ever recorded. Tsunami headed our way, maybe. Could be here any time."

Alex was in the common room reading the note Cyd had left for them on the table. "God *damn* it!" he swore, handing the note to Sam as he came out of the nav station. "Cyd and Nikki went ashore alone to hide the Sphere in the cave!"

Sam was angrily reading the note when the muffled sound of a tsunami warning horn came from shore sounding like a WWII air raid siren—which in fact it was.

***

5:20 a.m.

Nikki and Cyd, paddling their canoe into the harbor, heard the siren go off. Frightened, they watched as the island erupted in chaos. Residents and tourists alike began fleeing their homes and hotels and racing up the low-lying slopes of the nearby volcanos. Terrified screams of a tsunami coming filled the air in multiple languages. Women cradled babies in their arms as they ran. Others were slowed by the armloads of personal possessions they carried.

***

5:20 a.m.

Sam, returning from checking the ship's safe and finding it empty, grabbed his binoculars and trained them on the shore. In the early light, he saw the pandemonium as residents and tourists alike fled to higher ground, then focused on Nikki and Cyd climbing out of their canoe onto the harbor's floating dock. "They're going to be in that cave when the tsunami hits," he said, angrily throwing the binoculars aside.

"*If* it hits," Alex said.

"Ever seen what a big tsunami can do?" Sam said furiously. "It can level a city!"

Alex hesitated. "Or an island."

"Nikki said Boris told Max that the pool of seawater in the cave connects to the open ocean," Sam remembered, thinking out loud. "If Boris is right, and everything he and Max said so far has been right, that means the library is going to flood when the tsunami hits."

"And Nikki and Cyd are going to be in it." A chill went up Alex's spine as he headed for the door. "There's still time! I'm taking the dingy."

"Alex, stop!" Sam ordered. "Even if you reach them in time, you'll be as trapped as they are when the tsunami hits." He turned to his first mate who stood close by listening intently. "Tashtego, help me launch *Crab*!"

Alex followed them out of the room. "What if there is no tsunami?"

"Then I won't have to find out if that cave goes all the way through or not, will I?"

***

5:20 a.m.

Lt. Colonel Chen Li rushed from his bunk to the bridge on the Chinese frigate when he heard the siren wailing from shore. Captain Yang Zhongquan was already on the bridge when Li arrived, looking out to sea with his binoculars. The captain, dressed in an immaculate white uniform with shoulder boards that proclaimed his rank, had a small, round face that was as cold and impersonal as his ship. Li motioned that he wanted the binoculars and the captain handed them over.

Scanning the shore, Li focused on two women, apparently coming from the salvage vessel anchored nearby, paddling their canoe into the harbor. He was about to turn away thinking the pair in the canoe were just a couple of native girls when he recognized Cyd getting out on the dock, then saw the round fishnet bag that the other girl was carrying. His tiny eyes bulged with fury as the two women disappeared ashore before movement aboard the neighboring salvage ship caught his eye and he swung his binoculars in that direction.

Through his lenses, Li saw Sam and Tashtego emerge on deck to launch *Crab,* followed by Robert who had been awakened by the sound of the siren. Li's eyes bulged to the point they looked like they were going to pop out of their sockets.

The warning siren continued to blare as Captain Zhongquan was handed a written message from his radio operator warning him that a monstrous tsunami was likely headed his way. He threw the paper aside and started giving orders for his ship to immediately get under way.

"Ship stays here!" Li ordered. "Ship not move!"

Captain Zhongquan's dispassionate face turned red. "Tsunami dangerous! Leave now while still time!"

"The blue ball!" Li cried furiously. "They have the blue ball!"

"Ship safety my first responsibility!" Zhongquan argued.

The Lt. Colonel, with no experience or imagination for the sea, saw no danger in a hypothetical wave that might or might not materialize out of an ocean full of waves. In clipped, rapid Chinese he reminded the captain that while the naval officer was in charge of the ship, he, Lt. Colonel Chen Li of the People's Liberation Army, was in charge of the mission. Ignoring the captain's howls of protest, he grabbed the ship's microphone and over the loudspeakers ordered his squad of men to assemble on deck. Then turning back to the captain, he instructed him to launch a shore boat to take him and his men ashore. "Also have your troops standing by," he directed. "Will radio if I need."

Captain Yang Zhongquan, beside himself with frustration, watched helplessly as Li rushed off the bridge to join his men on deck. It took every ounce of willpower he had not to order his ship to deeper water the minute the fool of a Lt. Colonel was gone. Instead, knowing that disobeying a direct order from a mission commander would result in his arrest and imprisonment, he did nothing.

***

5:30 a.m.

Sam stood at the rail helping to guide his dented, yellow, bug-eyed submersible into the water. "Soon as I'm away, take the *Fortuna* out to sea," he instructed his first mate who was operating the hoist cable. "If you can get to deep water before the tsunami hits, you'll probably barely feel it when it passes under the hull."

Tashtego nodded. "After it reaches island, I bring ship back to pick you up," he promised.

"Counting on it," Sam said.

"I'm going with you," Alex announced as Sam started down the ladder.

"There isn't room," Sam said sharply.

"That yellow thing of yours has four seats, doesn't it?"

"It's not safe with four people aboard if we have to go deep."

"Cyd and Nikki are in a cave, not at the bottom of the ocean."

"It's your funeral," Sam shrugged, lifting *Crab's* top hatch.

"Room for one more?" Robert called. "I can help."

"You can help by staying aboard with Tashtego," Sam said, glancing ashore to make sure it wasn't already too late. "If something happens and we don't make it back, there needs to be somebody left to retrieve the Sphere and the library books, and make sure they don't end up in the wrong hands."

Robert nodded reluctantly, watching as Alex climbed down the ladder and followed Sam into the open hatch.

Tashtego released the hoist cable and the submersible floated free.

***

5:30 a.m.

Once ashore, Cyd and Nikki fled to higher ground like everyone else. Finding it impossible to run in their tight-fitting sarongs, they pulled the dresses off, threw on shorts and t-shirts that Cyd took from her daypack, then sprinted toward the safety of Boris's cave taking turns carrying the awkward mesh bag.

Chapter Thirty-Nine

CAVE OF THE MOON POOL

6:00 a.m.

A giant underwater wave raced eastward across the Pacific at the speed of a jet airplane. Tashtego had managed to get the *Fortuna* to open ocean and put over a thousand feet of water under her hull by the time the wave passed beneath it. As Sam predicted, those aboard barely felt a bump. But they saw it. Robert, Tashtego and the ship's two Bahamian crewmen watched as a white-frothing wave barely a foot high and stretching fifty miles wide on either side of the ship disappeared in the direction of Easter Island. Tashtego immediately brought the boat around to follow.

***

6:00 a.m.

Cyd and Nikki reached the mouth of the cave, struggled to pull aside the brambles covering it, hurriedly put them back from the inside and ran down the tunnels. Reasonably confident that the tsunami couldn't reach them here, the safety of their friends back on the boat worried them greatly. Arriving breathless at the Cave of the Moon Pool, they were startled to see Boris's solar gravity ship aglow with light and hovering in midair.

Nikki made her way cautiously around the ship, went to the wall of scrimshaw tablets that had the empty hole above it, and took the Sphere of Knowledge out of its mesh bag. Carefully, gently, she inserted the blue-shining ball into the opening. It was a perfect fit.

"That's that," she said, stepping back to admire the wall that now held the very thing the library was created for in the first place. "Home at last."

"We should get back to the boat," Cyd said nervously, unable to take her eyes off of Lucky's fusion tubes that were pulsing brighter and brighter. "Alex and Sam will be worried."

The solar gravity ship suddenly moved and they both jumped back as Lucky swung its nose in the air and pointed it straight up. Soundlessly, in their minds, they heard her say, *"Boris gave me a message to give to you."*

Cyd was stunned.

"Boris?" Nikki asked.

"He said to tell you he made a mistake letting Max create this library. He said your species is not ready for the kind of knowledge that the Sphere contains. He said you are not mature enough."

"Boris is dead," Cyd stammered.

"His body, not his spirit, not his soul," Lucky countered as the ship began to rise toward the circular light well in the ceiling.

Nikki was listening to the familiar voice of one of her guides that blew like a gentle breeze through her mind. "Lucky's taking Boris home," she whispered. "They're going back to where they came from so he can be reborn."

The nose of the gravity ship eased into the overhead opening and started to move through the narrow tube. Scraping sounds echoed down as it brushed against the lava walls. Halfway up, the shaft narrowed further and the ship got stuck.

Cyd and Nikki watched anxiously as Lucky backed down, turned sideways and tried again. This time it managed to squeeze through and a blinding light flashed down the shaft.

"Buen camino (Good way)*,"* Nikki murmured.

They turned to shield their eyes from the light, then gasped when they saw the water in the Moon Pool beginning to bubble and swell.

***

6:20 a.m.

The *Fortuna* was steaming back to Easter Island, but was still well offshore. Robert stood in the wheelhouse with Tashtego watching ahead for the tsunami to rise against the steep, submerged sides of the island when Boris' solar gravity ship streaked out of the collapsed cone of *Rano Kau,* the small volcano at the southwestern end of the island. Stunned, they watched as the ship shot upward in a vertical shaft of light, then disappeared into the heavens with an explosive boom.

Robert heard Lucky shouting *"Whoo-hoo!"*

"Godspeed," he whispered, smiling sadly.

***

6:10 a.m.

Lt. Colonel Chen Li stood looking out intently from the bow of the speeding shore boat that was taking him and his six men ashore. They were nearing the harbor when he spied Sam's yellow submersible wallowing along the surface toward the gaping, partially flooded entrance to *Ana Kai Tangata* (Man Eating Cave) just south of town. Li shouted to the sailor manning the helm to go after him. The shore boat's engine howled up as it raced toward *Crab.* Intent on the pursuit, Li did not see the giant wave forming behind him.

***

6:10 a.m.

Sam, looking out at the approaching cave through the spherical observation port on his side of the craft, prepared to submerge. He reached up and double checked that the hatch was dogged down, checked that life support was functioning properly, then opened the vents and flooded his ballast tanks. *Crab* sank below the surface and water rushed past his observation port.

Alex felt a jolt of anxiety go through him as the light dimmed and they sank into a blue aquatic world twenty feet below the surface. Without the wave action topside, *Crab* rode smoothly. The water darkened, but enough light still filtered down that visibility was good.

Sam engaged his thrusters and nudged the joystick forward to counter the unexpected pull of the sea that was rushing out to feed the wave building behind them. It was all he could do to keep moving forward and not get sucked back in the surge. Up ahead he saw that the partially submerged opening to the Man-Eating Cave was not deep enough for the submersible to get through. Staring out helplessly, his heart sank.

***

6:13 a.m.

Lt. Colonel Li heard a thunderous roar and turned in time to see a wall of water over a hundred feet high rising up behind him. The great wave, poised and foaming, held the huge Chinese warship in its curl like a toy boat. Li's mind went blank with terror. The wave broke, crashing down on the shore boat with the force of an exploding volcano before busily rushing ashore.

***

6:13 a.m.

The force of the breaking wave picked *Crab* up and flung her into the mouth of the cave like a bullet from a gun. The acceleration pressed Sam and Alex back in their seats. Illuminated in the craft's observation lights, the walls of the cave rushed by in the inky darkness. It felt like they were hurtling down a twisting, turning wormhole.

Sam cursed through clenched teeth as he fought with the controls to try and stay off the walls. Crab careened from one side of the cave to the other with the terrifying sound of crushing metal. The tunnel narrowed, made a sharp turn and there was a terrible rending sound as one of the submersible's front claws was torn off.

Alex braced himself against the overhead bulkhead with both arms, staring ahead like he was in a car that had just been driven off a cliff. Every time *Crab* hit a wall it felt like her shell was going to crack wide open.

***

6:15 a.m.

Water rushed up from the Moon Pool and flooded the cave so quickly Cyd and Nikki had no time to escape. They watched in terror as it rose above their knees, their waists and in seconds was above their chests. Struggling to stay afloat in the swirling tide, they watched as the walls of scrimshaw tablets rapidly disappeared underwater.

Choking and gasping, fighting for their lives, they saw the water suddenly erupt in front of them as *Crab* popped out of the Moon Pool and bobbed to the surface like a cork from a champagne bottle. Its hatch flew open, Alex stood in the opening and the two women screamed in relief.

"Anybody call for an Uber?" he grinned.

They frantically thrashed their way toward the craft as the water rose toward the ceiling. Alex hauled them aboard and they dove down the hatch. He followed and pulled the hatch closed, then struggled to dog down the latches with water rushing in around the edges.

Cyd and Nikki squeezed dripping wet into the cramped jump seats in back, as the last of the airspace in the cave disappeared. The incoming tide slowed and stopped. Submerged in an underwater cavern, they stared out through the observation ports. The Sphere of Knowledge was directly in front of them, secure in its hole, shining softly in blue light.

Sam repressurized the cabin, opened the vents and flooded his tanks as the tide turned and began to rush out. The bottom fell out of their stomachs as the force of the retreating tsunami sucked the submersible back into the hole in the bottom of the pool like it was being flushed down a toilet.

Hurtled along on the receding tide, Crab was almost impossible to control. Sam struggled with the joystick as the outgoing water bounced them off the tunnel walls. Every time they collided with the lava sides, Cyd and Nikki made tiny screams.

***

6:30 a.m.

The morning sun hung bright and hot over a calm and tranquil ocean littered with tsunami debris as *Crab* broke the surface. Its occupants gasped, looking out over the floating trash to the island beyond that was in shambles. Half a mile inland, the Chinese frigate lay on its side on the slopes of *Rano Kau* like a dead whale washed up on the tide.

Chapter Forty

January 28th

By the next morning, planeloads of food and medical supplies were arriving at the airport from the mainland. Alex and Cyd, happy just to be alive after all they had been through, went ashore as doctor and nurse to help with the sick and injured. Robert joined them to help reengineer the broken sewage and polluted water systems. Sam and Nikki went along to aid the islanders in locating their belongings, moving back into the homes that were still standing and to offer support wherever it was needed. Planes continued to come from Chile and by the end of the day the island was swarming with aid workers.

For five days the passengers and crew from the *Fortuna Explorer* helped with the disaster. Then boatloads of supplies and workers started arriving from the mainland and they were no longer needed. Easter Island had survived yet another catastrophe that nearly destroyed it.

***

February 2nd

Crab was back in her davits on the foredeck of the Fortuna looking like a coffee can that had been used for target practice. Sam and Tashtego walked around the submersible assessing the damage.

"Might need a few repairs here and there," Sam concluded. "Give you something to do on the voyage home."

"Humph," Tashtego grunted irritably.

That evening they were gathered around the table in the common room eating a delicious supper of fresh snapper that Tashtego had caught and baked for them when they heard a large ship arriving close by. They looked out and saw a U.S. Navy frigate anchoring in almost the same spot the Chinese frigate had been anchored. The American warship, crossing the Panama Canal from the Caribbean to the Pacific when the tsunami hit, was immediately ordered to sail for Easter Island to do what they could to help with the disaster. The American frigate was the same ugly gray as the Chinese frigate with the same armored sides, but considerably larger with a helipad on the stern. Its presence cast a dark shadow over the *Fortuna* and over the mood of its passengers having supper.

"What do we do now?" Cyd agonized. "We try hauling the library off under the noses of the U.S. Navy and all these aid workers that have shown up, and they'll think we're looting the island for sure."

Nikki took off her glasses and cleaned them on the tail of her t-shirt. "Cyd," she said, "remember the message Lucky gave us from Boris when we were in the cave?"

Cyd nodded slowly. "He said the human race wasn't ready for the technology that's in the Sphere. That our species wasn't mature enough. The image I got at the time was it would be like a parent giving an adolescent a loaded gun to take to school."

"Another thing," Robert said. "Fusion energy would likely put the fossil fuel industry out of business."

"And create a depression the likes of which the world has never seen," Alex surmised.

"Then let's just hand things over to the US Navy," Cyd insisted. "They're right next door. Let America take credit for cleaning up the environment and creating a pollution-free world."

"You put fusion energy into the hands of the U.S. military," Alex worried, "and it's no different than putting it into the hands of any other military. There won't be any environment left to clean up after they get done dominating the world with it or using it to blow it all up."

"What's in that cave is priceless," Sam argued angrily. "It's worth a damn fortune!"

"What concerns me most," Nikki said, "is doing something that is going to change the world overnight. I, for one, don't want the responsibility."

"It's simple," Sam claimed. "All we do is hang around under the pretense of helping to rebuild the island. That way we can take our time carting off the library in our backpacks piece by piece and nobody will be the wiser."

The logic was perfect; it was the perfect plan, and for a minute everyone agreed. Then the weight of the potential consequences settled back over them and their enthusiasm faded.

"So, what then?" Robert asked. "We just leave it all behind for future generations to find?"

They fell silent.

Sam was livid. "I didn't come all this way to quit and give up."

"Progress, at any cost, isn't progress," Alex suggested. "What we're doing is making a conscious choice to save the world from itself."

"And as far as quitting and giving up," Cyd added, "that isn't true. We've glimpsed the miracles of the universe and all that the future holds."

"Speaking for myself," Nikki smiled, "that's enough."

Sam stormed out of the room.

That night in their cabin Cyd got out of her bunk, climbed in with Alex and snuggled up close. "I have something to tell you," she began tentatively. "Don't know if you're going to want to hear it or not."

He rolled over and kissed her. "If you're worried about going home empty-handed," he said, "remember what we came for. We discovered the source of the lights. We learned fusion energy exists and that it's possible here on earth. We found Robert and dug him out of that cave-in.

I'm sure his parents will be thrilled. Robert told me he talked to Mateo on the ship's sat phone. He's not going to lose his leg, and he's expected to make a full recovery. Sounds like he was horrified thinking he might have told the Chinese something that put us all in danger, but Robert assured him everything worked out. He's taking Mateo home to meet his parents when we get back, then they're returning to Chile to start their own geological engineering and resource development company."

Cyd sighed. "That's not what I wanted to discuss."

"Please don't say you want to move to Easter Island."

"I want to move back to the ranch. I'm pregnant."

"What?"

She hesitated. "I'm going to have a baby, Alex. Our baby."

He nodded and fell silent as the idea sunk in. "Looks like I'm going to be a country doctor after all," he said finally.

"You're not mad then?"

"Mad? I'm thrilled! I couldn't be happier! This is amazing!"

She brightened. "We'll raise her to be a Montana cowgirl."

"We'll raise him to be a doctor."

"Sounds like we're going to need more than one."

"Two," he laughed, "at least."

They lay awake excitedly making plans, and after a while they fell asleep, warm and content in each other's arms.

The following morning Nikki told Sam she was going ashore and asked him to come with her.

"What for?" he demanded, still angry.

"Something I haven't found yet."

"Like what?"

"My grave."

Sam paled and followed her obediently out on deck. They boarded the dingy and motored ashore, weaving in and out between all the boats that had arrived to aid in the island's recovery.

In reading Max's journal, Nikki found his description of where he had built Whale House to be vague at best. He mentioned only that it was on a hill somewhere between the town and Boris's cave. It took a while, but after some searching, she eventually found it.

Leading the way up the slope to the clearing that overlooked *Hanga Roa* and the harbor below, she saw the top of a bone-framed teepee come into view. Running happily the rest of the way, she discovered the curved white whale ribs, bleached and weathered from the sun, still leaning in on each other as securely as the day they were erected.

Sam caught up with her. "I'm surprised the tsunami didn't do more damage up here," he remarked, looking around. "Probably the altitude."

"This is where Max and Iolana lived," Nikki cried in delight. "Where *we* lived!"

He put his arm around her and studied the long, slender ribs set in foundation blocks of lava. "Good bones," he concluded.

"I loved this house," she smiled. "I loved that you built it for me."

He tried with little success to imagine a life with her in this place.

Nikki moved away and began searching the area around the skeletal structure. She hadn't gone far when she stopped with a small cry. "Sam, over here!" she called. "I think I found it."

He joined her and together they stood looking down at a weathered whalebone tablet sticking out of the ground and leaning precariously to one side.

"You know the irony?" she remarked pensively. "It wasn't just this island where people died of the bubonic plague. Two hundred million people worldwide eventually died of it. And all from the fleas off of rats." She knelt down and brushed away the dirt and sand that covered the faded inscription carved in the bone.

"See?" she cried, looking up excitedly. "I kept my promise!"

"Promise?"

"That I'd 'See you soon'. I found you again, Sam, just like I said I would!"

Tears stung his eyes and he turned away in embarrassment. "I guess."

"You guess?"

He wiped at his eyes with the back of his hand. "Now that you found me, I guess you're stuck with me."

She stood and kissed him happily, then saw his expression darken. "What's wrong now?"

"Nothing."

"I know you're disappointed about having to abandon the library and leave the Sphere behind, but the water has receded and they're perfectly safe where they are. The trouble with miracles is you can't just turn them loose on the world without being responsible for the consequences."

He nodded reluctantly. "There are other treasures besides these."

"Then let's go home and find them," she declared. "The Bahamas are littered with sunken ships. Who knows what's laying around on the bottom of the ocean waiting to be found?"

"We'll be back someday," he vowed.

"Someday," she said. "Maybe."

About the Author

STEPHEN STEELE is a graduate of the University of North Texas with degrees in English literature and marketing. An avid sailor, swimmer and mountain biker, the author worked as a salesman, syndicator of television sports shows, builder and developer, ski instructor and cowboy. He lives in an 1800's Victorian home with his ruthless editor Beverly and a fly rod amid Montana's streams and rivers of ice and snow.

STEPHEN STEELE'S

THE TROUBLE WITH MIRACLES
BOOK 1 – BOOK 2

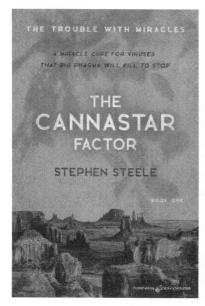

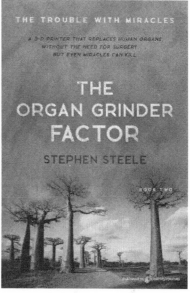

For more information
visit: www.SpeakingVolumes.us

MATT SCOTT'S

SURVIVING THE LION'S DEN
BOOK 1 – BOOK 2

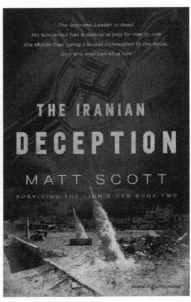

**For more information
visit:** www.SpeakingVolumes.us

STEPHEN H. MORIARTY'S

BILL DUNCAN MYSTERY
BOOK 1

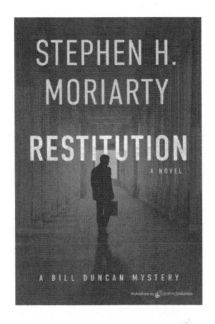

For more information
visit: www.SpeakingVolumes.us

  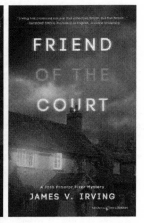

Made in the USA
Columbia, SC
21 October 2022

69775127R10171